the Soldier's Cross

Abigail J. Hartman

Ambassador International
Greenville, South Carolina & Belfast, Northern Ireland

www.ambassador-international.com

The Soldier's Cross

Printed in the United States of America

ISBN: 978-1-935507-38-3

Cover Design & Page Layout by David Siglin of A&E Media

AMBASSADOR INTERNATIONAL
Emerald House
427 Wade Hampton Blvd.
Greenville, SC 29609, USA
www.ambassador-international.com

AMBASSADOR BOOKS
The Mount
2 Woodstock Link
Belfast, BT6 8DD, Northern Ireland, UK
www.ambassador-international.com

The colophon is a trademark of Ambassador

To my God,

for His redemption.

And to my dad,

for encouraging me to the last page.

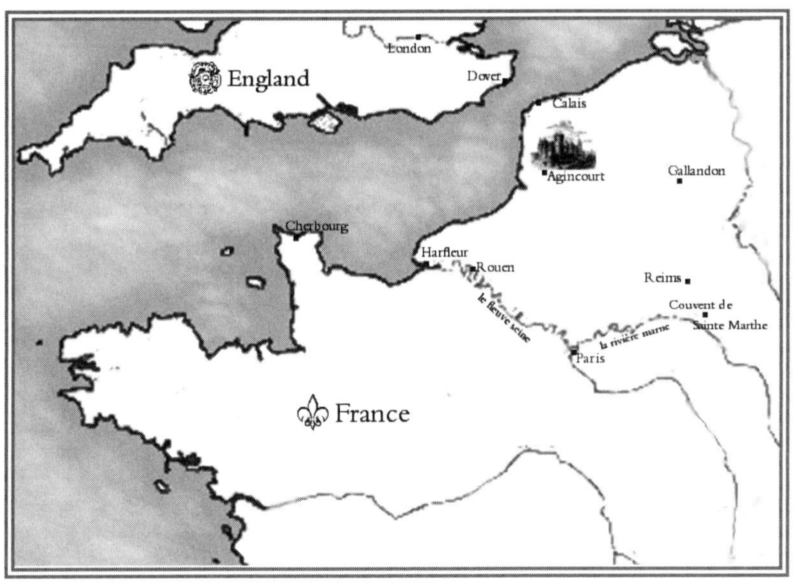

"Praised be God, and not our strength, for it!
What is this castle call'd that stands hard by?"

"They call it Agincourt."

"Then call we this the field of Agincourt,
Fought on the day of Crispin Crispianus."

—Shakespeare, Henry V, Act 4. Scene VII

1

THE WIND RAN ALONG the muddy-grey banks of the river, kicking up those bits of snow that had not fully melted and flinging them into Fiona's mouth. She paused to spit them out and squinted up at the black sky to catch the first scent of rain, and a slight mizzle began as she struggled onward again. It was not enough to be hampering and just enough to be vexing; she slapped her arms and rubbed them and blew into her palms as she walked, but still the colour sapped from her hands and left them a ghostly white, thinly veined in blue, and she could barely feel the presence of her chapped lips. Were those her own feet going up, down, up, and down on the turf in front of her? The only thing that she knew to be her own was her head, seated like a boulder upon her shoulders, and that she thought soon to fall off.

Night was coming on and the wind was picking up, though after having soaked through Fiona's clothes to her skin, the rain stopped. There were no stars and no moon, only clouds. Soon the Marne River disappeared into the blackness on her right; she got down on her hands and knees and ventured toward where it ought to have been, reaching out blindly to feel the slippery embankment or the water itself, but somehow she had lost it. She sat for a little while in the snow, clutching her small, metal cross for fear the wind would take it, until she began to feel drowsy.

Getting back to her feet, she shuffled along—in circles, for all she knew—for minutes or hours, and her hands began to come into contact with hard, rough things in her way. It was some time before her cold-slowed mind and numb fingers realized that she was walking among trees and her heart, already in her belly, gave a despairing thump. She must have wandered far from the Marne; she was lost in a wood, and even with the morning light she was not likely to find her way back again.

Fiona stood still and gazed about her; overhead, above the branching, witch-like trees, there was a stretch of dark blue several shades lighter than the darkness around her and a pale quarter moon now floated in and out of the clouds. It did not illumine her surroundings but only created a halo about itself and left the world below in gloom. The wind whistled around her, howling as it rushed between the oaks and yews and old, old elms; branches creaked and groaned like sailing ships. Now that she was not concentrating on the next step and keeping herself on the path, the night became frightening and full of evils that she would rather not face on her own. She kept on, her footsteps jarring her head and her already-aching shoulder.

The next moment—or perhaps it was the next hour, or the next one—her body contacted cold stone. She had walked into a wall much higher than her head and which stretched out on either side of her, and when she began tremulously to feel her way down the length of it, her fingers digging into the cracks and the moss and taking comfort in the presence of something man-made, she found something iron. Upon further investigation she discovered it to be a gate, but beyond it, inside the stone walled enclosure, she could see nothing. On the right side of the gateway her hands encountered what felt like a short rope dangling from an outcropping of stone, just about at the level of her nose, and she tugged on it experimentally.

A loud clanging immediately began above her head and she released the rope, but to no avail. It continued to swing and the bell sounded over and over; she shrank back against the wall but did not run. She watched as candles flared within the courtyard and light seeped out from under the door that she saw in the big, stone building inside, and soon three women were crossing the enclosure and coming to greet her through the gate. "Good evening, traveller," one smiled, as though it was nothing out of the ordinary to be called out of bed in the middle of the night to welcome a stranger. "Do you seek lodging here?"

"I-I-I-" stuttered Fiona through her blue lips, bewildered by the firelight in her face. "If it would not be too much trouble."

"It is no trouble," the nun assured her, swinging open the iron gate and reaching out to take Fiona's arm. Fiona sucked in a breath as the grip broke the numbness and sent pain all up and down her right side in spider-webbed patterns; the nun drew her fingers back and looked at them, finding them sticky with blood. "Saints," she murmured. "Come inside directly, my dear—what has happened to you? Come into the dining hall. Call Sister Marguerite, Annette, and quickly!"

Fiona was hurried into the convent and through a foyer and corridor to the narrow room that she took to be their dining hall. She had time to observe it as the nuns talked among themselves; it was decorated after the fashion of chapels, and Fiona felt the hundred pairs of eyes watching her from their lofty positions on the high walls as she came in. There was a great, black fireplace at the opposite end of the room as well, however, so she supposed this was not the sanctuary—or, if it was, it had not always been one.

Her guide seated her at a place close to the fire and called for another one of the sisters to light it. How warm it felt! Fiona thought she had never experienced such comfort, but the nun would not let her enjoy it in peace. She came and unfastened the pin that held Fiona's wet cloak to her shoulders and took it off, showing the red zigzag on the girl's right shoulder as well as her short, lopsided haircut. The nun gave another exclamation at that and touched Fiona's shorn head as if it were the most extraordinary phenomenon she had ever seen in her entire life, as well it might have been. "Well!" she said; it seemed the only thing she could think of to say.

After a moment she cleared her throat and returned to her brisk ordering of things, beginning to peel the cloth back from Fiona's right shoulder as she spoke. "What happened here? Were you attacked?"

"Only that I happened to be in the wrong place at the wrong time," Fiona replied ruefully, wincing at the woman's touch. "I was caught in a kind of brawl. I do not think it is very bad."

"No, the wound does not seem deep, but we will wait for Sister Marguerite before we decide. Here now, here comes Sister Catherine with some hot broth for you; you must be very hungry. How long have you been walking?"

Fiona could not clearly remember, but it seemed to her that this was the end of her first day. Time was not very important when one was concentrating on putting one foot after the other and thinking about how cold it was. She said so and the nun chuckled, setting the bowl of soup into Fiona's frozen paws.

"What is your name, girl? I am Sister Elisabeth, but there are so many nuns here that it will be of no consequence if you forget about me. If you stay here for any length of time, you may come to know us all. But now, your name?"

"Fiona, ma'am. It's very kind of you to take me in."

Sister Elisabeth waved her off. "As I said, it is no trouble whatsoever. Drink up your broth before Marguerite returns. Ah, does your shoulder pain you?" She watched as Fiona flinched in raising the bowl to her lips, the girl's hands shaking with exhaustion and a torrent of other sensations.

Fiona thrust her chin up and shook her head. "No, ma'am, I'm quite well. It's nothing very much."

"Well, here is Sister Marguerite now. Our guest has a wound in the shoulder, Marguerite; can you clean it?"

Marguerite was a thin, old woman, though still upright and with the appearance of a great deal of strength in her body. She did not touch Fiona's wound at first but only looked; presently she nodded. "Easily," she said, clearly and shortly. "I will go and bring my things while you finish your supper."

All the nuns but Elisabeth, Marguerite, and the young Annette, who seemed only necessary in that she fetched and carried what the older women wanted, left the room and returned to their beds. The other three worked at boiling herbs and binding them against the cut to prevent more bleeding, and though it stung, Fiona found that she could bear it without too much trial if she thought about the heat of the fire or the cold outside. They had just finished passing the bandage over her right shoulder and under her left arm for the last time and tying it off when another woman entered the room from a door half concealed on one side of the hearth; the nuns curtsied to her, and Fiona looked at her curiously. She was about Marguerite's age but neither as wrinkled nor as obviously strong; she was small, though not hunched, and only her eyes and the straight line of her mouth had any power in them.

"Who is this?" she asked, nodding to Fiona. Sister Elisabeth explained the situation as clearly as she knew it herself, and the Reverend Mother—for such Fiona took her to be—nodded. "Has her wound been treated, then? Good. You and Sister Marguerite may go back to bed now, but you should stay, Annette."

The two older nuns obediently left, and Annette retired to a place farther down the table where she could listen but not be in the way. All became quiet for a long, long time and Fiona thought she would doze off before the woman spoke. At last the Reverend Mother looked straight at Fiona and asked mildly, "What is your purpose, my daughter, in walking through the night in the cold, and alone? You seem too young to be a woman of the world."

Fiona felt a flicker of indignation, though her mind, which was working again after having been thawed, told her that it was a reasonable question. She looked into the fire and presently said, "I am not a woman of the world. But I would rather not tell anyone—just now—about my life. Please, let me stay and do not question me."

The woman continued to look at her. Her mouth continued in its stern, immoveable line for a minute, but at last it softened slightly and she nodded. "You may stay, my dear. I will not turn you out in the middle of winter. Perhaps in time you will be more willing."

Fiona did not contradict; she was too tired. "May I go to bed now?" she asked.

"Yes, you may go to bed now. Annette, show her to a guest room."

Annette stood and Fiona, stiff in every limb, did the same. She did not remember to thank the Reverend Mother, but the nun did not comment; she was thoughtfully watching the silver cross that swung from Fiona's fist as she walked.

Fiona followed the nun, who she thought was about her own age underneath the starkly black and white dress, through several corridors to where the guest rooms were. She looked about her as Annette led her into one, commenting under her breath, "It seems more like a room at Gallandon than a convent bedchamber."

"What was that?" Annette asked. "Did you say something?"

Fiona shook her head, dropping her gaze from the high ceiling again. "No. I was only thinking out loud."

"Ah. Well, here is your room; I will leave you to yourself for now and you can think aloud all you like. Do you need anything? Goodnight, then. I will wake you in the morning." She went out and shut the door carefully, leaving Fiona warm, full, and alone.

Crawling up into the high bed, which she soon noticed was harder than it looked, the girl put her head down and was asleep in minutes—the cross still in her hand.

☨

She awoke not much later, when it was still very dark and without the slightest appearance of lightening soon. She was very much alert, though, and from the quick pounding of her heart she knew it had been a bad dream that had awakened her; sitting up, she looked about at the block-shaped shadows in the room and wondered for a half second where she was and what had occurred to get her there. The necklace and cross reminded her and she sat back, somewhat more at ease, but still not ready to sleep again.

Presently she put her legs out of bed and stretched her feet to reach the floor, dropping onto it. The convent was still; she crossed to the door and opened it like a sneaking child, looking first one way and then the other down the hallway. Which way had she and Annette come? She forgot now but turned hopefully to the left and walked along the corridor and past a dozen or more doors, all shut, on either side. After a great many twists and turns through the convent, too many to keep track of, she stumbled into a large, rectangular room that could be nothing but the sanctuary. The ceiling was rounded and smooth high overhead, and there were archways to the right and left, separated by pillars with unlit candles mounted on each; there were windows up near the roof and one at the end of the room, letting in a little silvery light.

Hesitant lest someone catch her, Fiona took a few more steps down the middle of the room and paused. Nothing happened and no one appeared, for her footsteps were muffled by the carpet rolled down the aisle. She continued to one of the benches and sat down on it to rest and think, staring sightlessly before her and thinking, not about the chapel or the convent, but about the world outside and the little ornament she held. Then she stretched out on the wooden surface, cradled her head in her arm, and closed her eyes.

It was deep summer—deep, glorious summer—on the estates to the English side of the brooding, dark Welsh mountains. Golden sheaves of wheat waved merrily in a breeze, and the girl mounted in the twisted apple tree could see the forms of men and women working amid them. She swung her legs idly and watched them until her eye was caught by the appearance of a young man who had just begun to enter the shade of her tree; she sat up and, aiming through the film of leaves, threw down the russet apple she had been about to eat. It hit the ground a few inches from his toe, and he started back from it instinctively. She shrieked with girlish laughter, setting a flock of partridges flying from the ground cover, and the young man squinted into the foliage with a crooked grin as he picked up the apple. "Come down from there, Fiona! I want to talk to you."

"Come up here!" the girl cried, hugging her branch. "It's such a lovely view."

"No, no, you come down here."

Fiona obliged, scrambling down from her perch. For a moment her bare legs dangled a few inches from the ground, and then she dropped in front of the man in a heap. Picking herself up, she pressed the bruised apple into her brother's hand. "Good-morning, Giovanni; did you sleep well? It's so nice to have you back."

Giovanni replied with something suitable, but he was busy inspecting the handsome, red-and-green splashed fruit in his hand. Presently he tucked it behind his back and looked up. "Will you come for a walk with me, Fiona?"

"Of course," she replied innocently, suspecting nothing. She fell into step beside the tall young man, unconsciously trying to match his great strides. She loved to watch her brother's face as they walked, thinking to herself that he must, with his sandy hair and firm expression, be the handsomest man in the county. Theirs was a happy companionship, carrying over from the childhood that Fiona was just leaving, and the younger sibling regretted the elder's absences as one does the absences of a good friend. She was pleased with the prospect of having at least a fortnight to spend with him.

"Fiona," began Giovanni abruptly, stopping and once more fingering the apple between two fingers; "Fiona, you remember that the king is raising an army for a campaign in France?"

Fiona nodded, watching him curiously. She knew, slightly, of the plans brewing in London. The men of England talked of little else than Henry's promise to his people to unite the realms of Charles VI under his own rule, and at the dinners that were held at the estate of Giovanni and Fiona's father, the girl heard a great deal of the opinions of the lesser nobles. Sitting at her father's left hand, she would listen with interest to the talks and arguments of her elders until the heavy scent of mead and the heat of the fire made her too drowsy to listen further. Thus, she had gathered a reasonable knowledge of the latest news—Henry's commandeering ships in the Channel that would take his army to the French coast, the rising tally of men-at-arms, and the frosty relationship between the kings of England and France were all well enough known to her. "Yes, I know of all that; what of it?"

"The king is calling all able-bodied men to join him in his war—his 'sacred cause,' as he calls it." Giovanni snorted softly, raising an absent finger to stroke the small silver cross that swung from his neck. "Those who do not go are considered cowards."

Fiona felt the winds of the discussion turning foul, and she frowned. Giovanni remained silent for a few minutes longer, still contemplating his apple and playing with the heirloom lying on his chest. He continued, "It is but early July, Fiona; I still have time to join the army before it leaves for France. I will be heading for Southampton directly."

Fiona felt herself rooted to the spot, her heart stopped by the suddenness of those last words. It struck her in a brief moment how strange it was that a day that had but two minutes before been so cheerful and bright could now be as dark as a squall at sea. She cherished no hope of changing her brother's mind; she knew the tone he was using and knew that this discussion could end in no other way than he being as determined as ever to go and she, though devastated, convinced of the rightness of his actions. Still, she faltered, "But—surely King Harry has enough men as it is; *you* won't make a difference. Why should we concern ourselves with such far-off happenings?"

"If every man said that," Giovanni remarked with a mirthless smile, "no one would ever go to war. And as for far-off happenings, dear sister, you would find if you went out into the world that those things are not so far-off as you think."

"Then I'm glad I have stayed at home," Fiona cried with conviction. "Wars are nasty, brutal things, and I wish you did not have to be caught up in one. What does France mean to us?"

"It's the theory of the thing, Fiona. France, the *land* France, means very little to the king, I think—though the fertile southern regions are greatly needed. It's France the *idea* that we all want so badly, the France that dates back to the time of the great Edward III, the France that could win England fame and glory abroad if we were to capture her. Think of the power King Henry could wield if he sat on the French throne."

"I don't like France," the other insisted pettishly, "and I don't like you going off to war—*anyone* going off to war."

"Neither do I, Fiona. If left to me, I would as soon stay at home, but our king is the one to make the country's decisions and we are the ones to obey. I have thought and meditated, and I believe that this is what I ought to do."

Fiona could say nothing to that, so she asked instead, "Have you told Father?"

Once again Giovanni gave a little snort. "Ah, Father," he repeated, both contempt and sadness creeping into his tone. "Poor Father, who cares about nothing at all but his books and his scribbling and his wine. Father, who forgets so often that there has been a new king these past two years and who could not for anything keep it in his memory that there is a campaign being planned. No, I have yet to tell Father. Of course, he will raise no objections; a 'Well, well, go along then, my son,' is what he will say, and then he shall fall back to his scribbling and forget about it all in a trice."

Fiona knew this to be true. Her father's memory was quickly failing him, faster than his limbs, and he was, as he had always been and still more so, ever absorbed in his reading and little else. He had not married again after his first wife's death, as was expected; perhaps if he had, his health would be better. He was utterly harmless and Fiona had the affection for him that one might feel for a silly and slightly stupid, but loveable, child.

"No," Giovanni continued, "I knew you would care, so I thought to tell you first. I know you'll keep watch for me and miss me and laud me as a hero if I return—" (Fiona did not at all like his use of that *if*) "—and sorrow if I ..."

"No, no, don't!" Fiona shrieked, covering her ears. "I don't want to hear it; I don't even want to think about it! Don't talk so; it isn't right."

Giovanni half smiled at her. "No," he said doggedly, "my regrets will be all for you, sister. I feel my duty as a brother may be somewhat wanting."

"In what have you ever been wanting towards me?" Fiona scoffed.

"In not arranging a good marriage for you, firstly. Nearly fifteen years of age and still unmarried! It looks badly for you, does it not?"

Fiona had to agree that the fact that she was unwed did not reflect well on her character, but day to day she could not regret it, and she said so.

"Perhaps now, but I daresay you'll change your mind soon enough. If anything were to happen to me, I would be sorry to know that you had only poor, absent Father to look after you. In that I feel I could have done better."

"I still have time," said the younger comfortably. "Perhaps I will make some stunning alliance and raise the family honour to unheard-of heights."

Giovanni chuckled quietly.

"So? And in what more have you failed me, pray tell?"

The young man did not reply immediately but fiddled all the more with his ornament. Fiona understood the gesture, though, and waved a hand disparagingly. "Oh, that," said she. "You feel badly that you have not yet converted me, is that it? Come, Giovanni, am I so very bad? I can't see that I have a great need for your degree of fanaticism in the Church."

He looked at her firmly and quietly. "You are worse than you know," he said simply.

She sighed and looked away. On this point almost exclusively they did not agree and never could agree. Oh, Fiona went to Mass at the proper times and paid her tithes and listened listlessly to the priest on Sunday, but there her relationship with religion of any kind ended. She was, it seemed, too young and full of the present world for the concepts of sin and holiness and God to have much effect; when not plainly faced with the inevitability of death, how can one have a fear of judgment? If she was good enough for the priests and bishops, surely she was good enough for God.

"When are you leaving?" she asked in the hopes of changing the subject.

"Tomorrow. My travelling arrangements are made," he added, anticipating Fiona's first objection. "I have but to tell Father and I might leave, but I'll stay the night. I will leave early; will you still see me off?"

"Of course," Fiona returned eagerly. Knowing in her heart of hearts that it could be her last time seeing him, she would not have missed it had he been leaving in the dead of night. She frowned savagely; she would not think of such things. Most men did not die in battle, and Giovanni was skilled enough that he could surely remain alive. To accept the possibility of his death was to bring a cloud into the sunshine of her life, and that she would not have.

The two walked on together in silence after that until they were near the great house, and then Giovanni turned quickly to face his sister and said urgently, "Come, Fiona, you speak to Father for me, will you? You can break the news to him best."

Fiona agreed, but she knew that it was not because of worry for their father that Giovanni hesitated. She knew how much it pained him, as the firstborn and only son, to be forgotten and slighted by his sire; she knew he regretted that his reports were incapable of bringing either joy or sorrow. She, a woman, and thus accustomed to being treated as naught, was far more impervious to the lack of feeling in her poor father.

She left Giovanni in the kitchens and went to the library, where she was sure of finding the elderly man bent over a book, muttering things to himself and tracing the lines with a finger. She rapped on the heavy oaken door and then opened it without waiting for an invitation. "Father?"

The man sat up from the position that Fiona had guessed he would be in, his greying hair sticking up in odd little tufts around his ears, his eyes blinking like an owl's as they changed focus. He was, as usual, surrounded by dusty tomes and fading manuscripts, and so many quills of various points lay about him that it looked to Fiona as though a goose had been mangled there. A black puddle lay on the stone about his feet from where an ink capsule had been heedlessly knocked over.

"Oh dear," the girl sighed under her breath and would have moved forward to clean up the mess if her father had not waved a hand and stuttered anxiously, "No, no, no! I'll get it—don't trouble yourself!" He hastened to do so, but his efforts only made greater havoc. "Well, well, what is it, my dear? Eh? Something to tell me? I'm not hungry, if that is what you were going to ask …"

"No, Father, it's about Giovanni."

The man blinked at her a second as though trying to remember to whom that name belonged.

"Your son, Giovanni," Fiona prompted. "You remember all the talk about the planned campaign? Our king—Henry V, you know—is gathering troops to invade France, and …well, all the young men are going, and Giovanni thinks he ought to as well. He will be leaving for Southampton on the morrow to join the forces. He wanted to come and say goodbye."

"Campaigns," old Sir Madoc fussed, apparently not understanding the point of what his daughter said. "Too many wars, too much fighting, and it all comes to naught in the end; England cannot hold it all. Ah, dear. Well, well, get along then, Fiona. I have reading to do."

"But will you not say farewell to Giovanni, Father?" Fiona pressed.

"Eh? Who? Oh, yes, yes, well, send him in." But he fell back to his own world even before Fiona had left the room, and she knew that when she sent her brother in, their father's mind would once more be full of last century and would have forgotten all that his daughter had told him.

Fiona found her brother standing not far from the library door, rubbing his lip anxiously. He looked up when his sister came out, and his face was so clouded that Fiona asked sharply, "Did you hear us?"

But he shook his head. "Have you told him, then?"

"Yes, but I'm afraid he won't remember it. There's no need to tell him, is there, Giovanni? Come away and we'll go for a ride; you need not vex yourself."

"No," he replied firmly. "No, I have a duty to him. Wait for me in the courtyard, Fiona, and I will join you presently."

Fiona never knew what passed between father and son, but she knew from Giovanni's expression when he met her that it had not been very different from most times. She was sorry for her brother, but her mind was too preoccupied with thoughts of his departure to focus long on her father's faults.

†

The next morning was dry, despite predictions of rain, and Fiona found herself being awakened at an unholy hour by a maid. "What? What is it?" she moaned, sitting up wearily.

"Master Giovanni is leaving soon, miss," the maid whispered. "You asked me to wake you as soon as he was up."

Fiona then recalled yesterday's talk and flung herself out of bed with a speed that gave her a throbbing headache. She fidgeted as the maid dressed her, fearing that Giovanni would leave without waiting for her to say goodbye, and when the worthy servant went to brush and braid Fiona's tangled hair, the girl said impatiently, "No, no, forget that; bring me my slippers, Mary."

Thus she hurried out of her apartments, her long and unruly mane flying out behind her.

She found the young man waiting in the courtyard by his horse. "Whoa there, Fiona, slow up! I wasn't going to leave without saying goodbye."

Fiona did not heed him but flew at him and embraced him as tightly as she could. "Oh, Giovanni, *must* you go?" she cried.

He put his arms around her and patted her gently on the shoulder. He wisely said nothing, only held her for a long moment and then put her away. "Come, Fiona, be brave for me. It is not you who must march into battle, is it?"

Fiona hardly dared to speak, but at last she managed, "But you've always been so much braver than I. I–I'll be all alone, and I will be constantly worrying …" She could say no more without tears, so she fell silent.

"Yes, I know. The fate of the one who stays at home is so often worse than the one going abroad; I know that. But, my dear, you would not feel so empty and alone if you had *this* as I do." He once more touched the cross on his chest, "Nay, you scoff, but it is so. Think on it while I am gone, Fiona."

She wanted to reply angrily, to say that she would be able to think of nothing but the war in France while he was gone, but already tears were stinging her eyes and nose. It was hard enough for her to mouth a simple, "Yes, Giovanni." And then he was mounting and preparing to leave. Before he spurred his horse, she took hold of his breeches' hem and pleaded again, "Please don't go."

He touched her cheek a moment as though in regret, but he only said, "I must."

She nodded; she knew it was the only reply he could give now. She pulled from her sleeve a simple handkerchief, white with a crude red hem, and held it up to him. "Will you take this, then? I'm the only woman you leave behind."

He smiled and accepted it. "I will wear it into battle," he swore, and tied it around his arm to prove it.

"It will keep you safe." And Fiona hoped the darkness was too deep for him to see the glistening trails on her face.

Once more he said goodbye, and then he was gone. She heard for awhile the ring of shod hooves on the cobbles, but quickly the noise was indistinguishable from the other sounds of early morn. Standing in the courtyard, with the chill morning breeze piercing her clothing, Fiona had never felt so desolate or alone.

LONG, LAZY WEEKS DRIFTED into months after Giovanni left. Fiona no longer sat in the apple tree by the hour, for the serenity of the days made her think about things she would rather not have considered. Instead she stayed indoors, wandering here and there and giving orders to the servants as she met them in the hallways and kitchen; her father continued to wile away his days locked up in his study and so the household languished, and Fiona tried, as best she could, to set things straight while Giovanni was away. The servants had no particular liking for her, for she was inclined to be wilful and bull-headed even when she felt the pricking knowledge that she was wrong, but still they obeyed out of respect for her father and dead mother.

Once an acquaintance of Madoc's asked for Fiona's hand in marriage—an honest man some years older than she, of whom Giovanni would have approved, had he been there. It was no great compliment to any beauty of hers but was little more than an act of respect for her father and pity for her own unstable position; he himself had only seen her twice in his life. But in the end it did not matter what reason prompted the man to ask, for Fiona's father could not remember the request long enough to give a ruling, and so Fiona herself never knew. Thus she continued in her home, unmarried and with no prospects, hanging in the awkward place between childhood and womanhood.

The only times that her father left his cluttered room were when a banquet was held in the manor's great hall—for so they still were held, out of deference to the old man's friends and neighbours. Then he would sit at the end of the long table and nod off, waking but once or twice to say, "Aye, aye, 'tis all the wars. The wars …" before falling into a doze again. Fiona herself eagerly awaited these banquets because of the news and speculation they inevitably brought concerning the state of affairs in France. Anxiously she would listen, and at every tale of the starvation and diseases that were infesting the English troops, a greater part of her heart sank to her belly. She clung to the men's words as they spoke of the siege of Harfleur, the marches of the army, the terrible number of French soldiers and nobles that were pursuing them. And yet what tortured her thoughts most was the knowledge that even if Giovanni died, it would be months until she heard of it—if she ever did.

One such chill night in early October, while the fire roared on the hearth and smoke drifted through the hall, the men were speaking more heatedly than usual of England's troubles. Poor Sir Madoc was even less awake than usual but merely sat in his chair with his head lolling back against the headrest and slept steadily. The guests, however, were old associates of his and knew him well, and they let him nap undisturbed without a thought of being offended.

"If only the siege at Harfleur would end," a man further down the table said, pronouncing the French name with a harsh nasally accent; it was the third time he had said it that evening.

"If it lasts much longer, the king will have to return to England for winter," a younger man added. "There is no way that the army could make it to Calais in time for the storms; 'tis desolated as it is."

"The king will not return," another spoke up with conviction. Fiona craned her neck to see the speaker sitting further down the table; his face, like his words, showed a very definite character, certain of being right. "The king will not return without victory. If you had heard him speak to his people as I did, you would know—"

"Fah!" cried the second man, whom Fiona thought had drunk a little too deeply of his wine. "Idle promises to an over-eager people. Promises of kings are quickly made and more quickly broken."

"Hst," ordered a newcomer to the conversation, a Welshman through and through. "So it may be, young one, but kings have ears everywhere; be careful what you say."

All the participants in the conversation, as well as Fiona herself, remembered clearly the three nobles who had been arrested and executed for treachery by the king before the army left Southampton. It had all been done in a whirl—the uncovering of the plot, the judgement of the king, the punishment of the offenders—and the business transacted with brutal justice, displaying the powers of King Henry in a very clear and personal way. Such a decisive action early in his reign would make others think twice about speaking against him.

Properly chastened and perhaps a little awed, the man who had spoken now fell silent in order to nurse the insult. The reminder made all but the Welshman himself uncomfortable, and the talk floundered before turning to less sinister things; yet the small details of estates and the goings-on in London were not savoury to anyone, and they also fell flat. For a long space of time before the meal ended, the only noises were the crackling of the fire and the whine of dogs lying in the rushes.

After supper the men one by one took their leave of Fiona and her father, each careful to specifically address the lord of the manor, even though he never made any reply except a sleepy kind of snort. Then they left, their horses or carriages clattering away outside the house.

When the last man had gone, Fiona turned to help her father to bed. She had almost to carry him to his chambers, for he shuffled and seemed to sleep even while he walked and had no strength to hold himself up. Though she had no filial love for him, she was sorry for his dependence on others to help him do the simplest things; even lying down on his canopied bed was a struggle for his old bones. When she had made him as comfortable as she could, she left him murmuring things from the past and went out into the courtyard in which she had but a few months before said farewell to Giovanni. Finding that this spot brought too many hard memories, she pulled her shawl tighter over her shoulders and went out to walk through the estate.

Her feet took her to the lone tree that had so often been her refuge before. She stood just out of its shadow; black night stretched overhead and stars shone with an autumnal clarity. She heard nothing but the sounds of the wind running through the long grass and the far-off call of an owl, and somehow this separation from the world, which had once been so peaceful for her, brought a frightening sense of emptiness inside. She was overpowered with a feeling of loneliness, the loneliness of a man shipwrecked on a barren island, far out of reach of other humanity.

Fiona trembled and pulled her mantle over her face to block out the serenity of the night. The tree branches whispered overhead, brushing tenderly against her skin, speaking of past happiness. At its touch she remembered days in the spring long ago when she and Giovanni had played together here, careless of the world's problems. She remembered how they used to sit in the branches and how he would tell her fantastical stories and she would listen, wide-eyed and enraptured. Memories flooded over her, but even as they did so she knew with an overwhelming lucidity that she would never speak with him again. Summer had gone, and autumn had come before her time.

Fiona fled. She did not stop until she reached her chambers, where she flung herself upon her bed and pressed her face into the pillow. She longed to cry, but no tears came; there was only a harsh lump grating inside her throat, and she could not rid herself of it. At last, after many sleepless hours of tossing and turning, Sleep took pity on her and carried her away.

Even here, though, she was not free from her sorrow. Dreams haunted her, and visions of her brother pervaded her rest. She saw in her mind's eye the struggling band of Englishmen as they trekked through the rain over an unfamiliar land, felt their fear of attack, experienced their pangs of hunger and their weariness. They did not move as a body, as she always thought of armies doing, but rather they were like a horde of ants, weaving in and out of each other as they tried to avoid the bad ground, tripping and staggering as their limbs appeared to drag. Grey mud sucked at their feet, and many a time she saw a man go down and have to be dragged up again by a fellow soldier. Even those on horseback suffered from the rain, for often their horses stumbled and fell, and a few drowned in the mud before their masters could save them.

For a moment as she looked on she thought she caught a glimpse of Giovanni amid the foot soldiers and opened her mouth to call to him, but, as so often happens in dreams, she could not do so. He was once more lost amid the swarm of men, and Fiona woke up in tears.

This was not the last of her dreams; she had many more like it. They tormented her sleep so greatly that she dreaded going to bed, and only sheer weariness at last compelled her to shut her eyes at night. When news reached her via their dinner guests that the siege of Harfleur had at last succeeded a few days previous to their last banquet and that the king had reformed his troops and was continuing on to Calais, she no longer felt the panicked worry. Instead, a chill crept into her belly and she felt her fears confirmed.

Days passed and her father's condition worsened. The doctor confined him to his room but said that if Fiona would feed him properly, he would not grow worse. So Fiona did as he instructed and spent her days in her father's chamber, looking after him with care; dinners were no longer held in the hall and she felt cut off from the world. Whenever a maid or a manservant brought something to her, she shuddered at the sound of the heavy door slamming behind them as they left. It was the sound of a cage door being shut on her.

True to the doctor's predictions, the old man grew better. He was able to sit up in his bed, but he was not allowed any books lest the strain be too much for his eyes (for the windows were kept strictly covered and the room was dark), so he fidgeted and muttered a great deal. A day later he was allowed to get up and walk about the room with a servant's help, and he spent much of his time in a chair by the fire. There he would doze, and sometimes he would wake up with a start, blink at his daughter, and grumble, "Well, who are you, then?" And Fiona would explain to him yet again. "Hrmm," was inevitably his answer, and he would mutter about it until, again, he fell asleep.

Sometime in mid or late October—she was losing track of the days as well as the hours—she gathered the courage to ask the doctor how long Madoc had.

"Oh, awhile," the man assured her, looking on her kindly. "Don't be worrying about him."

Fiona could not express to a stranger her half wish that her father would either recover amazingly or die soon, so she nodded wearily.

Time dragged in the heated room. She left only one or two times during the day to tell the servants what to do, for though she would leave her father sleeping soundly, he would inevitably awaken while she was gone and fuss for someone to be with him.

The doctor was the only person who visited them; her father's friends had abandoned him, and Fiona herself had few enough acquaintances. She could not read as her brother and father could, and so she, like the old man, dozed in a chair before the fire during the long hours of the day.

On the fourth or fifth day since he had been confined to his room, Fiona's father sat in his chair and stared blankly into the firepit. He had not dozed off once that morning; she watched him carefully, hoping that this was a sign for the better. When she spoke his name he did not answer but twitched his head and muttered one word: "Fiona." She guessed, though, that this was meant not for herself, but for her dead Italian mother. Her heart sank and her fingers curled around the wood of her chair. Twice she leapt up and tried to peer from the window to see if the doctor had arrived, but he did not.

Noontide, marked only by the entrance of a maid with a platter of food, came and went, and there was no marked change in the old man's appearance. His chin had sunk onto his chest, but his eyes remained open and occasionally his lips would move soundlessly around that same name. Fiona brushed a damp bit of hair from her forehead, breathing unsteadily.

At last, about an hour later, he fell asleep. Fiona also relaxed in her chair and was able to nod for a few minutes, but her constant dreams woke her with a start not long afterward. "Father?" she whispered; the doctor had warned her against letting him sleep for long periods of time. "Father, wake up."

He did not respond to her voice, but it was not until she laid a hand on his thin shoulder that she understood why. There was no life in his skin, no pulse in his neck. She dropped her hand as though burned. She stared; the room cavorted wildly, and she only knew that she had to get out. She ran for the door, which stuck for an instant before giving way, ran down the hall, ran until she reached the kitchens, where all the household servants were assembled. They all straightened up silently as their mistress flew into their midst and every one of them knew the reason for the violent intrusion.

Fiona stood just inside the kitchen door, her eyes darting over their faces. Wavering, she raised one hand to point upward; two male servants immediately jumped into action and ran past her in the direction of her father's apartments while Mary came forward and supported her. "I'll be all right," Fiona managed. "Just sit me down—there." She crossed her arms on the rough table and laid her head on them, too tired to move.

She was not sure afterwards if she dozed or merely let her mind wander, but when she finally gathered strength to raise her head, the rest of the servants were gone. "So," she said, her voice cracking, "I'm all alone."

The funeral, held the next day, was a quiet affair; because the priest had not been able to perform the last rites, few would admit friendship with the old man's soul. The frosty earth closed over the coffin and the few men who had come to pay their respects dispersed, and Fiona, the blood pounding in her temples and every inch of her body weary from nervous strain, sought to calm herself by a walk along the dirt path that passed in front of the properties. The cool air nipped at her face and sought to take away the clinging heat of her father's chamber, but the feverish warmth remained inside. It was not so much death itself that frightened her but rather the void that her brother's departure and her father's death left. Everything was different and wrong because of it. She was lost and without guidance in what suddenly seemed to be a hostile world; she was without covering on a bitter night.

Fiona took a deep breath and shut her eyes. Her youthfulness clung to the barest scrap of hope she had left, that Giovanni would soon return and once more fill the place of a protector. "I will be brave," she murmured to herself. "He will find me brave." For a moment longer she communed with herself before rising and pacing hurriedly back to the house.

AS SOME MEN DRINK to drown their sorrows, Fiona worked to drown hers. Her work before had been half-hearted, if still effective, but now she flung herself into managing the household with a feverish passion that wearied her mind as much as her body. She never spoke of Giovanni, and the servants, taking their cue from her, kept silent about their absent master. They wished for his return, for they all loved him, and yet to question Fiona's authority was the furthest thought from their minds and they allowed the young girl to command them as dumb oxen do their master. It was fortunate for Fiona that they did so, though she never considered it; she would have been impotent in the face of a mutiny.

Two days after her father's passing, Fiona had another dream worse than those that had preceded it. She saw first a forest and then caught a glimpse of a castle rising near the skirt of it. There came a field, and beyond it stood another bit of woods with another smaller castle. Between the stands of trees were arrayed two armies—prepared for battle, she thought. The armour of the one, a magnificent army indeed, shone even without the help of the sun, which was hidden behind thick clouds; the latter was a sorry looking bunch of archers and foot soldiers. The men of both sides stood up to their ankles in mud, the horses' hocks became sucked into it, and the rain continued to pitter-patter down upon their helmets and breastplates.

At some unseen signal the band of archers in the latter army let fly their arrows and the cavalry of the other began to charge, and in but a few seconds all was havoc to Fiona's dreaming eye. She was as lost among the chaos as the soldiers themselves must have been; she thought that it was strange how the heaving of the muck was heard even amid the men's cries, and she saw that both horses and men seemed not to charge, as they first had, but rather to wade and then to wallow. There seemed more mire than blood in the battle.

Of a sudden Fiona also found herself trapped. The grey sludge opened up beneath her to swallow a foot, then a leg, and so on until she was sunken up to her neck and could barely draw breath. The pressure on her arms pinned them to her sides; the mud pulled her further down and began to fill her mouth and her nostrils and choke her—

Gurgling, Fiona awoke to find herself in utter blackness and as confined as she had been in her dream. Something covered her face and she thought she was suffocating, but after a moment of panic she found that it was nothing more than her coverlets, which had become tangled in her sleep. She sat up in bed and raised a hand to her pounding heart.

"They grow worse every night," she said aloud. Her voice sounded hollow in the darkness, and she shivered. Lying back down, she forced herself to close her eyes and tried with all her might to think on peaceful times and circumstances, but even as she thought them the knowledge that they were fantastical or long past only sharpened her desolation. At last, sometime early in the morning the beat of her own heart lulled her to sleep again.

On the morrow Fiona accepted her maid's suggestion that she take the carriage, in the company of a manservant, to the nearby village to refresh herself, and set off some three hours before noon. The day was clear enough, with a huge sun hanging crisp and distant in a clear, robin's-egg blue sky and the last few oak leaves twirling down to the frosty ground, and on a road that held few memories for her she found that she had the capacity of being happy. Jolting along the deeply rutted path, Fiona watched the window of landscape and took comfort in the manifestation of the seasons' constancy. Winter, she mused, would follow autumn, and spring would follow winter, and summer would follow spring, whether or not there was a campaign in France. The knowledge was strangely comforting.

Once in town, she was surprised by the loud and constant clanging of the church bells. Indeed, now that she paused to listen, Fiona heard many more both near and distant. Curious, she joined the crowd of people who stood discussing the latest news in the square. There was a moment of awkwardness as they, glancing at her clothes, fell silent and made way for her, but as she stood blushing amid them, their own eagerness to hear of their king's victories distracted them and the gossip continued.

"They say twenty-thousand French died," a woman somewhere in the crowd affirmed. "And King Harry lost nary a man."

"Pshaw," scoffed a farmer. "The king lost more men than *that*."

But the other villagers only cast him many disparaging glances and continued with their talk, which was somewhat more effusive than accurate. "Imagine the king winning so soundly against such odds!" someone else contributed.

"Where's the wonder? 'Tis plain as day their armies 're no match for ours."

The crowd murmured in agreement and there came a lull in the discussion. Fiona took the opportunity to ask a neighbour what they were speaking of. "Haven't you heard?" he replied, visibly shocked. "The king won a battle; with his forces all starving and exhausted, he routed a French army as nicely as you could ask to see it."

"When was this?"

The man did not rightly know the answer to that, but, not caring to admit as much, he said, "Naught but a few days ago, at a place about four days' march from Calais, a field near a castle called Agincourt. The account is circulating about the country now. Fancy you not hearing about it," he repeated, peering curiously at her. "'Tis all anyone is talking about." He retired once more to the general gossip and no longer appeared at all inclined to answer Fiona's questions. At last, though, when she plucked at his sleeve and asked twice how many of the English soldiers were killed, he returned to her reluctantly and answered, "No one's sure of the numbers as yet; they say the Constable's losses were ten times Harry's."

Seeing that her companion was only intent on embellishing the king's role in the victory, Fiona retired and listened in silence. The man who had previously remarked on the superiority of the English soldiers now replied to someone else and said, "Well, I suppose the king will continue on to Calais; what else can he do with the winter storms coming?"

"Aye," added Fiona's companion; "and with such a demonstration, I say that French madman-king will lose what heart he had and sue for peace within a fortnight." The mass cheered his speech and he flushed red as a turkey's crest and nodded proudly to himself.

"Does this mean our men will be coming home?"

All eyes turned to seek out Fiona, and she immediately wished with all her heart that she had kept silent. No one seemed to want to answer, but at last her neighbour, bolstered by the recent acclaim, answered her with a mere, "One would think so." The throng nodded as though the man were a font of wisdom, and then, obviously made somewhat uncomfortable by Fiona's pronouncement, they separated and went about with their daily business.

Embarrassed but encouraged, Fiona returned to her carriage and ordered the driver to carry her back home. She no longer thought about the scenery as they bounced along; her mind was focused on thoughts of the battle. It seemed clear enough, she reasoned with herself, that few of the English soldiers had been killed; surely there could be no cause for undue worry over Giovanni. He was healthy and fine; no French soldier stood a chance against him. He would be coming home soon, and life would be restored to its former summer.

Happier days passed and Fiona began to speak often of Giovanni to herself and the servants, as she used to. He was coming home, she repeated, aloud and to herself; Giovanni was coming home to take care of her, and there would be no more worry about battles and campaigns. No one in the household dared dissuade her, but they all had their doubts. Each one of them often had occasion to go into the village, and over the next few days they heard more reasonable numbers from the battle. As usual, the first reports had been greatly exaggerated in favour of the victor; now rumours were circulating that at least five hundred Englishmen had died. Compared to the number of French who were slain, this number was nothing—save to those whose husbands, fathers, and brothers made up the tally.

As for the king himself, his plans were still relatively unknown. It was clear that negotiations with Charles the Mad were still going on from Harry's seat in Calais, but as to their effectiveness, little was known. From town gossip, the servants soon learned that many of the soldiers were being shipped home again and the dead soldiers' bodies being restored to their families for burial, but they pretended to be deaf and dumb and said nothing of it to their mistress.

Thus, they were less surprised than she when on the morning of All Saints Day a cart with a weary driver and horse clattered across the cobbles and into the courtyard. An exclamation of joy escaped Fiona's lips as she glimpsed it from a window, and though her maid tried to hold her back, she was outside before any of the servants could stop her.

But it was not Giovanni who was climbing down from the seat; it was a lean, gaunt looking man who seemed both physically and mentally weary. His mouth hung slightly open and his sallow eyes drooped as he regarded the fresh-faced girl in front of him. "Sir Madoc?" he asked at last, his voice harsh for so thin a body.

"He-he is dead," Fiona wavered. "I am his daughter." Her heart was already pounding and she guessed with a sick dread why this man had come.

The man seemed to want to hesitate, for he deliberated and then asked what seemed obvious: "You are the mistress of the house?"

Fiona nodded. "But—please, do you bring news of my brother? Where is he?"

The messenger shook his head jadedly and leaned on the side of the cart. "He fell at the Battle of Agincourt, mistress."

Time stood still. For a moment, as when her father had died, Fiona could say nothing. Her lips moved, but no sounds came out; she sank down on the cobbles, staring at the hands in her lap. Those few words seemed like a doctor's needle, bleeding her of warmth and emotion so that she could not even cry or scream or doubt this man's word. "Tell me," she said at last.

The man was obviously drained from his task, poor fellow, and he had no wish to speak of the battle, but he obeyed. "He was a foot-soldier, madam, and they fared worse than the others. The mud—it had been raining for days, and the mud drew us in like a monster. Many drowned, as did your brother."

"*Drowned?*" Fiona repeated, raising her eyes. To hear that Giovanni, her beloved brother, had been killed in battle: that was a blow too great to be sustained, but at least if she knew that he had died by a lance or a sword stroke … there would be honour in such a death. But to drown? To drown like an unwanted puppy? The word echoed in her mind.

"I am sorry." The man bowed his head, and by his tone Fiona knew that he truly was.

She pressed her hands to her face, shivering from head to toe. Her misery lay heavy in her own stomach; she wanted to vomit it away, but it was not a sickness to be gotten rid of so easily. With difficulty she rose, and with a nod of acknowledgement she staggered back to the kitchen entry.

"Madam!"

She turned back and looked at him wearily. He gestured halfheartedly to the cart, and Fiona realized with dismay what it carried. She was repulsed yet horribly fascinated; she let her feet take her around to the back of the cart.

"My Giovanni," she whispered. "Oh God, why have you done this to me? Why have you done this to me?"

The body on the straw seemed merely to sleep. A few blemishes marred his flesh, but the mud had been washed away by a stranger's hands and there was no blood on him; only his armour told that he had been in battle. As Fiona gazed on him, she saw a ragged bit of cloth tied about his upper right arm: her own handkerchief, the red of the hem bleeding onto the white cloth, one corner waving like a banner in the breeze.

"Oh God!" she screamed to the clear sky. The messenger flinched. "Oh God, *why? Why have you done this to me?*" She tried to say something more, but her voice gave way and her body shook with sobs. She had to have the man help her inside and hand her over to two of the servants, who carried her to her bed and laid her on it. Darkness—a darkness that was red and not black—swept across her eyes.

SHE SLEPT THROUGH THAT day and night and awoke early in the morning, before the sun was up. She crawled out from her bed and dressed herself haphazardly, as Mary was not there, and went down to the kitchens. A huddle of servants stood about, discussing, she gathered, what to do with Giovanni and whether or not to wake her.

"Where is he?" she demanded.

Everyone jumped and looked guilty. A boy, not more than nine years old, scuttled past her and ran for the barn; two stable-hands also hurried away, leaving the kitchen servants looking nervously at one other.

"Where is he?" Fiona repeated, her frustration rising.

Mary came forward and took her mutely by the arm, leading her to the door of Giovanni's old bedchamber. "Are you sure you ought to …" the maid began, but Fiona jerked her arm away and went in.

They had laid him out on the bed and redressed him for burial. His armour was intact, she saw, save that his helmet was missing; the bronze greaves and the gold engravings glittered, having been newly polished. His jaw had only a few patches of stubble where the barber's razor had missed. How proud and noble he looked, thus arrayed! Fiona half expected him to get up and laugh at her for being fooled by his guise. She turned away bitterly until she could recollect herself sufficiently to look at him again.

"Come away now, mistress," Mary urged from the doorway.

Fiona shook her head silently. This was to be her last time gazing on him, and, as with his departure for Southampton months ago, whatever pain it brought must be endured for the chance to say goodbye.

Goodbye. She realized now that that was what she had come to say. Hand shaking, she reached out and brushed her fingertips against Giovanni's pale cheek. *Oh, Giovanni, if only you had stayed here! Why did you have to leave me? No one ever meant more to me than you; why did you go?* She bit her lip against the flood of tears that hastened to rise.

What made her think of the family heirloom just then, she never knew. Later she thought that it must have been the void in her heart that made her recall her brother's words that he had given her just before he left, that if she had the cross as he did, she would not be so empty inside. Eagerly she reached for the ornament, which should have been lying on Giovanni's breast, but it was not there. There was no chain about his neck, though she could see the worn red line on his flesh where it had rubbed and torn.

She whirled to face Mary. "Where is it? His cross, the cross he wore; where has it gone?"

The maid, who had but a vague idea what it was that Fiona was referring to, could but stare in shock. "I-I do not know, m'lady; mayhap the servants removed it when they were dressing him."

"Ask them, ask them!" Fiona urged, her voice increasing to a feverish pitch. She clasped her hands together in a frenzied manner and her small frame shook violently, her whole being so unlike that of a normal girl her age that Mary, who had not been in the household more than two years and did not know her well, was quite frightened of her. The maid hurried away and Fiona awaited her return with apprehension. Giovanni had worn that cross for as long as she could remember, and many times when they were young he had told her stories about their mother, a pretty Italian immigrant, and how she had given him the necklace when he was six years old and instructed him to explain to Fiona, then but a baby, what it meant. Fiona had never accepted the tales as truths, but that cross was as linked to her brother in her mind as his very face. If it was gone....

Mary returned a few minutes later, creeping meekly into the room. "Please, mistress, they say they never saw the cross."

Fiona cried out angrily. "Search the house, then; the chambers, the kitchen, the courtyard! It must be found."

The maid scuttled off again and Fiona followed, anxiously overseeing the search. The house was turned upside down and back, then upside down yet again; but the cross was nowhere to be found, though she drove the servants all morning. At last Mary compelled her to eat a late dinner, and in the afternoon there was the funeral to arrange. This latter point was left primarily to the care of the steward, for Fiona's feelings were still too raw to allow her to speak easily of burying her brother. She sat at the long dining board and looked the man in the face as he made suggestions, but she shut her ears to his actual words and only occasionally found it in herself to nod or shake her head.

The necessary evil was performed at twilight. Last rites had been given to all the soldiers before battle, so without that to keep them away, a number of men who had nominally been Sir Madoc's friends came to pay their respects. If she had had it in her own power entirely, Fiona would have gladly driven them off the church grounds; what right had they, who would go back to their business tomorrow not a bit disquieted by Giovanni's death, to try to share in her sorrow? To attend a man's funeral merely as a bow to propriety was nothing more than an aggravation to the wound.

Fiona's anger against these men, however, was in some ways a benefit, for it kept her from a public display of sorrow as her brother's body was taken out of sight forever. She stood as tall as her height would allow, her face pale and stony and, as a guest later said, quite eerie in the light of the torches, while the priest spoke the necessary invocations. The service had never seemed so long before; every minute that the ceremony lingered brought fresh sorrows. She had never known such a feeling of relief as when all was over and she could return home, though *home* was cold and cheerless and little more than a mere residence now.

"Will you be all right, mistress?" Mary asked with concern before she left Fiona's chamber that night.

Fiona glanced up from her study of the dying embers in the fireplace and tried to force a smile; she felt the ghastliness of the effect. "Yes, Mary. I'll let you know if I need you." After all, with Giovanni gone, she knew that the dreams that had haunted her would leave. Worry had caused them, and now there was nothing more to fear for him.

"How glad I would be to worry about him again," she said aloud to the empty room. "Anything is better than this despair."

The heat made her eyelids heavy and the crackle of the popping wood dulled her senses so that her thoughts became jumbled between Giovanni's last words to her, the missing cross, her late father, and her brother himself. She felt herself falling asleep before it actually overpowered her, and her last thought was gratefulness for being able to forget the world.

For a time, it seemed, her sleep was peaceful, and it was only sometime past midnight that dreams infiltrated her subconscious. Unlike the former times, she knew as the images appeared in her mind that she was dreaming and not caught in a nightmarish reality. The scene that appeared in her eyes was like the battle that she had dreamt of last, with the mud and the rain and the death all around her, but it was as though she was viewing a close-up of two opposing soldiers in that same battle. One of them was a sandy-haired youth whom she thought, in a detached way, that she knew, and the other was dark-haired and taller and unknown to her.

When she first saw them, the mind in her dream thought they were wrestling like clumsy bears from the way they struggled and stumbled against one another; soon, though, the dream-Fiona was able to see that this was not so but that the thick mud was attempting to pull them both down, and it was all they could do to keep upright. In a moment the shorter man managed to pull away, but, whether by accident or design, the other moved after him and grasped at the ornament that hung about the first soldier's neck. He wrenched at it, the light-haired youth stumbled forward, and then in the same moment the chain snapped, both soldiers staggered precariously—Fiona's dream-self attempted to reach out and steady them—and the one whom she thought she recognized fell forward into the quagmire. The mud eagerly swallowed him up and would not allow him to regain his footing.

Fiona opened her eyes. She was not in a sweat as usual, nor was her heart pounding; she was quite calm. With regained consciousness the dream was clear to her, and with a slight flutter in her belly she knew what it had meant: it had shown her the fate of Giovanni's cross, and what was left now but to regain it? Thus she decided and then rolled over and fell asleep again. It was not until that morning that the full import of the dream struck her—that, if this dream was as true as her others, some French soldier was in possession of her brother's cross and that the reclamation of the heirloom would mean sailing to France. And yet these thoughts did not dissuade her but only made her angry and stubborn and more set on her task than before.

She rang for Mary, and when the maid arrived Fiona asked, "Has the king returned from France yet, do you know?"

Poor Mary, who had dealt with a great deal in the past two weeks, no longer felt at all surprised by her mistress' bizarre questions. "No, mistress, I think he is still in Calais. But," she added, as she recognized the familiar look of frustration in Fiona's face, "I daresay he'll be coming home soon. So the people in the town are saying."

Fiona set her chin in her hands, her hair falling in disorder over her shoulders, her dressing gown rumpled, and her bare feet swinging above the floor like a child's as she sat on the bed. "How long is a trip to London at this time of year?" she asked presently.

"Oh, at least three days, mistress, if the carriage doesn't upset, or a wheel get stuck in the mud."

Fiona shivered at the last word. She frowned, allowing Mary to lead her to the dressing table and set her down on the bench. Her thoughts continued on the line of her questions, but because she was silent, the maid hoped there would be an end to the subject. Just before Mary had finished braiding her hair, however, she went on as before, "If I wished to see King Henry about … an important matter, but he was still in France, who would I arrange an audience with?" She seemed more to be pondering aloud than asking the servant a question, but Mary hesitantly suggested,

"A duke or earl, I should think; perhaps one of the king's brothers."

Fiona made no reply for a time, but at last shook her head. "No, *they* are all in France as well. Who rules the country," she continued musingly, "when the king is away?" She remained silent until Mary had finished her preparations then sat for a little longer looking at herself in the foggy, crude mirror. It was not a new experience for her to see herself every morning when she got up, for as the new housekeeper she had taken residence in these chambers, which had been her mother's, on her thirteen birthday, but it still interested her to see that pale, freckled face that was her own peering back at her from the glass. This morning, however, she looked at herself and was surprised to find shadows under her eyes and lips that sagged into a frown at both corners, a face that looked older than her few years. She tried to smile, but the expression became distorted and she turned away.

After breakfast, which she did not feel like eating at all, she called the house steward into the dining hall. "Edwin," she began, "if I were to sell the estate and the servants, how much might I gain?"

Edwin, who was a work-worn but cheery fellow in his declining years, expressed no surprise but was all business. "Would the horses and the carriages be sold as well, mistress?"

After considering a moment, Fiona replied with more confidence than she felt, "The larger carriage and the black charger may be sold."

The steward whistled through his nose and worked the numbers on his fingers while Fiona tried to calm the fright that beat in her head. She was not sure what she would do should Edwin try to cheat her and hoped that his long ties to the family would keep him honest if nothing else would.

At last the man looked up and pronounced his number. Fiona, who knew nothing of such matters, could not have said whether it was reasonable or not; she merely nodded. "What if I were to free the servants?" she suggested impulsively.

"Hmm … Hrmm…." Edwin peered thoughtfully at the oak beams overhead. He dropped his head again and gave a price not much less than the first. "But where would they go if you were to free them? Sometimes, m'lady, it is easier to be a servant and be safe under one man's lordship than to be at liberty in the world and prey to all."

Fiona could once again do nothing but consent. "I can put you in charge of these affairs, then?"

The steward smiled, showing a set of teeth that were whiter than was to be expected in such a harsh face. "Of course, madam," he bowed. "Your family's property is safe in my hands."

Liking his manner, the fifteen-year-old girl trusted him and expressed it with another nod. "That will be all," she concluded, but her attempt to sound like a mature head of the household failed.

When Edwin had gone, she crossed her arms on the table and laid her head on them with a sigh. It would be a relief to be rid of the property; she knew nothing of buying and selling, the discipline of servants, the planting and harvesting of crops. If left under her hand, she had no doubt but that the whole of the estate would lose its worth. Once more she felt the vulnerability of a woman without father, brother, husband, or friend. The weight of responsibility was too great for her to carry, and she knew it. She was but a girl, a girl who should have had a husband to watch out for her and protect her and servants who feared that man's voice and thus would do her bidding. Without a strong lord's hand, the servants would rebel.

These thoughts consoled as much as frightened her, for they allowed her to rest in the decision to give up this place. It still pained her to walk through the rooms with Edwin and appraise them without bias when she had memories of every one. The very floors made her think of Giovanni and how they used to chase one another throughout the house or play at dice before the fire in the great room. The thought of another woman wearing her mother's jewellery, which she could still remember glistening around the olive throat, was painful; the knowledge that soon someone else would be sleeping in Giovanni's chambers was almost too great to bear. Even thinking of another man reading in her father's study hurt.

"Mistress?"

Fiona blinked, surprised out of her reverie over a toy lamb that had been hers. "What? Oh, yes, of course. I'll be right there."

SHE NAIVELY HOPED THAT the process of selling the estates could be concluded in no more than two days, but on the morning of the third day, when Edwin heard her express this wish, he laughed good-naturedly. "Two days? Luck will have been with us if we can finish this business in a week."

"A week?" Fiona stared aghast.

"Aye, mistress. These things can take months, in fact."

Nothing ever goes as one wants it to, and so Fiona was learning. She wanted to leave as soon as possible for London; her trip could not be delayed, and this much she said.

"Perhaps," Edwin began delicately, "perhaps you might leave the estate's affairs in my hands and make your journey, and I shall handle it all for you. Would that be acceptable?"

Fiona was young, but she was not quite a fool. Her eyes narrowed. To leave a servant, even one so helpful and willing as Edwin, unattended for many days was inviting trouble; if and when she returned, she was sure to find the property in disarray and the steward off with her money. She sighed aloud without thinking.

"Oh, I see now," the steward said, his broad face creasing into a frown. "Yes, you're wise not to trust a man who seems to want to help; they're the ones who turn on you at the last minute. Well now, what you have to decide is which is more important: your journey or your property."

This seemed sound advice and not what one might expect from a thief. Still, the prospect of fortune does strange things to men; was that not the very cause that the lords in Southampton had attempted to betray the king three months prior? A man, Fiona thought to herself, could be perfectly friendly and helpful and devoted one day and, when faced with money, turn traitor the next without so much as a moment's notice.

On the other hand, her thoughts ran on, *what does money mean to me? Am I to admit that money means more to me than Giovanni does?* One more thought of the silver cross hanging from her brother's neck was enough to make up her mind.

"I will leave the estate in your hands, then," she said, her voice rather more timid than usual.

The white smile flashed again. "Very well," said Edwin, visibly pleased. "Shall I tell John to ready the coach?"

Fiona glanced out at the position of the sun. She was not sure of the location of villages along the way and wondered where they would sleep, but she was unwilling to express her ignorance, so she merely said, "We will leave in the morning."

†

The next day Fiona awoke to the sound of the coach wheels ringing on the stones outside her window and the voices of servants as they packed. Mary had not yet come in to wake her, but she found herself too alert to go back to sleep, so she rose and had the maid dress her. As she went down the corridor in the direction of the dining hall, she glanced once or twice into the rooms on either side. Most were bare, for the servants under Edwin's direction had begun to move things out.

The old nursery was the last room she looked at; it was cold and empty, black ashes lying on the hearth and devoid of all the familiar childhood toys save for one roughly carved hobbyhorse that sat in a corner. Fiona impulsively stepped inside the room.

"Your breakfast will be ready soon," Mary objected half-heartedly.

"I'll come in a minute," was all Fiona replied, and she shut the nursery door in her maidservant's face. When the servant's footsteps had receded, she ran to the little rocking-horse, knelt beside it, and flung her arms about it in a burst of passionate weeping. She felt a kinship for the little toy that no one wanted anymore, sitting all by itself in the big bare room. The big painted eyes were mournful on the wooden face and they seemed to say, "What has happened? Everyone loved me, and now I'm all alone. What has happened? Can you tell me?"

For some time Fiona indulged her girlish desire to cry, but it soon became clear that if she did not leave soon, someone would come and find her like this. She caressed the toy once more as she rose, whispering, "Things will get better for you. Things will get better for you...."

The preparations for the journey were soon finished, for Fiona would be taking little with her. She was going alone except for the coach driver; though Mary may have felt some little guilt over this arrangement, she was certainly glad not to have to go with her mistress. As for Fiona, she was so terrified that she could eat little breakfast, and that which she did threatened to come up again. The prospect of riding alone along provincial roads combined with little knowledge of her destination, the chaotic and dirty city of London, would have been enough to make her shrink from the journey had it been for any other reason; as it was, she swallowed hard, steeled herself, and entered the coach.

Only Edwin and Mary were there to see her off, and neither looked as downcast as one ought at a leave-taking. As the coach rattled out of the gates, Fiona leaned out her window and strained to gaze at the place once more. She had a curious fear that this would be the last time she would see it, rather like what she had felt when Giovanni left. She collapsed back onto her seat and shut her eyes, and despite the discomfort of the coach, she was able to doze off.

The sun had only been up for an hour or so when she awoke and straightened in her seat, blinking against the light. There was no one to ask about their location, so she began trying to guess from the landscape. The scenery did not change much from time to time; though it was but early November, winter was already upon them and everything was buried in a deep white blanket. Stiles could sometimes be seen peeping from the banks, and when they passed villages Fiona could see the thatched roofs of the cottages brushed with snow. She saw the sunlight glittering through the icicles that clung to the tree branches and played at trying to spy the red holly berries on their snowy bushes; once she caught a glimpse of a crowd of children clipping mistletoe and holly branches with which to decorate their homes, and when the coach rolled by them they all stopped their task and waved cheerily. One of the girls in the group, not more than eight years old, was seized by a sudden wave of merriment and ran after the carriage, holding up a holly branch within Fiona's grasp. And Fiona found as she accepted it, the contact lasting for but half a second before the coach pulled away, that she could smile and laugh back at the child without awkwardness.

Soon, however, Fiona's spirits sank back into moroseness and her thoughts preceded her to London. She was unclear what she would do when she did arrive; to seek an audience with the king, even if he had returned from Calais, would be like aspiring to stand in the throne room of God Himself and talk to Him—it could not be done. And yet she knew that there was a ban on ships travelling to or from France, so that without written permission from the king himself, there was no way she could cross the Channel.

The coach jerked and flung her back against her seat. Every single part of her body was aching already, and it was still morning of the first day; she groaned at the thought of how she would feel when the journey was done. "Oh dear," she said aloud, or tried to—a hole in the path shook the carriage again so that her teeth chattered over the words. She rearranged herself on the wooden bench that was but sparsely covered in cushions and tried to attend to the countryside again.

By mid-afternoon the body of the carriage, which had appeared small at the outset, seemed to have shrunken. The smell of horse filled the car so that Fiona could think of little else, and the small window of fresh, clean air no longer seemed enough. She leaned out as far as she could, but the scent still overwhelmed her. Her head spun; she had never taken a long trip in a coach and saw now why others avoided it as much as they could.

"Coachman? Coachman!" she cried up to the servant driving the horses, but he could not hear her over the commotion of the horses and the vehicle's rattling chains and metalwork, and she was obliged to ride on without stopping.

Fiona was glad that evening came so early, for she was certain that if she had had to ride for another hour she would have been sick. The coach pulled into a little village by the wayside and stopped outside the local inn. Fiona's muscles ached so terribly that when she went to step out of the coach she stumbled and nearly fell in a mud-puddle, had to stand leaning against the entryway to regain the feeling in her limbs, and could not even long for a soft bed to lie down in. No fat, comfortable tick, she was sure, could ever soothe these cramps. As for supper, the thought sickened her. The strong aroma of stew and coarse wine reached her nostrils as she paid the innkeeper for a room, and she had to turn away to avoid unleashing her stomach's contents on the man's boots.

Her pains kept her up most of the night and no position could lessen the throbbing of her newly-tested muscles. She began to drift off in the wee hours of the morning, but in what seemed only a few minutes a maid was shaking her by the shoulder and drawing her back to a consciousness of her own body. She rubbed the sleep from her eyes and stood, only to give a yelp and come crashing the floor as the fire in both legs rekindled. There she crouched for several moments, biting her lip; the sensation in her muscles was that of two rough materials being scraped mercilessly together over and over. She had to crawl to her pile of clothes and don most of them from where she sat on the floorboards, and when she had to stand it was like torture.

It took her longer than it ought to make it downstairs, clinging to the rail as she went. The coach and driver waited for her outside. "Breakfast, ma'am?" the innkeeper suggested as Fiona eased her aching limbs across the room.

She replied with something not quite ladylike; how could she put food in her stomach when that organ was as uncooperative as the rest of her?

"It's a long trip to the next lodging," the man pursued, eager for the few pennies more it would put into his pocket. "All day riding on an empty belly? 'Tis not suited for a lady."

Thoughts of horse sweat and dung rose in Fiona's mind along with thoughts of a revisited breakfast on the walls of the car; it was not appealing to her. Still, the man would not leave off urging her until she had accepted some cold pheasant turnovers and a loaf of bread for the journey and laid her coins on the counter. Then he smiled and rubbed his hands appreciatively and thanked her and bid her God-speed as she left.

"A'right, mistress?" the coachman asked from his lofty seat; he was not one of her father's servants but had been hired for the journey, so Fiona knew nothing of him. She replied in the affirmative. "I say, ye'd best not be eatin' too moch," he added, glancing at the handkerchief of food she held; "a coach like this can jolt a grown man's belly out." His curious accent flattened the vowels of his words in a way that Fiona had never heard before, and despite her aches and pains she managed a wan smile.

She struggled into the carriage and the driver cracked his whip over the horses' backs; out of the village they bounced, the belly of the car swaying between the wheels. Fiona, feeling even more ill than she had the day before, dozed on and off but woke whenever they crashed over a particularly large rut; with the state of the roads, these came in intervals of about fifteen minutes. Yesterday's sunshine had melted the snow and flooded sections of the path so that twice before noon the wheels became stuck and the coachman had to extricate them. Fiona shivered every time she heard the sound of the sucking mud underneath her.

The sun passed its zenith and Fiona began to feel an emptiness in her belly that did not displace, but only added to, the former discomfort. She stared miserably at the packet of food in her hands, knowing that it would only make her feel worse, but then wondering if that was possible. Just as she had decided that it was not and that it would be best to eat, the car once more lurched and flung her against first one door and then the other. The driver cursed and she leaned out the window to see what had happened.

"Stuck in the mud again, ma'am!" he called from where he stood ankle-deep in the mire next to the back right wheel. He jerked his thumb toward the nearby set of houses and added, "I don't think we can reach the next village afore sundown at this rate; best to stop here for the night and get the horses reshod, what?"

"But it's only just afternoon!" Fiona cried. Much as she disliked travelling in a coach, she was eager to reach London as soon as possible.

"I don't think ye'll be wantin' to ride at night, tho'," the man replied, somewhat out of his Irish temper. "And I don't moch care for the idea of gettin' the horses and the coach stolen by robbers."

What he said was true, but Fiona was aggravated by his way of speaking to her and her own patience was wearing thin. "It is I who am paying you!" she cried angrily, flushing to the roots of her hair. "And whose coach is this?"

"Yours," replied the driver, "but 'tis my neck you'll be riskin'!"

"And my own," she snapped hotly. "'Tis too early to stop; we'll go on."

He muttered vindictively under his breath as he heaved the carriage out of the muck and climbed back into his seat, but Fiona could not hear what he was saying. She slumped back into the car and glowered out the window, not liking the look of the black clouds on the horizon but unwilling to retract her command.

They had no more trouble with the wheels, as they were passing through a forest where the sunlight had not penetrated, and Fiona began to feel that her decision was a wise one. Still, as the coach kept rattling and the trees kept stretching out before them and the sun kept getting lower, her doubts returned.

Once the coachman hauled the horses to a halt and turned around to say, "And if ye are wantin' to go back, well ye'd better thought of that back when I advised it, so don't go botherin' me about your hindsight." And before Fiona could retort he had straightened himself and called for the brutes to keep moving.

By early evening she was sure of the foolishness of her order. Men and beasts seemed to lurk behind every bush, the shadows stretching across the forest floor took the shape of monsters, and even the horses began to lay back their ears and shy. She meekly ate her turnovers while keeping a frightened eye on the road, waiting for the ambush that was sure to come. When a creature cried somewhere in the deeper woods, she was so nervous that she dropped her supper on the floor of the car and had to feel for it again in the darkness.

The hours drew on and the moon, not yet obscured by the storm rolling in, gleamed on the path in places where the foliage was sparser. The dead leaves rustled on the ground, sending shivers up Fiona's spine. Indeed, of the three—horses, mistress, and driver—the coachman seemed the most at ease despite his apprehensions, for the two times that Fiona gathered enough courage to lean out and look at him, he was sitting as straight as before and allowing himself no anxious scans of the area. For a moment Fiona felt ashamed of her own cowardice—but when a dog howled to the south, she flinched anyway.

Nothing dire happened in the next two hours and Fiona managed through sheer exhaustion to fall asleep. It was not yet morning when she opened her eyes, but they had come out of the woods and she guessed that the sun had not but an hour or so before it rose. The driver pulled the carriage up beside a creek to allow the horses to drink and she alighted shakily, still able to pronounce with more pride than she felt, "See there, your neck is safe enough."

He only glowered at her, his face sour as curdled milk. His expression seemed to say, "Oh, aye, but there's still plenty o' time for a robbery afore morn!"

Finding him disconcerting, Fiona passed the time by walking beside the edge of the path in search of winter flowers. It occurred to her as she shook the snow off a chain of bryony that her thoughts had been little occupied with either Giovanni or the cross since yesterday; she had been more concerned with the state of her own body. Guilt washed over her at the realization, for she considered her task as much an avenging of her brother's blood as a simple retrieval of the heirloom.

"I must not," she murmured to herself; "I must not let anything distract me from my charge. Mary, Mother of Jesus, bless my mission!"

"Horses are ready to go," the man growled. "If'n ye want to waltz around playin' at makin' daisy chains, tho', ye be free to do so."

Despite his quaint accent, at that moment Fiona despised him with all the passion a girl of fifteen can feel. She flung down her chain of bryony and went back to the car with as vehement footsteps as she could produce with such shaky legs, and she did not speak to him for the rest of the trip.

NEARLY FOUR DAYS AFTER it had left Fiona's estate, the coach, bespattered with mud and its horses flecked with foam, rolled into the great city of London. Fiona could not gather an accurate image of the town because of the duskiness, but she was awestruck by the sheer greatness of the place. Everything was large: the buildings, the streets, the churches, and most of all, the Tower itself that she could but barely see from the city's gateway. She was surprised to see that people were still roaming the streets even though the watchman was calling out a late hour, and she swallowed her pride enough to ask the driver, "Why do they not go home?"

The man snorted; *he* had not forgotten his pride. "Home? What a naive little lass ye are! They haven't got a home, that's why. The streets're where they live."

Fiona subsided into the car, content to look out the window and wonder in silence. She had never seen so many people together, so much humanity in one place. It was like a summer fair at home but multiplied several times over.

"Well, here's the inn," the man interrupted grudgingly. "And the nicest one to find in this part o' England—not Ireland, mind. I doubt even you will ha' much to grumble about 'ere."

Fiona was too hungry and tired and sick of the smell of horse and the feel of mud to think of a suitable response, so she gave him a sleepy glare and crawled out of the car. Inside, she felt smaller than ever before; the room was crowded and most of the occupants were men. A large fire at one end of the inn kept the place warm and half-lit but also hazy from the smoke so that Fiona had a hard time finding her way about.

"Well now," began the innkeeper when applied to for a room, his brow furrowing, "I think we can find you a room. The inns are filling up around here; everyone wanting to be here when the king comes home, I expect. If you are," he added, "then you'll have some time to wait; he's not expected for another week at least."

Fiona assured him that she was only here on personal business. "Good, good," he nodded, but the way he looked at her shrewdly through his black eyes said that he would be glad to hear more of the business that brought such a young girl to London alone. He did not press the matter but led her upstairs to a front room that had a small window overlooking the streets but little else to recommend it. "I hope this will be all right."

His tone said that it was all they had, so Fiona nodded and paid. "Well," she said aloud after he left, shutting the door behind him, "at least I'm in London."

The thing to consider now was what to do next. Here she was in London, a girl without the least knowledge of the world and with money enough to make her prey to the dissolute men of the city, and she had a feeling that she would not long survive in this big place. With no comrades to turn to, gossip was to be her best friend, telling her the things she needed to know—perhaps not with full accuracy but with details enough for her to grasp what was necessary. Having determined this, Fiona went down the next morning to breakfast and instead of sitting in a darkened corner, away from the others, she tried to position herself as close to them all as she could.

"They crawl about like worms and when you cut one up, two appear," a wiry, middle-aged man on her right remarked.

"I would have thought the Wycliffe's burning would be enough to dissuade them," another replied. "But men will cling to their purpose with a will when they believe themselves to be right."

"Or are possessed by devils."

A third man jerked his head negatively. "They are stubborn and resilient, I'll grant you, but they're not demons. Confused and mistaken, if you will, but not Satanic."

"Oh, aye, stubborn they are," the second man replied comfortably. "Stubborn even when they're feeding the flames with their own bodies."

Fiona, seeing that they were not discussing anything of import to her, glanced around to the other parties in the room; one was playing at dice, two others engaged in no conversation at all, and the fourth was discussing the state of the city, crops, and other such layman's topics. She returned to the talk of heretics, as it seemed most likely to develop into a conversation about the king and the campaigns.

"The Church has her hands full keeping track of the heretics that spring up. Not just here, either: in France and all across Christendom, too."

"Aye, but what do you expect from France?"

Fiona guessed, from scraps of conversation she had picked up from her brother, that the men were discussing the underground, heretical sect of Lollardy in England. Giovanni had talked about them a great deal, but she had never been interested in religious matters enough to give more than an ear and half a mind to him. As far as she knew, they were radicals who denounced the excesses of Rome and who had incurred the harsh judgement of Henry IV, whose son now continued the persecution.

"—King Harry."

This last bit of a sentence brought Fiona back to reality with a start. She turned to her companions and listened carefully to catch their talk, which was less animated than before. They appeared to be talking of the king's return from France, which was expected sometime in the next three or four weeks. There were reports circulating constantly of Henry's ship having been spotted off the coast, but thus far they had been false alarms, and the people were growing impatient to see their victorious king. More and more of the middle-class Englishmen came to London each day, waiting for a glimpse of the returning Ares.

Since the conversation was not heading in its proper course without help, Fiona gathered her courage and prompted the discussion with, "I wonder that the King is willing to leave his country for so long."

The three men turned and looked at her in momentary surprise before one of them laughed, as if he could not think of another suitable response. "If kings were as cautious as you or I, lass, wars would never be fought nor won."

This was not the reply Fiona wanted. She continued, "But what of the civil matters? They still go on even in wartime."

The man looked as though he was not sure that they did, but he replied vaguely, "Oh, kings always leave a few trusted men to govern."

"And since Agincourt, the Duke of Gloucester has been dealing with those matters," the thin man contributed.

Ah! Now here was a bit of information that might help. "Oh, yes, Good Duke Humphrey. He was wounded in battle, wasn't he?"

The third man, who had been watching Fiona closely ever since she joined the conversation, bestirred himself and rumbled, "Aye, wounded in the leg. They said it was a nasty lesion, too, and bled copiously; the King sent him back to England as soon as possible. They say he limps still. Ah, when one thinks of the injuries a soldier receives in battle—all those cuts and slices, arms and legs hewn off...."

Fiona shuddered but clung to her purpose. "He's not in London himself now, is he?" she interrupted.

"No, in Dover. The sea air works wonders on open wounds, or so they say."

At this point the man who had spoken just before shoved back his chair and rose, towering over Fiona. For a minute she was terrified that he would do something to her, but he only stepped away from the table—perhaps disgusted by the thought of sharing it with a woman—and the conversation, apparently no longer interested in his companions' talk. As he moved from the board, Fiona was surprised by the strange way in which he walked but chalked it up to a trick of the firelight until she let her eyes wander to the man's booted feet; one, though clothed like its companion, was skewed to the right and dragged on its side to give him a curious, rakish stride.

She caught herself staring too late. The man also had noticed, and his eyes narrowed to slits in his rough face. He gave her a long, hard look, meditating on whether or not to speak, and then turned from her; but in a minute he returned again and, stepping closer to her chair, murmured, "A girl on her own should take care where she looks, no matter her intent."

Fiona blushed and dropped her eyes to her lap, feeling the hairs on the back of her neck rise. She was ashamed despite the fact that his tone, while not friendly, was neither offended nor menacing, and there was no one to speak up for her; the two other men only glanced away with impassive faces. The man left and she retreated from the table to a corner with her little store of information, not daring to remain where she was to gather more. There she sat for a good hour and a half and would have gone on sitting there for the rest of the day, though the others had long since left, had not one of the barmaids taken it upon herself to come over and smilingly suggest a few places in the city that Fiona might enjoy walking in. Fiona thanked her but declined.

"What, you be going to spend your whole time in the great city of London cooped up in a little inn? Come now, mistress, take a walk; 'tis not a bad day for one, winter though it is." The maid smiled widely again and darted away before Fiona could manage a response.

So, feeling very small and out of place, Fiona wrapped a shawl around her shoulders and hesitantly left the smoky inn. She stood on the grey street and looked about her for some time, trying to get her bearings and wondering how she would find her way back to her lodgings and how she would manage not to get lost in such vast an ocean of humanity. She closed her eyes and took once step forward, then another, and then another....

...And when she opened her eyes, she was standing in a crowd of people all moving in opposite directions. It was so disorienting that she nearly fell over; the only thing that stopped her was the fact that with so many counter-currents of people, she had no room to do so. She managed to locate the red sign that hung over the inn door and took care to keep in sight of it as she joined the majority of the mass in moving toward a set of shops.

It was these shops that brought Fiona her first taste of London's delights. She admired beautifully dyed cloths and silks imported from Italy, Cathay, and other far-off places; she gazed in awe at the delicate designs on a goblet at a silversmith's; she frankly coveted a jeweller's handiwork (which would have been considered only third-rate by a highborn lady); and she procured a small ivory-hilted knife that could be easily hid in her dress. She enjoyed herself so much that she moved farther and farther away from the inn, every now and then casting an anxious glance at the sign.

At noon the bells in the nearby cathedral all rang, sending a flock of grey-tinted birds flying from the tower. Her belly rumbled, but when she thought of going back to the lodging-house, she was reminded of the lame man and found the hunger pangs were not as bad as before.

"Can you spa' a coin, mistress?"

Fiona started from her thoughts and saw a young lad, not much shorter than herself, standing at an alley corner looking at her with a quaint expression of hunger and mischief. He wore mud-stained breeches and a torn white doublet, and his black boots were badly in need of a shine. Her heart went out to him, and she obligingly pulled out her money purse to shake out a few coins. In but a second, the lad leapt out, snatched the bag out of her hand, and made off into the dark alley like a bolt of lightning. She cried out and pulled the hem of her skirt up out of the dirt to run after the boy, but a powerful hand grabbed her arm and jerked her with enough force to send her falling back to splash her petticoats in a puddle.

"Let him go," her captor advised, "or you'll find more gone than just your purse."

Drawing herself out of the water, Fiona stood with her underclothes dripping and her shame mounting. Only her first day in the city, and already she had lost her coins to an ungrateful waif! "Oh!" she cried, forgetting herself and turning toward the man. She was too wretched and angry to form any other syllable. "Oh!" she said again.

The man moved out of the sunlight so she could see him properly. She noticed first that what had appeared to be a great deformity of his lower face was actually a dark, full beard, and then it came to her that this was the man from the inn.

"Oh!" said she for a third time, but with a different tone.

"Well? You had tongue enough at the tavern."

"I-I-" Fiona fumbled. "I'm sorry I stared then, sir. I-I hadn't meant to offend."

His eyebrows flickered up as if in scorn. "It was not for that reason I warned you. London is an inhospitable place when you are unprotected; that is all."

Fiona could see that now, from the boy's thievery to the man's jerking her and throwing her into a puddle, but all this she did not say. She stood shivering with anger, not cold, and the water dripped off her clothes to splash on the stone pavers. "I—thank you, sir," she managed at last, as he seemed to expect a response of some sort.

The man gave a noise like a snort and remarked, "You're a very foolish girl to be traipsing around the streets of London. No one would miss you if you disappeared—no one *would*, would they?"

Fiona pulled together a few shards of sensibility and gasped, "I don't see as that is your business, sir."

He nodded. "Well, at least you have some spirit," he conceded unwillingly. "But you're still a very silly creature. You ought to have a man to take care of you. Come back to the inn now; 'tis nearly an hour since noon."

"Why should I?" Fiona demanded brashly. She did not want this man, or any other person, to see her walking with her wet, heavy petticoats slapping against her boots, and she did not care to be told that she needed someone to protect her. Did she not know it herself? But there was no one. "Why should I?" she repeated.

The man regarded her in silence for several seconds then merely said, "Can you see the inn sign from where you stand?"

She looked around her with a rise of fear; the scarlet emblem was nowhere in sight. She was disoriented and could not have said whether the inn was to her right or to her left, and as she turned back to the man to swallow her pride and allow him to lead her back, he was just disappearing into the crowd. "Saints!" she ejaculated, and flung herself against the tide of bodies to pursue him.

She soon caught up and came alongside him, panting and tottering. He cast a sideways glance at her, saying, "So, you changed your mind."

Fiona said nothing and followed him meekly back to her lodgings. As they came up to the inn door, the man swung about and said, as if he had only just thought of it, "There are ruts and hollows all over London's streets and it is not unusual for newcomers to step in them."

He meant, Fiona guessed, that the sight of her gleaming wet boots and muddied hem would not attract any ridicule, and she felt grateful. But then she remembered that it was he who had made her to stumble into the water, and she felt another twinge of irritation. "I ought to go and see my coachman," she said stiffly, and, drawing back as he went inside, she turned to the building that was the inn's stables and hurried toward it. Here was where the drivers slept, to be near the horses in case of thieves or fire, and she found her hired coachman in the room partitioned off behind the stalls. He sat with his feet up on a bale of hay, holding a mug of poorly brewed ale in his fist, and he did not stand when Fiona entered; perhaps he had already had more of the drink than was good for him.

"Have the horses been well looked after?" she asked first; it seemed proper.

The Irishman twitched his nose and frowned. "I know the care of horses, mistress," he replied bluntly.

Fiona ignored his tone. "We will be heading for Dover in the morning," she said, "so see that the horses are ready."

"Dover!" the man stared. "Why, I havena been paid for my trip here, let alone Dover! I be hired for your carriage, which means I take pay for my trouble."

Fiona felt a quiver run through her and she choked. The importance of her lost purse suddenly struck her; how could she explain that she had no more money to pay for her own food and lodging than she had to pay this man? She swallowed hard and quavered, "I have no more money."

"Indeed! Then ye have no more coachman, for I cannae drive ye on a mere promise of money. Ye shall have to find ye'r own way to Dover now."

Fiona was shocked at being so spoken to by a man so far beneath her. The other men chuckled underneath their breath and she heard one comment on her soggy skirt; she flushed scarlet, but nothing rose to her lips that she could say. She faltered, angry, but the coachman's face was impassive and there was nothing she could do to make him understand her situation, for he had been too long in the world to trust the word of a nobleman's daughter. She left the stables without another word, shamed.

The barmaid met her inside, her smile as pleasant as ever. "Well, did you have a nice stroll? I say, the wind's put some colour in your cheeks. Oh, step in a puddle, did you? Ah, happens to everyone; this time of year, 'tis quite impossible to avoid it. The maid upstairs will help you change so as you don't catch cold, and I'll get a bowl of stew ready for you—off you go, now!"

Fiona was bundled upstairs, changed, and bundled back down again. She spent the rest of the day inside, for the lame man went out directly after dinner and she feared running into him again beyond the inn doors. Under the maid's advice, she had a rest and then returned to the main room to watch the few remaining men play at dice and argue over trifles. Thus she wiled away her time until the supper hour drew near, and the bearded fellow returned, striking up a conversation with the same two men as before. With the rest of her hours spent avoiding him religiously, Fiona found that the time to retire came faster than expected.

THE MAID WOKE HER early the next morning, as ordered, and she ate alone just as the sun was creeping in at the foggy, smudged windows. She had already been out to the stable, and not only had the coachman been true to his word in saying he would not take her, but he had made off with both her carriage and her horses. She sat with her head on the table and listened to the dull throb inside her temples, thinking, or trying to think, of a way to get to Dover and the Duke. The thought of walking occurred to her, but she was sure she could never make her feet take her so far; going home posed the same problem over an even greater distance. She thought of hiring a new coach with the promise of later pay, but while it might work in another town, there was little possibility of finding such a man in this corrupt place. Her only bit of jewellery left was an emerald pendant of her mother's that she was saving—if possible, to keep; if not, to use as a bribe to see the duke. No other ideas occurred to her, and still she sat hopelessly in the same position. *If these*, she reflected bitterly, *are the kinds of blessings the Virgin Mother bestows, I can do better without them.*

The sun was up and other lodgers were beginning to come in for their breakfast. Fiona raised her head to look at them, hoping one might have a face that showed a kind enough heart to be willing to grant her this kindness. She saw a balding man who wore a frivolous kind of hat of last year's fashion to cover his smooth pate; a well-dressed couple, the woman looking arrogant and the man asinine; about half a dozen persons of unremarkable appearance; the lame and bearded man of yesterday, looking as grim as ever; and the gaunt gentleman with whom the last always conversed. It was an unpromising assortment of individuals.

"No, no, sir!" cried the bearded man, quite loudly and adamantly. "I tell you, I cannot; I am leaving directly."

"Leaving, eh? Where to?"

"Dover, sir."

Fiona sat up straight; if she had been a dog, she would have pricked her ears. She forgot herself and came rushing from her corner, hands clasped eagerly. "Oh!" she cried, as she always seemed to be saying to him; "oh, *are* you going to Dover?"

The man was obviously shocked, too shocked to say anything.

"Oh, please do take me! I was just on my way there, but my driver has gone off with my coach and I have no other way to get there. Say you will!"

"Girl," the man began, regaining his voice, "you are a defect of Providence. I cannot say whether bad luck follows you or you follow it. What makes you think I would be willing to take you to Dover?"

Fiona was not sure, but she had found an opportunity and would not easily let it go. "But if you are going, it cannot be much trouble for you to take me along. Out of charity, do!"

"And what if I feel no charity toward you? I have gotten you out of one scrape already; why another?"

But it appeared that he did not, in fact, mean it. He regarded her for a long moment after he finished talking, eyebrows shoved down into a thoughtful scowl; his companion leaned forward and said good-naturedly, "Come now, you are both going to Dover, after all. As she says, you would have no trouble carting her along with you." The bearded man did not look as though he were paying attention to the words, but when the other had finished he seemed to make up his own mind and, jerking his head at Fiona, relented with, "All right then, girl, you can ride in my coach. Nay, stay your flowing gratitude, I do not want it! Keep your tongue between your teeth and don't be chattering on like some saucy squirrel. Be off!"

Fiona backed away, delighted despite his wrathful tone. It took awhile for her joy to abate enough for her to consider the detriments to be had in a two or three day ride with that man. He was sour as green apples, and besides that, he was a man. What self-respecting woman would ride in a stranger's coach? She had returned to her state of depression by the time the man came to collect her and was as disinclined to talk to him as he was to talk to her. They sat in the car on opposite sides and corners, each looking out their window without a word.

"Well," remarked the man finally, "this is an awkward situation."

Fiona said nothing but shifted closer to the wall of the compartment. They bumped and rattled along over rocks that made her teeth chatter and ruts that made her jolt out of her seat, adding to the discomfort by sending the two falling onto each other's side of the carriage. Fiona took to clinging to her window edge, vainly trying to keep some distance between herself and the man.

The other cleared his throat as they were going over a smoother stretch of road, these being the only times one could be heard in the car, and remarked, "You see now why you would have done better to seek other means of transportation."

She would rather have had some more comfortable means of travel, but at least this would land her in Dover. This last she said aloud, somewhat coldly.

"And what makes reaching Dover so important?"

Fiona hunkered down in her corner and pretended not to hear, as they were once more going over a rough section. Her companion later repeated his question, and she replied, "Personal business."

"Marriage?" the man asked bluntly.

She cast him an appalled glance, but quickly returned to her perusal of the landscape and did not answer.

"So then, you do not want to talk. Well enough, I suppose; you should not be too eager to talk to strangers." After a pause, during which he seemed to want a response, he added, "My name is David."

It was polite to return the favour, so she said, "Mine is Fiona."

"Ah," he murmured, as if somehow this enlightened him. He seemed to want to say more; after some hesitation, at last he shook his head. "It will keep," he said to himself, and spoke no more.

David's horses were, without a doubt, finer creatures than Fiona's, and they reached Canterbury an hour after nightfall that day. She was exhausted, her own trip having done little to harden her body and her worries having tired her mind, and even her escort began to nod off before they came into the town. The change of sound alerted him, and he directed the driver to head for one of the less expensive inns.

"I will be paying for your room, of course," stated David, and though his tone was that of a question, it was clear that he did not consider it one.

Fiona opened her mouth in pride, but the scrap of common sense that she had made her close it again. She was hungry despite the uncomfortable travel and would be destitute enough after he dumped her in the city; there was no reason for her stomach to be pinched now. She let him pay for both her room and her food, and she shut her eyes against the sight of the cold, metallic coins being placed, for her sake, on the tavern counter. She was not insensible of the favour he was doing her and yet could not bring herself to thank him aloud for it. She thought of other things instead.

Nine or so hours later, they were back in the coach and rumbling along in the darkness with the coachman straining to see the potholes in the path. Fiona was regretting that David had paid for her breakfast at all; she was feeling more ill than usual and twice thought with horror that her light breakfast was going to come up in her companion's lap. She managed fairly well until daybreak. The sudden glare off the snow, however, was too much, and she felt the bile rise in her throat and lunged for the door.

David, startled, called the carriage to a halt and held the door open for Fiona as she stumbled out into the ankle-deep snow. Falling to her knees, she crouched thus in the bushes and threw up more than she thought she had put in during the past twenty-four hours. The action did much to settle her stressed stomach and in a few minutes she crawled back into the coach, her head lowered in disgrace.

David said nothing at first but signalled for the coachman to drive on. "I hope you are feeling better," he then remarked.

She turned an even brighter shade of crimson and murmured, "I'm sorry."

"No need. Riding in a coach is no easy task for the weak of stomach."

Needless to say, this did little to lighten Fiona's shame, however David meant it. She was sure that she had had more embarrassments since she set out from the manor than she had experienced in all the previous fourteen years of her life, and she would have been grateful to be able to say as before, "I'm glad I've stayed at home." She shut her eyes and concentrated on an image of Giovanni's cross.

Around noon David carefully unfolded a handkerchief of titbits left from his breakfast: sausages, biscuits, bits of bacon rolled in dough, and a ripe, luscious apple. Fiona's mouth watered and her belly, so recently emptied, growled in protest.

"I would offer you some dinner," he was saying, "but I suspect your belly would not care for it."

She was at this point suffering no other ill effects from her sickness than a foul taste in her mouth and a continued sense of shame, the latter of which kept her from protesting. She could not keep herself from staring, though, and her stomach roared louder and louder. At last David raised his eyes and regarded her with one eyebrow crooked and his lip curling up in what could either have been a smile or a look of derision. Silently he offered her a biscuit, and she snatched it from him and devoured it.

In the mid-afternoon Fiona began to smell the sea air, and soon Dover showed itself on the horizon. She leaned out her window and strained to see better; she glimpsed the silvery bodies of gulls flying along the cliffs, the foaming, grey ocean meeting the sky, and the grey stone walls of the castle rising up proudly from the snowy hill.

"Careful," David remarked dryly. "With your luck, you're likely to fly out the window."

The sun was still up when they reached their destination. David ordered the coach halted on the outskirts of the town as though he did not want to be seen riding with a woman, and he opened the door for Fiona. Before she climbed out—he seemed rather in a hurry for her to do so—she paused to say politely, "Thank you for the use of your coach."

He twisted his mouth to one side and replied with his usual ill-will, "Well, I can't say it was a pleasure, but at least your bad luck did not happen to upset the coach and set robbers on us. Now go on and find some other poor unfortunate to curse." But before she walked away or the coachman drove the horses on, he held out his fist to her and said shortly, "For your journey home. Do not waste it." And when she dumbly held out her palm, he dumped a handful of groats into it.

As the carriage door shut and the horses trotted on, leaving Fiona alone once more, she stood in the road and stared down at the coins she held. They were new, she reflected idly, or almost new. There were not many of them but enough to hire a coach and driver to take her back home when her business was complete, or to the sea, if she was granted her request. She closed her fist around them and raised her head higher than before, beginning her walk the rest of the distance into Dover.

SHE ARRIVED. THAT WAS the first thing to be considered, she thought. The state of her arrival and what she was going to do now both came after this first thought, and the fact that she had arrived took precedence over them both. The first stage of her mission was completed, and the second stage would commence on the morrow. For the moment, she decided that it would be best to try to enjoy her position while her mind was not needs being occupied by sickness, lame men, urchin thieves, coachmen, and the lost ornament.

She found herself lodgings, parting jealously with one of her groats, and used the little bit of daylight left to take a walk along the cliffs. The salty smell and the fresh, chill breeze off the sea soothed her spirits, and the beauty all around her made her almost forget her purpose in coming. The chalk turned golden in the dying sunshine, and the ocean far below her was darkening into a grey-green, the crests translucent as they rose and foaming as they fell again. The gulls were coming to rest on the shelves of the rock face, a few still circling and diving and screaming overhead. Fishing boats bobbed close to shore, not allowed to venture far because of the king's ban on private sea travel in the Channel. It was all just as she had always pictured the White Cliffs, the one place that she had ever dreamt of travelling to.

Fiona slept better that night than she had in over a month and wholeheartedly agreed with the physicians who declared sea air to be the best medicine in the world. Her appearance for breakfast was late, and when she arrived downstairs she was almost cheerful—but not quite, for the thought of her pending interview, if interview there was to be, would not leave her alone.

"The Duke of Gloucester is staying at the castle, is he not?" she asked someone later. They nodded and Fiona felt her spirits rise; perhaps now, at last, she was getting somewhere.

Late in the morning she left her lodgings and walked the ridge to the Constable's Gate. It was a cloudless day and across the sea she saw the dark coast of France looming on the horizon, and the realization that she, though standing on England's shore, was within sight of the mainland of Europe surprised her. This rocky island was not so isolated as she had always believed. England and her enemy were separated only by a thin strait; nothing else lay between them.

As she thought, she drew closer to the wall that encircled the ancient city of Dubris; now she halted and peered up at it in awe. From a distance the castle had seemed small against the infinitude of the sky, but now it seemed to reach up and sprawl out over the peak of the hill with such imperial strength that Fiona felt lost and as small as an ant beside it. She found the east gate with difficulty and approached it querulously.

"Halt!" ordered the closest guard, a fine looking young man with bright blue eyes and a mouth chiselled into a mocking grin. "What is your business, mistress?"

Fiona glanced nervously from one man to another; they were all looking at her with bored curiosity. Overhead, other soldiers marched slowly along the walls as they did their rounds of the castle. "I'm here to speak with Duke Humphrey," she replied faintly.

"What, now?" The man leaned forward to hear better.

Fiona repeated herself, looking wretched about the whole thing.

"Oh, yes, everyone comes to see the Duke. Is he expecting you?"

Slowly, she shook her head.

The bright blue eyes narrowed. "How much money do you have then, lass? If you have enough, it might buy you an audience. If not, well then, you had best be running along now."

So, as she had expected, it had come down to money. With burning cheeks she recalled the stupidity that had cost her her purse in London. "I have one shilling left," she said, holding out her money bag.

The soldier and his companions laughed good-naturedly and waved the limp cloth away. "No, no, 'tis not enough," he replied with the same spiteful curl of the lip. He was about to order her away, but his eye caught the gleam of polished stone on Fiona's chest, and he twisted his head to one side like an impish bird. "What's the pretty bauble around your neck, then? Come, let us have it." He held out a hand for the necklace.

"No!" Fiona cried, too startled by his manners to stop and think about her reply. Something pushed her hard in the small of her back so that she stumbled forward almost into the soldier's arms, and his gloved hand caught the pendant as it swung and pulled it forward.

"Ai, emeralds! Why, this would fetch a pretty farthing. I tell you what, lass," this as he let her go; "I tell you what: an audience with the Duke in return for your jewels. Now come! Think about it a moment before you rage; 'tis not an unfair deal. Why, if you consider how much more Gloucester is worth than those stones, you're getting the better deal by far! What do you say, then?"

At that moment, Fiona wanted nothing more than to spit in the soldier's face and run away, but that wicked smile brooked no opposition. She unfastened the chain in silence and held out the pendant, dropping it in the sparse snow at his feet a moment before he reached out to snatch it away. "Let me see the Duke now," she said quietly, struggling to keep her composure.

The man twitched a shoulder in reply and leaned over to whisper something to one of his companions. The latter nodded and slipped away inside the building. In the space of time that followed, the soldier stared coolly, his companions continued pacing, and Fiona kept her head down and looked at the ground between her feet. The time seemed interminable, but at last the fellow returned and said a word to the blue-eyed man, who was apparently of higher rank, and he crooked a finger as a sign for Fiona to follow him.

Once beyond the gate, the two walked through the ramparts and came out in a great stretch of lawn that, Fiona now saw, took up the greater part of the walls' interior. All was coated in some layer of snow, the trees stark and the stones bare, but she guessed that it was a beautiful place to see in the high seasons of the year. They crossed the moat, whose water was thick and brown, and passed through another barricade and another lawn before entering the castle itself. With so many layers peeled off, Fiona found that the abode was not as grand as she had at first feared, though it still towered over her head.

"Come now, do you wish to see the Duke or not?"

Fiona dropped her eyes from the sheer walls and hurried to catch up with her guide. A great many winding staircases and twists and turns and large rooms followed until she had no idea where they had come from or even whether they were on the topmost level or the bottommost; she knew that if she were made to find her own way out again, she would be left wandering about the castle for days in search of an exit. The soldier no longer had to tell her to keep up but once ordered her not to follow so closely.

At last, with a suddenness that left Fiona blinking dazedly from the transition into bright sunlight, they came out onto a kind of parapet where a man—a nobleman, to judge from his manner of dress—sat with his back to them. A servant stood by him with a platter, and a scrawny hound sat with its long, pointed head in its master's lap, but they were the only others on the wall.

The soldier announced their presence with, "My lord? The woman who asked to see you."

The man turned to face them, and Fiona was surprised to see that the Duke of Gloucester was much younger than she had been expecting. He had a pale, pointed face with a thin nose, large eyes, and lips that seemed to want to twitch at all times. The middles of his ears curled outward and came back to his head again at the tips, and the hat he wore did nothing to improve their appearance. His expression was that of a kind and well-meaning man, but his eyes spoke of an indecisive nature. He was, in all respects, an unhandsome man.

He stood and faced her, leaning heavily on one leg as though his other pained him. He smiled pleasantly, his lips still twitching, and waved a hand for the soldier to leave. When he had gone, the Duke beckoned Fiona forward and said, "Well, well, you want to speak with me about something?"

The meeting was without any of the ceremony that she had expected. There were no great halls hung with tapestries, no trains of noblemen, no pomp, and nothing fine about it at all. Fiona was not sure whether to be pleased or thoroughly taken aback. She came forward and the bitch-hound raised her head and curled her thin, grey lips back in a snarl, her hackles rising as thick tendrils of drool flooded from her open mouth. Fiona halted.

Shoving the dog back with his wounded leg and wincing as he did so, Gloucester once more called her forward and then collapsed into his chair again with a groan shoved from between his teeth. Fiona obeyed and came to stand before him. "What is your name, then?" he asked, his nostrils widening in a heavy breath. He seemed to be trying to recognize her from among the regulars at court.

"Fiona, my lord; daughter of Sir Madoc of Wales."

"Ah, yes," the man replied, as though he had already known this. "You have something you wish me to do for you, I suppose?"

"Yes, my lord."

There was a space of silence while Gloucester, digging his fingers into the folds of his hound's skin, waited expectantly. When the pause became too long he prompted, "Yes?"

Fiona hesitated a moment longer before remarking slowly, "They say you were wounded at Agincourt."

A flicker of something passed across Gloucester's eyes, but he only nodded.

"My brother died in that battle."

"Then he died an honourable death," the Duke assured her with the same kind, twitching smile. Fiona found that the expression was not so repulsive as she had thought at first, for the man truly seemed to feel for her and was not merely speaking diplomatically.

Fiona closed her eyes for a moment, listening to the crying of the gulls and trying not to think of her brother drowning in the thick, bog-like mud. "They sent his body back for burial," she continued, trying to keep her voice from wavering, "and all was as it should have been, but he was missing the heirloom he always wore: a silver cross."

Gloucester frowned. "Perhaps it fell in the battle," he suggested.

She thought back to her dream, clear as the summer sky in her memory still, and slowly shook her head. She guessed wisely that the Duke would not believe her if she claimed a vision, so she went on, "I want to request safe passage to France."

The Duke leaned forward in his chair, his eyes seeming to pop out of his head. "Passage to France?" he repeated incredulously. "Girl, private travel between England and France has been forbidden by the King for all but warships. I am sorry, but I can by no means grant you this."

For all his appearance of vacillation, Gloucester sounded determined. "Oh, but you don't understand!" Fiona cried out, taking a step closer and laying her hand on the arm of the nobleman's chair. "I must find it; I cannot live without it! You cannot understand how much it means to me. Please, grant me this!"

The Duke's lips twitched still more at her plea, but he said again, "I am sorry. I have not the power to break a law of the King's. Perhaps if you will remain here for awhile until King Henry returns, I can arrange a meeting for you."

Fiona fell back, her hopes crushed. She had not, she knew, ever really expected that passage would be granted; she was only a woman—a girl, at that—and her purpose sounded foolish. She had hoped, though! She cast down her eyes and turned away.

"Is that all?" Gloucester enquired gently. She nodded, and he gestured for the servant at his side to lead her out.

She was let out by the Constable's Gate, from which she had come in, and the blue-eyed soldier glanced up as she came into view. "Ah, and how did you fare, little lass? Have anything more for us?" And he looked so pointedly at her that Fiona grasped his full meaning. She did what she wished she could have done before: she walked slowly up to him and spat full in his face then whirled and ran away before he could gather his wits about him.

The run and the fresh air did not renew her spirits as before. She was flung into another bout of bitterness and despair and spent the day huddled miserably on her tick. Her thoughts were divided between how she would get home and how she could ever make herself live without Giovanni's cross. Her estates were as good as sold now; where was she to stay? All her plans had been dependent on her reaching France, and now she was even more lost than before.

With David's coins still lying warm in her pocket, Fiona had no trouble procuring a coach and driver to take her home. *To the manor,* she corrected herself; *it will not be "home" much longer.* Her stomach muscles firmer, the ride home was not as great a trial as before but no pleasanter. Her meeting with Humphrey had sunk her morale to the lowest degree, and her eyes stared blindly out the window of the car as she bumped along; she did not care to notice the landscape anymore.

Two weeks and a day after her setting out, the sweating, white-flanked horses heaved the muddy coach into the yard of the manor and Fiona limped from the car. She glanced pessimistically across the yard, but there was no evidence of any new inhabitants; at least Edwin had not sold the place out from under her. Inside, the story was different. Nearly everything was gone, from furniture to books, from tapestries to the last of her mother's jewellery to the old hobby-horse that had stood in the nursery. The halls echoed back her voice and felt cold as a tomb.

"Oh, mistress, you're back!"

Fiona turned to see Mary standing in the doorway to the kitchen, looking more startled than pleased. She looked the same as ever, and Fiona wondered how the past two weeks, which had seemed like an eternity to her, had not turned the maid's hair white and her face wrinkled. Strange to think that not even a month had passed since she had last been in this house. "Yes, Mary," she replied wearily. "Where is Edwin?"

"In the kitchens, ma'am. Oh, how was your trip, ma'am?"

The other shook her head viciously. "I don't wish to discuss it," was all she said, and then she pushed past the servant and walked to the kitchens. She found two of the house servants there in addition to Edwin, all grouped about the table and talking idly as was their wont. They all bowed and greeted her when she came in as though happy to see her though their expressions said otherwise. Fiona was too tired and drained to care; she beckoned for Edwin to follow her and left the room.

"I see the selling off of my father's things is going well?" she questioned as they entered the dining hall. Her voice did not sound like her own in the emptiness.

Edwin smiled proudly. "Yes, everything is going quite well, mistress. I trust your journey was—"

"How many of the servants have you sold?" Fiona interrupted. "And did you leave my brother's chamber alone, as I requested?"

The steward looked questioningly at her but only said, "About half, mistress. And no, mistress, the young master's rooms (God rest his soul) have been left as they were. If I may enquire, my lady, do you plan to leave the manor again soon?"

"I don't know, Edwin. I'm not sure; I—we shall see."

"Ah, well, the best thing to do is rest," he returned cheerfully. "Weeks spent riding in a coach is no enjoyable adventure, to be sure."

"No. No, it isn't. That is all, Edwin."

As she lay in bed that night, listening to the scraggly branches scrape across the walls outside and the wind howling down through the mountains, she decided that she would have to force herself to live without the cross. The very thought of it tormented her, but she had nothing else to do. She would go on living her life as before, trusting to Time to soothe the wound; surely Giovanni would have wished nothing more. Yet still, even after this conclusion, she tossed and turned and could not help but think of her brother's unavenged blood.

Long after midnight she fell asleep and dreamt the same dream as she had the night of Giovanni's burial. She was awakened by the maid shaking her and saying, "Wake up, mistress! 'Tis nothing but a bad dream."

Fiona's eyes flew open and she sat up, casting about her wildly. "What? What was it? Why are you waking me?" she demanded.

"You were screaming as though the very devil were after you, mistress," explained Mary, crossing herself as she spoke of the Evil One. "Do you not recall?"

Fiona only stared at her. She remembered her dream but nothing more. There had been nothing frightening about it, as far as she knew; certainly there had been nothing to wake her up in a sweat. She shook her head and rose, allowing the servant to dress her, and then she went back to her brother's room to be sure that Edwin had kept everything as promised. All was as before: his clothes hung in the wardrobe, generally colourless and unfashionable; his books lay on the floor on the far side of the bed, all coated in dust, some still lying open to passages; the mantelpiece over his hearth held various treasures, including a gold locket that held a rough sketch of himself as a toddler. The casement was opened and a chill breeze swept through the room, stirring the canopy's curtains. Everything was just how he had always kept it.

Fiona took the locket and slipped it into an inner pocket along the seam of her dress but left the rest of the room intact. She could not bear to think of selling her brother's things, nor could she imagine another man reading those books or sleeping in that bed or wearing those clothes. If she moved, these would come with her; if she continued her search.... She shook her head and went out, shutting the door softly behind her.

At the proper time, when the church bells were ringing, she went to Mass. She had not done so for a long time, but if she were to continue her daily pattern of life, this habit must be reinstated. She walked the short distance alone—the presence of the servants grated on her nerves. Upon arriving a little late, she took her seat at the back of the chapel and kept enough out of the way that no one would be obliged to look at her for long, but in sight of a few so that those in the neighbouring manor houses would see that she had come and not consider her a perfect heathen. God was not of great importance in a person's life, but Mass could not be done without.

As she sat there, listening with only a glancing interest to the priest's Latin readings that even he himself probably did not understand, it happened that the low-lying winter sunlight shot through the windows and fell in multihued shafts upon the carving above the man's head. It was of a body, whose face she could not see, hanging on a cross like that that Giovanni had worn. The figure had always struck her as being coarse and unpleasant and a strange thing to hang in such a beautiful minster, but now with a thrill all over her body she took it as a sign from a divine somebody: she was to continue her search.

In the middle of the service, Fiona rose and left.

"I am leaving again," she announced that day to Mary and Edwin, "and I doubt if I shall be coming back."

Mary gawked, but Edwin only smiled and looked as though he thought the plan a good one. "Where are you going this time?" he ventured to enquire.

headiness of the scent. Owen kindly held out a hand to steady her and she accepted. He led her to the back of the room, where a man whom she guessed to be in his mid forties, a younger man of about four-and-twenty, and a grey-haired seaman sat sharing their mead. They glanced up and hailed Owen as he came, and the first man raised a brow at Fiona. "Who's this, then?" he asked bluntly.

"She would like passage on a ship," Owen replied for her. A look passed between himself and the other man, and the latter's brow twitched again.

"Really?" he hummed. "What is your name, girl?"

"Fiona, sir," she said meekly, more than willing to let the burly Owen do her talking for her.

"And your father?" She gave her family name and he seemed pleased. "Ah, a Welshman, was he? Well, that makes business easier. Owen, pull up a chair for the girl." The two other men made room for her and her companion, casting curious glances at her as she sat. The first man introduced them, waving a hand to the younger man and saying, "Llewelyn, my son and namesake, whom you may call Llew, and that seadog over there is my first-mate, Carag. Owen here is my son-in-law. Now, where is it you wish to go?"

Fiona glanced from one man to the other, but they did not have the look of conspirators. All were honest-looking, open-faced men, and she began to feel that they could be trusted; the powerful seas demanded honesty of men. "I need to get to France," she said finally.

"Yes, I thought as much," Llewelyn nodded. "And I suspect you know of the ban your king has put on sea travel?"

"I would not have come here otherwise."

A hint of a smile flickered across the captain's mouth. "The king has commandeered all sea-worthy vessels," he continued.

"What makes you think I have a ship?"

Fiona looked at him hard, her brow furrowing, and said presently, gesturing to Owen, "He would not have brought me here if there was nothing you could do for me. And you seem the type to outfox such an edict," she added impulsively.

Llew gave a sharp, barking laugh and then smiled, stroking his stubble. "Ah," was all he said at first. Then he continued, "You would pay?"

"I have money," Fiona assured him. "How much would you want?"

Llewelyn glanced at his companions as though seeking their advice, then named a price. Fiona balked at first but silently turned away and drew her purse from her dress, counting the desired amount and casting it on the table. "Take me to France."

The captain considered the money in silence, still running a finger across his jaw thoughtfully. Presently he scooped the coins into his hand, took Fiona's wrist in his other, and dumped them into her palm again. "I shall never let it be said that I took pay from a woman for giving her safe passage where she needed to go," he said quietly. "Come along, men; the ship needs readying. Carag, show the lady where she can rest for awhile."

The three men left and Fiona, following Carag mechanically, stared at the coins in her hand. Perhaps not everyone in the world was self-centred after all.

She slept till late into the evening, and then Owen was there to wake her. "The ship's ready," he told her and bade her follow him along the wharfs. It was dark and she relied on him entirely for guidance through the maze, but still when they reached a certain point he turned and, holding out a handkerchief, said, "The captain asked that you be blindfolded before we bring you aboard. No offence meant; but should you turn out to be a spy, he doesn't want you knowing where our beauty lies at anchor." He smiled apologetically, his teeth flashing for a second.

After the bandage had been tied about her eyes, Fiona clung to Owen's hand and trembled lest she lose her footing and fall into the harbour; the sound of the water lapping at the docks was not very comforting. Once she did slip, one foot sliding into the water, but the seaman lifted her up (she thought he would break her arm) and set her on shore again without a word. She gasped a thanks, and the noise he made in reply sounded like a laugh.

Soon Fiona was placed in what she guessed was a rowboat and they began to move across the water. With her eyes shut and the ground beneath her feet no longer solid, she felt as dizzy and disoriented as a newly fledged bird. She heard the clatter of two wooden objects touching, a man's call overhead, and then Owen was helping her up from one direction and another pair of hands were helping her from another and she was at last deposited on a surface that reeked of fish and mould.

"Ah, there's our passenger!" cried a voice somewhere above her and straight in front of her. "Owen, get that handkerchief off the lady's face. There now."

Fiona's eyes were unbandaged and she found herself sitting on the deck of a ship directly in front of the captain's feet. He helped her up and swept a hand to indicate everything around them, saying, "Well, here she is. Not much to look at, but she's sturdy enough."

Pushing her hair back from her face, she looked around. The brig was indeed not much to look at—nor smell, either—as she was but a small craft built for fishing. Her timbers creaked with the movement of the waves, her one sail snapping eagerly in the fresh breeze as though she were straining to be out of port. Fiona could not see much, so she trusted the captain's proud words and hoped the ship would hold together out in the Channel.

Fiona was blindfolded again and deposited in a cabin below decks while the ship heaved out to sea, lest she recognize the English coastline enough to guess where the boat had lain hidden away. Her belly rocked with the vessel and she was already feeling the effects of sea travel. When they were far enough out she was allowed to come back on deck and watch the progress, as much as she could see in the darkness, so long as she kept out of the way. It was a clear night for November and the wind was brisk, and the ship maintained a slight, steady larboard tack.

"Why were you so willing to give me passage?" she asked the captain after he had ordered the other sail hung out and stood idle at the bow.

His eyes twinkled and he shrugged. "The best fishing is on the western coast of France," he explained. "Many an evening we set sail for those regions, spend the night fishing, and lie concealed in the coves till the next night. Then we sail home; so we make our living. This is but a quick trip for us."

"What if you are caught?"

"I don't think we will be," he replied flippantly. "King Harry is too busy with his affairs in France to notice a small fishing boat here." And then he was called away by Carag, so Fiona could not question him further.

The ship glided through the open sea for no more than an hour or so, and then they switched tack and moved along with a stretch of French coast on their larboard side. It was altogether not a long trip, but the night silence prolonged the minutes so that the voyage seemed interminable. At last, however, they were bobbing off a secluded shore with the rowboat ready to be lowered. Before she got in, Llewelyn led her down to his cabin and showed her their position on a faded, splotched map. "Where are you going, exactly?" he asked.

Fiona could not read the map to point out Agincourt upon it, but she said its name simply and waited for the man to show it to her. The captain's eyebrows shot up and he looked at her curiously, his keen eyes searching her face, but he said nothing until they had gone back on deck. Just as she was being helped over the side, he seemed to make up his mind; he came over to her and said in a low tone, "Why are you going?"

"I have to," she replied stubbornly. "For my brother."

After a moment, the captain continued, "I have a wife and two daughters; for their sakes it is very hard for me to let you do this."

"I must," Fiona repeated. "You are no more than a stranger, anyway; why need you worry about me?"

Llewelyn shook his head but allowed her to get into the boat, saying only, "I still think you a very silly woman."

The dinghy was released and the rowers dipped their oars into the water, pushing the craft away from its mother vessel. For a time the only sound was the quiet splashing against the wood as it moved through the water, and then after a space of some minutes there came the noise of the boat's underside scraping across the rocky shore. Owen and Llew helped her out and had hardly said goodbye before they were shoving the craft back out into deeper water and leaping aboard.

THE NOISE OF THE oars soon disappeared into the lapping of the waves on the shore, and Fiona felt a rush of loneliness as she stood on the rocks in the dead of night with not a soul in view. "Well," she said aloud to test her voice, but the sound echoing on the boulders sounded like little ghosts all around her, and she shivered. How had Giovanni felt on first setting foot on French land? Fiona wondered if he had been homesick at all and if he had missed the green, lush, fairy-haunted hills of England when his boat had hit the mainland. How forlorn the crags and rocks seemed when compared to the shimmering white cliffs of Porte Dubris!

At this point, Fiona realized from the surf licking her shoes that the tide was coming in and that she would soon be trapped there if she stayed where she was. Stumbling and feeling her way blindly, she moved to her right, which she thought must be east. From the captain's directions, she knew that she was to keep the sea on her left at all times until she reached Abbeville, at the head of the harbour where the river Somme emptied into the Channel. From there on the Welshman's instructions had been full of "northeast by east" and "tacks" and other such sea-talk so that Fiona had understood about a quarter of it, and she determined that it would be best, upon reaching Abbeville, to simply stop and ask directions on to Agincourt.

Fiona crawled on her hands and knees over the unforgiving landscape for about an hour in the darkness, receiving more than her fair share of cuts and bruises before she discovered a place where the ground began to slope upward. Following this, she struggled up and at last found herself, or guessed herself to be, no longer below but on top of the precipice. The French sea cliffs were really nothing more than hills compared to the rocky faces of Britannia, but Fiona took care to continue on all fours and move slowly to avoid a tumble over the edge. It seemed an eternity, going this way, until the sun finally began to peek over the horizon before her. By its light she rose and looked about her to determine how far from humanity she was, and she found that though the coastline was populated by small fishermen's huts, there did not appear to be many large towns to worry about in this part of her travels.

She did not afford as much interest as she had feared from the rural citizens, who assumed her to be a fisherman's wife or daughter, or a woman of disrepute heading for a larger town. Occasionally a squall-worn fishmonger would glance up from his mending of nets and watch her with a kind of languid curiosity, and once Fiona stopped a woman to beg a bit of bread from her, but otherwise she was not forced into any contact with the people. She began almost to enjoy her solitary walking, surrounded by a landscape that she saw now to be pretty, though not what she was used to. A constant wind beat against the coast, ruffling her ill-kept hair and keeping the waves dancing down below, and the brine-loving grass swayed happily in it. The sun hung in the clear eastern sky, tickling the seaside with her rays. The gulls shrieked and dove and flew high to drop a hard-shelled sea creature on the rocks, their silver wings reflecting the light.

This continued for some time, but soon Fiona's feet began to ache from the abuse and her legs were not long in following suit. The wind now became an irritation, for she had to walk against it and it chilled her to the bone; the sun created a glare off the ocean, the salt stung her eyes, and the gulls' cries sounded repeatedly in her ears so as to give her a headache. She caught the skirt of her dress in a patch of briars and tore the hem, falling headlong just a foot from the edge of the cliff, and nearly began to cry as she got back to her feet. The knowledge that she still had to walk the length of France to reach her destination made every step slow and heavy. With barely a glancing familiarity of the country that she was crossing, she could not even look forward to the next town.

"Hey there!"

The voice was a girl's, and Fiona glanced up from her contemplation of her steps. A cart full of barrels had pulled alongside her, and on the bench up front sat a white-haired man and a rosy-cheeked girl who appeared to be a little younger than Fiona herself. The girl was regarding her curiously while her companion continued to stare straight ahead. "Where are you going?" she asked, pulling the mare to a halt.

Fiona was terrified of showing her ignorance, so she waved a hand before her to indicate her heading in that direction.

"Are you going to Cherbourg? Papa and I are headed there ourselves. Would you like to ride with us? It won't be very comfortable, I daresay, but anything is better than walking on foot all that distance."

Glad as she was of a chance to rest her heels, Fiona hardly even thought of being suspicious. "Thank you," she replied, trying to keep the tone of relief out of her voice. "'Tis very kind of you."

The lass shot her an odd glance and Fiona realized with a grimace that her accent was anything but French. As the cart began to jerk along again, the man still saying nothing, the girl chattered on, "My name is Marie, and this is my father. Papa is blind," she added in a low tone.

"Blind I am, but not deaf!" said the man, raising his head and speaking with a clarity that made Fiona jump. "Watch your tongue, girl."

Marie humbly subsided for a few moments, but hers was not a disposition to keep silent long. Soon she was continuing, "All the barrels back there are salted fish; I suppose you can smell them. My brother and Papa catch them and then my mother and sister and I salt them, and then usually Charles (that's my brother) and Papa take them to the city, but Charles is laid up with a fever today, so I came along instead."

"So much the worse for me," grumbled the old man.

"Are you from these parts?" Marie went on, undaunted. "I suppose not; your clothes are too fine for that. What is your business in Cherbourg, then?"

Thinking rapidly, Fiona replied, "Looking for someone."

"Oh?" the girl turned and looked at her, barely turning back in time to keep the cart from rolling into a ditch. "Is it a lover?"

Her father groaned audibly and a wan smile flickered across Fiona's mouth. "No," she said, "just someone."

Marie seemed fascinated by Fiona's accent, for soon her curiosity got the better of her and she asked in her own slurred French voice, "Where are you from?"

"By the Virgin Mother," ejaculated her father before Fiona had to reply, "keep your questions in your head, Marie! I should have thought your mother would have taught you better than to ask a stranger and a guest such things. Keep your eyes ahead of you and your lips shut now."

"My eyes are ahead of me," Marie protested, forgetting the curious foreigner for a moment.

"The rattling of the barrels back there says otherwise; and do not be wagging your tongue at me, girl."

Marie obeyed and set her gaze on the mare's broad back, only now and then letting it drift toward Fiona with a bright-eyed interest. The English girl was glad of her Mediterranean heritage and the dark olive skin that thinly veiled her nationality, but she knew that if even this empty-headed rural French lass guessed she was an outsider, she would not long survive elsewhere. She kept her ears open and had ample opportunity during the trip to pick up on the girl's accent, which she later imitated to the best of her ability.

The trip to Cherbourg, which Fiona discovered was at the tip of a peninsula jutting into the Channel, should have taken them a day and a half at least, but by Marie's reckless driving the mare was hauling the cart into town some hours after the sun went down that day. The feel of the place was like that of London—large and grey and full of merchants and their wares—and Fiona dreaded being separated from even the brusque fisherman and his magpie daughter. She felt the lump in her clothing protectively; her purse was still safe.

"Are you leaving?" Marie's father spoke, apparently having heard her begin to get down from the cart. "Ah, well, I wish we could offer you lodgings, but I am afraid the back of the cart serves that purpose for us."

Fiona would little have minded sleeping next to the barrels, which Marie and her father did to keep them from being stolen; she did not care for the idea of giving money for lodgings to a Frenchman, to one of those who had killed her brother. But the fisherman's words were not an invitation, so she merely said, "Oh, I will find somewhere. Thank you very much for the ride."

Marie waved cheerfully as Fiona headed for lodgings, but she was soon swallowed up in the darkness. It was only by the light and noise within the foggy windows that told her which building was the inn; she stepped inside and was greeted by a heady scent of smoked meat and ale and crackling wood. She glanced about her warily but found it to be not so different from an English tavern, save that the voices that rose in the room were thick with

French accents. Barmaids flirted with guests, men argued over their drinks, mice occasionally skittered across the floor to poke their noses into pools of spilled ale and nibble at scraps of meat: the picture was becoming familiar to her.

Once again, Fiona was pleasantly surprised in that few people took notice of her. Only one man with a loud voice and amber liquid dribbling down his beard eyed her a little too closely, but as she took him to be drunk it was of little consequence to her. She paid her board and kept clear of the others as she ate, and they in turn left her alone.

With walking in the dark being so difficult, Fiona allowed herself a few extra hours of sleep the next day and rose about an hour after Matins—if they had Matins in this stretch of land. She saw Marie and her father in the marketplace as she went through on her way out of the town, but she did not stop or wave a greeting; it would look too much as though she were hanging about like a common beggar, asking for money or food or the use of their cart again. She burned with shame just looking at her torn and muddy skirt and her calloused hands, rubbed raw by clinging to the rocks along the shore. A passer-by might think she had been raised in a sow's wallowing place, and she had not yet lain aside enough of her pride to realize that this had its benefits: no one talks to a sow.

The minutes stretched into hours as the sun moved along, smilingly oblivious, through the sky, and Fiona's shoes wore down until she could feel the soles of her feet rubbing the ground through the last bits of leather left. She stood undecided in the path, and then she cried to the world at large, "Oh, what good is it now?" and tore off the footwear, hurling them over the nearest hedge. With her skin worn and her clothes muddied, it was vain to try to keep a fine appearance. She hobbled miserably along, avoiding pebbles where she could and bruising herself where she could not.

When she crossed her first river that day, she regretted her decision. It was but a creek and no more than calf-high at its deepest point, but the flowing, shimmering water looked as cold as ice even before she set foot in it. She stood on its banks and shivered and at last gritted her teeth and splashed in. "Oh! Oh!" she cried. "Oh! Oh, 'tis cold!" She kept on, however, and tried to get to the other side as fast as possible, but the riverbed was coated in rocks and she was constantly stumbling and sending water flying even as she attempted to keep her skirt above the surface. When she at last crawled out, her feet like blocks of ice dangling off her legs, her dress was soaked mid-thigh and she was forced to walk along the road with the hem slapping against her.

Thus she went for over two hours, the weak sun doing little to dry her out but merely continuing to grin stupidly from the sky. No kind-hearted French lassies stopped and offered her a ride today; a fisherman rattling along in his cart even paused to laugh at her sorry state before driving on and leaving her humiliated. Fiona grew tired of the sound of her own dress smacking against her skin; she grew tired of the unbearably firm feel of the ground under her heels; she grew tired of how endless the road and the day seemed before her. And while she cursed it in her heart, the sun smiled and smiled and seemed to move as little as it had the day Joshua commanded it to stand still.

Evening at last deepened and Fiona took refuge in a little fishing village of no consequence and no name. There was not even a tavern, so she crawled wearily under a cart whose wood was tainted with the scent of seaweed and slept there till morning, only to be awakened by the wagon moving off from over top of her.

She opened her eyes and found herself lying on her back in the middle of a dirty, thin road that was hardly worthy of the name. The sky was clear overhead, the weather holding charitably, and the sun was shining straight above her.

Straight above her. Fiona sat up straight with a hand clasped to her aching head, casting about her wildly. The day was half gone and she was only just awakening—a half day's walking lost. "Oh, you!" she said aloud, shaking her fist at the luminary suspended in the heavens. "You want to play games with me, do you? Well, you shan't thwart me; oh, you can keep taunting, but you won't stop me!" She got to her feet in a burning rage, beating the dust from her stiff dress.

She doubled her pace that day, scorning her weary feet and her chapped skin. The wind pounded and tore at her and her eyes continued to smart with the particles of salt and dust that pricked them constantly, but her anger made her resilient and she stumbled on. This mindset carried through the next two days, and she walked late and arose early; towns and villages blurred together in her mind, and it seemed to her that the faces of the workers were all the same.

At last, on the afternoon of the fourth day she reached a wide and quick-flowing river that a peasant boy told her was called the Seine. She remembered from Llewelyn's map that this was the river that fed the great city of Paris and also that on either side of the harbour which the river emptied into lay the twin cities of Honfleur and Harfleur. Standing on the west bank near the former, the blackened stones of Harfleur's walls seemed stark and naked against the grey water of the Channel. Still, she appeared to Fiona to be a proud town; how long she had held out against the English forces, refusing for so many days to give in and lay down her arms! Fiona felt a kind of grudging respect for her.

Turning her eyes back to the clear water rushing past her toes, she surveyed the width of the river doubtfully. Though she had had her fair share of rivers to get across in the past few days and had not caught cold yet, it was clear that this was no creek to be waded across. It was deep and the current picked up large stones at the bottom and tossed them along as though they were light as feathers; Fiona could easily imagine being pulled off her feet and drowned in the tide. She walked the scrubby bank for some time, but the river seemed to continue on at the same rate and breadth.

There was no hope for it. Bunching her skirt up about her knees—though she had long since realized that it was a useless cause—she took a deep breath and plunged in, first to her waist, then to her chest, then up to her neck until the water swirled into her mouth and ears. She flailed her arms wildly like a drowning pup and went under, pummelled by the current that seemed to have tripled its strength. She was tossed about for what seemed like an eternity, her arms and legs encumbered by the weight of her dress, and the only clear thought in her head was, *Here it comes; I'm going to die*. Strangely, the thought was not panicked at all, but easy and coldly certain.

And then in a rush the river, as though it disliked the taste of her, was spitting her up so that her head broke surface and she could cling to the root of an old tree that was growing out of the bank. Spluttering and coughing and dizzy from her ride, she crawled out on the bank and lay still for a minute. At last she managed to sit up and look about her, only to find that she was back on the west bank and had been carried some length down river. She spat out a wad of river mud and got to her feet undaunted.

She was not quite foolish enough to try for another swim across, and she wisely turned to some other means of transporting herself to the other side. There was no ferry, nor a bridge, nor any kind of boat-like object available, and to build any of these would take more time and labour and knowledge than Fiona possessed, so she paced the bank impatiently like a cat wishing to get over without getting its paws wet. She paced and thought and paced some more until her eye lit upon a large branch that curved over the river and hung low to the ground on the opposite bank.

"Well," said she from between clenched teeth as she cast about her and began to strip to her under dress, "I am not going to be stopped by a bit of tainted French water. I've gotten thus far, haven't I?" And she began her ascent, her dress thrown over her shoulder as she shimmied up the trunk. In actuality, her bold words merely belied a deep fear of falling and breaking her neck; the old apple tree back home had had branches growing near to the ground, and climbing into it was child's play. This colossal work of nature was another matter entirely.

And so a girl dressed only in her petticoats spent nigh on half an hour clawing her way to the proper branch and then a further ten minutes working up the courage to move out over the water. Her legs began to bleed and twice she had to save her sodden dress from destruction, but at last she gained the other bank and gave a sigh of relief as she rested on the grass. The water bubbled before her and sounded distraught, but she could not even manage a triumphant laugh at its expense. It was over; she had conquered the mighty Seine River.

†

Since first spotting it, Fiona had been irrepressibly drawn to the walled fortress of Harfleur, and though it was mid-evening and the sky was darkening quickly she persevered until she was just outside the city. She lay the night in a loose bale of hay, the wet cloth that clung to her making it impossible to sleep until about an hour before the cock's crow. Then she dozed, but the piercing rays of the sun woke her far too soon.

Her first sight on waking was the light hitting the dark stones of Harfleur, and it seemed like a sorcerer's castle from the Scottish fairy tales she had heard when she was little: black and ominous against the sky, which was cloudy today. The fortress, though ravaged, was still beautiful in a proud way: beautiful in its history, somewhat in the same way that Dover Castle was. But not, Fiona added to herself quickly, as beautiful as that.

She rose from her makeshift bed, peeling her skirt from off her dust-caked legs and trying to put it in order. Wearily drawing the straw from out of her hair, which she thought she would never get properly brushed again, she got to her feet and looked about her in the light of day. The strip of land outside Harfleur, where the English must have camped, was spotted with patches of burned grass from the soldiers' campfires, and the earth was marked from where they had stood and charged and been shot down by the French crossbows. Everything seemed to tell of the battle that had been fought there, though rains had since quenched the fires in the city. As Fiona turned, she saw with a horrified revulsion that the bale on which she had slept was encrusted with dried blood; she turned away.

Over the days, Fiona had managed to feed herself by begging bread from the more kind-hearted women of the towns, but today she had to make do with what she could find to eat in the woods lining the river. The citizens of the town, she guessed, would be wary of strangers and not likely to allow her within their gates, and she did not wish to draw over-much attention to herself. She was sorely tempted to eat the glossy red berries that grew in the holly bushes and on the bryony vines, though even basic herbology had taught her that they were poisonous; their pretty, brilliant scarlet hues made them look twice as delicious as anything else she had ever tasted in her life. Looking at them while she chewed on thick roots made her belly rumble.

From now on, the path she took showed signs of the presence of an invader. Whole fields of grass still lay trampled on the cold earth from where the army had passed; trees along the way had been hacked at to provide firewood; an occasional grave marked the way, and these grew more frequent as she progressed. She felt sorry for the families of those who were buried in foreign soil, and she was thankful at least that Giovanni lay in rich English earth back home. A chill crept into her soul at the thought and she walked faster.

She reached the river Somme on a cold day thick with rain, slept the night on its western bank, and crossed the next day as the sun was peeking over the horizon in a still-cloudy sky. Her body no longer felt like her own; her feet were numb from the cold, her skin dry, and her belly shrunken, for on this side of the Seine the French were not so willing to share their food with a stranger. She managed to scrape together a meal in Abbeville, though she later felt sick remembering just what she had eaten, and procured directions to Agincourt from a tired old man who was too fatigued by life to care what her purpose was there. Two more rivers were crossed, nameless to Fiona, and she finally, finally came in sight of the castle of Agincourt.

The layout of the land was as it had been in her dream, save that there were no armies facing each other today. The old castle and the commune of Tramecourt lay diagonal to each other, separated by the pass in which the French and the English had fought, and Tramecourt stood out in the open with its large chapel easily seen even from a distance. Agincourt lay in the western patch of woods, her ancient stones chipped and worn by age but her towers still standing tall above the trees. She kept watch like a guardian angel over the pass; it was little wonder that she had given her name to the battle fought before her. As Fiona walked down slowly into the plain, she felt her hackles rise as the castle's shadow seemed to loom across the field over her.

The rain of the past few days had once more made the ground thick as pudding and just as stable so that the girl had to keep careful watch where she put her feet. She could well imagine the charging French horses, as much laden down by their tack and armour as their riders, breaking their legs in the changing bog; she could almost hear their desperate screams piercing the air, accompanied by the soldiers' shouts as they too sank in the mud and drowned under the weight of encasing iron. *How many had actually died by sword or lance?* she wondered. *How many of them had fallen in honour?*

She found a charred log and sat down on it with her head in her hands, feeling the drumbeats at her temples. She thought of the Duke of Gloucester's pronounced limp and obvious pain; she thought of the graves she had seen along the wayside; she thought of Giovanni's face, pale and still; she thought of the different tallies she had heard of English dead. "How many are grieving over what happened here?" she whispered to the earth. "How many are mourning the loss of a loved one? God did not even spare the nobles." They said both the Earl of Suffolk and the Duke of York had died here, spilling their blood on unfamiliar soil.

Victory or no, Fiona thought the name of *Agincourt* a blight on history's page.

THE FIRST DROPS OF the storm began to spatter on her lips and cheeks, and she left the field lest she get caught herself in the mud. The tears in her eyes and the thick sheets of rain blinded her equally; she groped her way along until she reached the road heading southeast. Her mind was not clear and she knew not where she was headed, only that she could not stay a minute longer on that plain, or her sorrow would get the better of her. Her subconscious hoped to find a town where she could sleep the night, and she let it guide her.

She had no idea how many days she had been on the road since landing on the west coast of Normandy, but when she limped into the town of St. Pol-sur-Ternoise she was muddy and ragged and had she been able to catch a glimpse in a pool, she would not have recognized herself. Her tresses had been caked in dust so that the rain that dripped off their ends was a dark brown; her ankles were swollen from the distance travelled; her thighs itched with the walking and the rub of coarse fabric. She was a sight to behold as she dragged herself into the tavern, and behold her the residents did.

It was not long after she had settled herself in a corner with a mug of ale clenched in her trembling hand that one of the men cocked his head, drew a little nearer, and asked the obvious: "You're new here?"

Fiona raised her eyes with difficulty from the leg of meat she was grasping between her teeth, nodding slightly; she was too exhausted to care what happened to her.

With the initiation over, most of the others also came closer and eyed her with interest. "Where are you from?" asked one, and

"What's your name?" came from another.

"Fiona," she replied to the latter, dropping her head to her flagon again. The former question was repeated, and she answered with the first thought that came to her heavy mind. "I was a lady's jester." As soon as the words were out of her mouth she balked; whatever had induced her to say that? She had seen a jester but once in all her life.

The throng was pleased with this answer, however, and a man sitting at a neighbouring table cried, "Give us a trick, then!" The motion was endorsed with such vigour that Fiona could not have resisted had not a skinny, pasty youth, trying to be witty, stuttered, "But my good man, do you not know that that would be a *foolish* thing to do?"

The others booed him from the inn at this lame witticism, but it saved Fiona from a public performance and she wished the boy well with every ounce of her being. When the voices had dulled down, the questions continued. "Run away from your mistress, have you?" a maid asked with a look of scorn, most likely jealous of the attention being shown this grimy waif.

"Who was your mistress?" another added before Fiona had a chance to deny it.

"I-I-" she faltered, shrinking away. "Well … do you mean the last one or the one before her?"

The fellow closest to her guffawed mightily and his companions followed suit. "The last one, the last one!"

"Lady Anne," Fiona replied, quicker this time, "of Nowhere Precisely."

"Nowhere Precisely? And how does one get to be lady of Nowhere Precisely?"

"Oh, it's quite easy to be lady of Nowhere Precisely," said she, thinking fast and remembering something that Giovanni had teasingly said to her long ago. "You see, it's so small and of so little consequence that no one minds if you make yourself lady or lord of it."

A fresh burst of laughter met this, for the people of St. Pol were badly in need of something or someone to laugh at and this girl was just right for the purpose. "I should like to find Nowhere Precisely and become lord of it," someone remarked, and the others agreed whole-heartedly.

The banter continued for some time, Fiona's eyelids growing heavier and heavier all the while, until the addition of an apparently well-known young man to the lodge distracted their attention. Finding herself suddenly left alone, her admirers having scattered with almost enough force to create a breeze, she leaned out of the shadows to catch sight of the newcomer. He did not appear from what she could see of him to be French at all, but neither was he English; his complexion she could not see for the tricky firelight, but his hair was as fair as the summer sun and the crafting of his face was not what she was used to. She might have thought him handsome, but the eyes that swept the room were as cold and as bright a blue as the soldier's who had kept watch at Dubris Castle. She did not like him.

He spoke clear and perfectly enunciated French so that she could hear his talk plainly, but it lacked the twang of French. He was, however, turning the flow of discussion to the Battle of Agincourt, and his way of speaking of it showed only disgust for the English; Fiona watched with a kind of repulsed fascination as his thin lips curled back in derision and the light flashed off his teeth. "'Twas not the English who were the victors, anyway," he was saying to no one in particular, pushing the words between his teeth with a harsh accent; "'twas the mud." He leaned forward in his seat and pinched the closest barmaid, who jumped and shrieked in surprise. Once again the man laughed, shooing her away and continuing, "An exact rendition of what those poor English soldiers sounded like as they were drowning."

Tears stung Fiona's eyes as a few of her companions chuckled. "How can he make so light," she whispered, "of a place where so many died?"

The man's ears seemed to prick up and he turned toward her corner, scanning the shadows with those blue eyes and saying, "What was that?"

She blushed and drew back, murmuring, "Nothing, sir."

"Ah," was all he said, but though he seemed to ignore her after that, she continued to feel his gaze piercing her skin.

In awhile the men began to rise and leave for their homes, save for those who were staying the night and a few whose habit it was to gamble until the wee hours of the morning. The blue-eyed man was one of those to stay, but Fiona made sure to keep clear of him and stayed in her corner. The hours stretched longer and still he did not leave; she dared not pay for a room, for a deep fear that she could not express had taken over her heart and she was afraid even to walk past him. The men sank deeper into their ale as the night grew older; seeing a clear path to the inn door, Fiona moved for it.

She was never sure how, but in a moment he was there, right at her side, holding the sleeve of her dress in an iron grip. "You wished to say something to me earlier, little girl?" he asked coolly.

Fiona cowered. "I—no, no, my lord," she gasped, attempting to draw away. The man only took her by the arm and drew her to a table, sitting her down.

"Are you afraid of me? Not unwise. Tell me your name." Then, as she kept silent and merely sat quaking across from him, his eyes narrowed and he snapped, "Has the Devil got your tongue?"

"F-Fiona," she stuttered; how she wished the floor would

open and swallow her away! She thought of David and longed for him to be there, for no matter his curtness, she knew he would have helped her.

"Fiona," the man repeated, hissing the name as he drew a finger down her cheek. She began to pull away in earnest, and his hand closed around her wrist. "Fiona," he said again, looking down at the skinny arm in his grasp. "You see how much larger my hand is than your wrist, Fiona? You see how I could snap your body like a twig?"

Fiona saw, and she was terrified. Though she pulled away, he would not release her; though she gave a weak cry, no one else in the room seemed to notice. The man was pushing the table out of the way, still holding her wrist, and she blindly reached for the little dagger that lay concealed in her dress. She was unskilled in the use of weaponry and her hand shook, but the blue-eyed youth was not expecting the sudden slash across his face; he swore and let her go, swiping at the stream of blood coursing into his left eye, and Fiona fled out the door and into the evening.

She could not hear him following her, for though the night was clear and just washed clean by another shower, the sound of her own pounding feet filled her ears and deafened her. Something in her whispered that she was running blindly, that she would soon be lost or fall in the darkness, but she was too afraid to look out for her own interests. The night seemed like a bosom friend when compared to the stifling darkness of the inn.

The harsh bark of a dog made her run faster, and the sound of the mongrel flying after her brought a shrill scream bursting from her lips. She covered her head and fled for a stand of trees, her heart pounding, her breath coming hard, her heels seeming to strike craters in the earth. The hound soon went back to its own place and the emptiness behind her was quiet, but her terror persisted: every whisper of breeze in the dry branches above her brought new strength into her shaking legs, and every stirring of a twig along the way made her heart fit to burst out of her chest.

The voice in her head was proven correct very soon. Fiona's foot caught a rock and she smashed her shin against its craggy edges as she sprawled across the forest floor. Moving a hand down her leg, she felt blood beginning to ooze out of the jagged wound, the pain just beginning to start and her calf to throb. She did not stay long to nurse her injury, however; the brushing of a leaf against her face made her scramble back to her feet with a cry and move on, pushing her way through the deepening woods. Her ankle hurt with the same lightning-quick twinges that she had felt when, at the age of six, she had broken it in a rabbit hole, but for the first time in her journey she showed something like courage: she clenched her teeth and pushed forward.

After some time the moon came up, but it played hide-and-seek behind the clouds and only illumined the way for a minute at a time before disappearing again. Shadows played across the way, creating sprites and forest imps out of scraggly, leafless bushes. Some winter bird screamed overhead, and Fiona shuddered as the element of superstition got the better of her. Was this not the kind of night that the Evil One picked to prowl about on? What if one of his minions should reach out from behind that tree and drag her away to the spirit realm? She crossed herself and forced her lagging feet into a run once more.

The rain picked up again at this inauspicious moment, thunder rolling somewhere to her left—or was it her right? She had lost all sense of direction. With few leaves to catch the rain, it pattered down and splashed on Fiona's face like dozens of fairies all laughing at her, and her clothes seemed to drag her down. Whenever she stopped, however, a sound like a man's breath at her back spurred her on again. Two sounds rang over and over in her ears: that of the rain splashing on her own skin and that of her heels hitting the ground beneath her. It hardly seemed as though she was moving of her own volition; she seemed to float above the ground, save that her body felt as heavy as a ton of weights. A dry sob tore at her throat.

She might have been running all night or it may have only been half an hour, but some time in her flight Fiona's numb body detected a change. She no longer seemed to be floating and the sensation of moving forward was gone; rather, she seemed to be falling into a bottomless pit. She was sinking, sinking, sinking for what seemed like an eternity, and then with a shock that brought her senses alive again she felt water encompassing her head. She gurgled into the liquid prison and reached out straight over her head, groping for something like clean air, but the rain and the darkness above made it hard to tell the difference between river and forest.

Later, she was unsure as to whether it was she herself that tore the last of the ivory buttons from her dress and set her free, or whether it was the current, but with the burden gone she was able to fight for the surface and struggle onto the opposite bank. The dark form that was her clothing glided down the river, and along with it went the locket that she had so carefully preserved; it was drifting to the riverbed, far out of reach.

Even with a river as well as such a length of distance separating her from the inn, she still would not allow herself to rest in the cover of a holly bush. *Go on, I must go on!* Her heart beat and her head pounded in rhythm with the words. Thorns pierced the soles of her feet, her wound tingled from the sudden dive into the frigid, rushing water, and her whole frame longed for relief, but she was powerless to stop herself. She still felt the man's hand around her wrist, and his words echoed in her mind. She knew what would happen if he caught her, and the knowledge kept her going.

Dawn came and she hardly noticed. In some ways it was a disadvantage, for now she could see the things that were causing her pain but could no more avoid them now than she could in the dark. Daylight did not make her afraid of being seen, though; shame at the thought of anyone catching sight of the thin, half-naked girl stumbling and tripping through the woods was the furthest thought from her mind. She had only enough sanity left to think of the blue-eyed man and the burning in her chest.

Trip and stumble she did, that day and night and the next day and the next night. She was not running constantly all that time, but she stopped as few times as possible, for the first time she did she thought she was going to die where she stood. For all she knew she was running about in circles, for the forest never seemed to change; the bare trees continued to loom overhead, oblivious to her presence, and the cloudy sky hid the position of the sun. Night and day were scarcely different to her; both were dark and seemed never to end. Not even the periods of rain and dry meant much to her, for she remained soggy in both, as there was no sun to dry her. Thus she had no way and no interest in measuring the time that lapsed; for all she knew she would continue to run forever, or until exhaustion took over and she died here, all alone.

In time—if time still existed—she left the forest and crossed a meadow and then reached a patch of nondescript land whose scenery she did not stop to consider. This gave way to a kind of swamp land, which she only recognized when she was waist-deep in the mire and had to spend some little while extricating herself. She could not even smell it—her nostrils stung and she was only aware of the scent of rushing blood within them—and with a renewed pang of fear she wondered if she were dying. It occurred to her that she did not want to die. It was the first time the thought had come to her in all its burning precision, and she began to cry as she crawled along on all fours, thick with mud. Her head was light on her shoulders and her hand slipped; she tumbled down a slope, smashed her head on a rock, and fell, her eyes darkening, into a mound of straw.

THREE TIMES SHE CAME out of her separate universe enough to hear voices around her and once to feel a great weight that appeared to be attached to her being moved, but when she did there was always pain—she was glad when she could slip back into darkness. The fourth time, however, she realized that that weight was her own body and the sheets of iron on her face were her eyelids, and she knew there was no going back to her other world again. She twitched a finger and found that it moved under her command, and with a great deal of effort she was able to open her eyes into slits.

She thought at first that she was in a cage. The room was certainly very small and the walls seemed to move of their own volition; indeed, her first thought was that she was caught in the Wind itself. She was lying on something soft and warm, covered with something of the same material, but her head was too heavy to be moved. She continued to lie there and twitch her fingers and try to move her toes, which were not as cooperative as the former.

Suddenly one wall was drawn back and a piercing deluge of light rushed in, stinging her eyes and bringing a rasping moan from her half-parted lips. She tried to say something more, anything more, but her tongue was swollen and motionless in her mouth.

"Well then, is she alive?" a brisk, ice-fringed voice asked above her.

Fiona listened with interest for the reply, and it came from a rounder voice on her left. "Oh, I believe so," it said, and something warm probed her throat and her wrist. "Yes, the pulse is quicker now; I think she should be moving soon."

A liquid, spicy and hot, trickled over her lips and down into her mouth. When it moved over her tongue she was sorry to find that it was neither wine nor ale but some pungent drink that she had never tasted before; still, it made it possible for her to move her tongue. She did so, pushing it out and running it across her lips.

"Ah, you see?" the round voice seemed pleased. Fiona felt her right arm being lifted and rubbed gently from shoulder to wrist until the life returned to it, like the ice over a stream giving way with the first warmth of spring. "Give her some of the tea again, my lord," the voice instructed as he worked on her left arm, and once again the drink was poured into her mouth. With its bitter aroma she felt the blood stirring in the rest of her body; her heart began to beat again and her legs were no longer great slabs of rock tied to her waist. She found also that her eyes would open all the way and her vision was less hazy.

"How do you feel, girl?" the voice asked. Turning her head with difficulty, she found that it belonged not to a short, fat little man, as she would have expected from the voice, but to a stringy-looking man with the appearance of a sapling. Yet he waddled like a duck despite that, which made him odd and—if she had been less tired and hurting—comic. She thought he was a monk, from his habit.

Fiona tried to reply that she felt better, but that which came out was an indistinct gurgle and a flood of saliva mixed with tea. The man smiled kindly and wiped her face without a word, and she was too tired to feel very embarrassed.

A hand took her by the jaw and turned her face to the other side of the bed—she realized now that it was a canopied bed that she was lying on—where she saw another man with a sharp face. "Come now, girl, can you speak?" he asked, and his voice was not as benevolent as the monk's.

"Oh, hush, my lord; let the poor thing rest before you question her. Let us away for breakfast now and leave the girl to sleep awhile." The monk patted the younger man's shoulder firmly and the latter released Fiona with a last annoyed, searching glance. The two left her alone and, weary of thinking, Fiona slipped off to sleep again.

☨

It was early morning, she thought, with the sun just creeping in and a bird chirping outside. A sweetly humming noise encircled her with a melancholy, beautiful tune that reminded her of her mother and the times in her childhood when she had been sent to sleep by a lullaby and a kiss. The sound tasted of summer and smelled like azure and daisy-scented wind. She turned toward it, but it stopped and the noise of rustling skirts replaced it.

A hand brushed across her forehead and Fiona blinked open her eyes. When the world came into focus she saw a young woman with large, dark eyes and a soft smile sitting beside the bed, one hand laid against Fiona's face and the other adjusting the coverlet. "Who are you?" Fiona asked; the noise was cracked and rough.

The other only shook her head and rose, patting Fiona's cheek affectionately and slipping mouse-like from the room. She had not said a word, and yet the English girl could not find it in her to be surprised—silence seemed to express the stranger's nature. She lay back and looked up at the canopy, letting her foggy mind drift. It was warm and comfortable here, and that was all she cared about just now; her brain was too weary to think clearly about anything.

In a little while the door opened again, but in place of the woman of earlier, the odd, monk-like man entered. He beamed his pleasant smile, saying, "Awake! Good, good. Can you speak?"

Fiona nodded but did not attempt it. The man came over and gave her another drink of the spicy stuff, continuing, "Can you feel your right leg? You had a nasty cut there; I could see clean to your bone." He pulled back the blanket and Fiona raised her head to look at the white bandage encircling her calf; she gave a muffled cry and fell back as the man began to probe at it. "Yes, it hurts," he said matter-of-factly, beginning to unwind the cloth. "But at least that means the feeling is coming back to you now."

The girl found that small comfort. She tried to look away, but her eyes were drawn to the incision in her leg as the monk peeled the last, clinging bit of bandage from the open wound. She shuddered at how starkly red and white it was, noticing the grotesque way in which the skin curled up on either side of the injury, and she felt her weak belly churn. How was it that the man seemed so at ease as he washed his hands and pried the wound? He took a bottle from the side table and poured some of the amber contents onto a cloth, took a firm hold about Fiona's ankle, and dabbed the wet fabric against the cut without warning. She cried out, bringing her teeth down hard on her lip and squeezing the blood from it; if the monk had shoved her entire leg into a fire, the pain could not have been worse.

During the process, someone else entered the room and came to press their hand against Fiona's forehead, gently pushing a rag between her teeth to keep her from grinding them together. Fiona's eyes were too glazed to see properly who it might be, but her hearing at least was clear and she heard the monk saying, "Ah, my lady. Yes, that is good—" as the cloth was inserted in her mouth. "These bone wounds are always the worst, eh? I only hope enough dirt has been removed; why, when they brought her in I could hardly see the wound for the mud!" He gave a half laugh, then added, "Hand me the bandages, would you, mistress? Ah, thank you."

Fiona felt the cloth passing around her leg, the fibres seeming to claw at the open flesh. She whimpered miserably around the obstruction in her mouth, wishing she could die or at least return to oblivion; it seemed as though these people delighted in torturing her. She heard the man saying that it was over, but it did not feel so. Her leg seemed about to fall off her body entirely.

Another voice entered the conversation, the cold voice of—was it yesterday? Fiona could not rightly remember. "How is she?" it asked, and the tone spoke more of irritation than care or concern. "Is she better?"

A hand took the cloth from her jaw and the monk replied, "Well, the wound is as clean as I can get it. If it becomes infected, though—"

The other seemed to wave away the physician's words, and the voice was sharp as he said, "But can she speak? Is she able to answer questions?"

Oh, questions! Thoughts! Fiona turned her face toward the wall. Would they not leave her alone? The ice in this man's voice stabbed her skull like a thousand needles and she wished he would be silent; she did not see that they had a right to stand by her bedside and discuss her as though she were an ailing horse.

"I think," she heard the monk saying tactfully, "that a few more days are needed for her recovery before she will be up for a questioning. Now, my lord, you leave her to the care of myself and your wife, and she will soon be whole again. Let us leave her to rest, shall we?"

The man blew a heavy breath through his nose as though he did wish to wait any longer for a full explanation, but it appeared that he submitted, for the room grew silent and Fiona drifted into another period of unconsciousness.

This pattern continued for several days with her dozing on and off and dreading, even in her sleep, the daily cleansing of her wound. The silent woman was often there when she awakened, and as Fiona's sight cleared she surveyed the lady's face curiously. She was young, only a few years older than Fiona herself; her hair was a gold-streaked brown, her eyes the same, and her face was distinctly oval with pale, almost translucent skin. She almost always smiled, even when doing something as tedious as embroidering a dress or a sheet or a covering for a banquet table, and never once spoke. She was pretty in an ethereal kind of way, as though her soul itself were shining through her frail body like a star. Fiona liked her very much.

As for the ice-cold man, whom she learned through listening to the monk talk was the lady's husband, her opinion of him was quite different. She never heard him speak without the noise stabbing into her brain like a knife, and she had only seen him once, for she shut her eyes and pretended to sleep whenever he entered the room. The promise of an interrogation from him sent chills up her spine; what would he ask? What would happen to her? The questions took up a great deal of her waking hours, those times when she was not thinking of beautiful England back home and missing it. The days were long and the time dismal until the monk—who, she had since learned, was not a monk at all but merely a physician named Francis—allowed her to get up for the first time.

Swinging her bare legs out from under the covers and into the shockingly chill air, Fiona was for the first time ashamed of her scanty clothing. Dressing a limp body being so difficult, they had only managed to slip on a white underdress some sizes too large for her that left her feeling naked as she sat on the bed before the doctor. Seeming to sense her discomfort, the lady waved the reluctant physician from the room and herself helped Fiona to stand and take her first tottering step. Flashes of pain seared her leg up to the middle of her thigh, and she soon began to lean on the other's shoulder so greatly that the latter could hardly hold her up. In less than thirty seconds Fiona was forced to crawl back into bed, her head aching and her body weary.

"I will be up soon," she whispered aloud, her eyelids beginning to close again. She longed to be mobile, to be able to get out of this soft, warm cell and to be of some worth to herself again. It hurt her pride terribly to be thus reliant on those around her.

The lady smiled in reply and brushed the hair back from Fiona's forehead with her hand before retiring once more to her domestic occupations.

In about two weeks' time, though it seemed to her like two months at the very least, Fiona was well enough for the master of the place to have his desired questioning of her. He came to her room one cloud-strewn day about an hour after dinner, when she and the lady were sitting near the blazing hearthfire and Fiona's clumsy fingers were remembering the use of a needle, and did not stand upon ceremony. He stood beside the mantelpiece and demanded immediately, "So, girl, what is your name?"

Fiona dropped her needle in surprise and spent some time searching for it among the ashes as she replied, "Fiona, my lord."

"And what were you doing on my manor grounds?"

She recovered her seat and sat blushing—or perhaps it was only the heat that sent the rose to her cheeks. "Please," she said slowly, "I didn't know it was your manor."

The man shrugged one shoulder. "Be that as it may, a trespass is a trespass. Do you even know where you are?"

Fiona shook her head, dropping her eyes to the hands now lying idle in her lap.

The other laughed harshly, calling for a servant to fetch some well-worn map from his study. It was brought, a rough scrawl on a watermarked parchment whose writings she could not have read even had she been literate. The man jabbed a finger at the paper, saying, "*Here* is where you are: a swampy, worthless scrap of land in the northeast region of Champagne. You follow?"

She frantically tried to call to mind a clearer image of the French nation, but none came. She nodded hesitantly, but he accepted it and flung the map away for a servant to pick up. "So," he continued, "that is where you are, in a little land of no consequence called Gallandon. And I am Pierre, the lord of Gallandon, and as such a man of very little consequence to all but myself. Ah, yes, and this is my wife," he added, swinging a hand toward the pale lady. "Leah." The name came out blunt and frigid, bereft of any title, and he seemed to glance at his pretty wife with scorn as he said it. He turned back to Fiona. "As I was saying, you are a trespasser, a vagrant, and—" a slight pause "—a woman of questionable background and character." Fiona began to protest, but he cut her off with, "*Therefore*, it is a kindness for me to make you a servant in my household."

Fiona sat with her mouth gaping. Leah stirred at her side but continued to embroider with her eyes fixed on the patterns the thread was making; her smile was gone and her eyes were not glittering. "A-a servant?" Fiona gasped. This was a great blow—worse than death or being turned out to the cold of the mistral winds. All her life to order her own servants about with careless ease, and now to suddenly become one? To one of French blood, no less? The shame sat like a stone in her belly, and the saliva in her mouth turned foul.

"A maid to my wife," Pierre nodded. "You can learn to … translate for her." Again came the curious look directed at the mute lady. He waited for a reply but received none; he cleared his throat, bowed slightly to Leah, and left the room. Fiona listened to the sound of his footsteps receding down the corridor like the sounds of Death himself.

After a moment Leah laid a hand sympathetically on Fiona's shoulder, but Fiona shook her off and rose. Her gesture was clear, and the mistress of the place bowed to her wish and let her alone. The chamber was empty save for herself now, and the crackling of the fire filled the silence. She did not cry—tears never got her anywhere, and they were powerless to ease the ache inside—but merely lay down on the bed and stared above her unblinkingly, searching for something warm in a world that had turned cold and hostile. Her thoughts drifted and her eyelids fluttered, her eyelashes resting against her cheeks.

Late in the evening she woke from her doze as a maidservant brought her a platter of food for her lonely supper; she was not yet well enough to join the larger party in the banquet hall, and for this she was glad. She stared at the steaming venison, the red meat thick and juicy, and the fluffy pudding-like concoctions and other foreign substances before her, but she had no stomach for them. The very thought of continuing to eat French food was revolting to her, and she carried the platter to the window and flung the contents out for the winter birds to eat.

If she was to choose between servanthood and death, she would choose the latter. A swift death was preferable to the slow, agonizing death of starvation, but her knife had been lost in the river along with her dress; this was the easiest way to go.

In the morning she was already beginning to feel the effects of her decision, but she bravely—or foolishly—sent her breakfast out the window; so too went her dinner, and she felt ready to faint as Leah took her for a short walk about the manor. Twice she stumbled and was forced to lean on the other for support, and Leah's face showed concern as she led Fiona back to her quarters.

"I'm only tired," Fiona insisted, guessing the thoughts that were passing through the other's mind. "I will be better soon."

Against her better judgment, Leah did not call the physician but trusted to the girl's word. Again the two sat together and embroidered in silence—the one because she had nothing she wished to say, the other because she was incapable of saying the things she wished—and Leah seemed not to hear the insistent rumblings of Fiona's belly. Twice darkness passed across Fiona's eyes and her head felt as though it were ready to float right from her, but she shut her eyes to steady herself and kept on at her sewing with shaking hands. Presently, however, she was forced to say, "I think I need to lie down; my—my leg is hurting."

Leah glanced up, searching the girl's face pointedly. Noiselessly, for her movements were as silent as her voice, she gathered up her tools and set them by the bedside then disappeared for a few minutes. When she returned she was carrying a leather-bound tome with beautiful scribes' etchings on the pages and covers; she held it reverently, for books were rare and precious and not to be handled lightly, and her face seemed to glow brighter than ever as she brought it to her chair and laid it on the bed.

"You can read?" Fiona asked incredulously, her curiosity besting her hunger. Leah nodded with a faint colouring of the cheeks, and the younger girl almost asked for her to read aloud before she remembered and closed her mouth. It was not the words that the French lady had brought the book to her for, but the jewel-coloured engravings, done in the modern style, that marked the pages. Fiona sat up a little straighter and studied the pictures like a bright-eyed child, wondering how many years of painstaking work went into the making of this manuscript; her father had spent much of his money in the collecting of these works, but he had never taught either of his children to read—Giovanni had struggled and laboured and had come to learn for himself, but Fiona had never had the patience to study the strange etchings on the page. She had always loved to look at the pictures though, and often her brother would read her stories from the big book that he read oftenest of all.

At that moment Leah was called away by a servant to fix some crisis elsewhere on the estate, and Fiona was left alone to smell the musty, inky scent of writings and wonder at the meanings of the engravings. A servant brought her food as the afternoon drew on to evening; she was so absorbed in turning the yellowed pages and tracing the floral designs that she reached for the food without thinking, and a meat pasty was halfway to her mouth before she remembered her decision. She was a little sorry now, for she would have liked to have more time to look at the book, but she sighed aloud and crawled out of bed. For a moment she stood wavering at the window, looking down at the ground already coated with snow. Was it worth it? The aroma of good, hearty food tickled her nostrils and she almost gave in, but at the last moment she grabbed the platter and hurled the contents.

"FEEDING THE BIRDS, ARE you?"

Fiona jumped and spun around, dropping the silver plate to the floor with a clatter. Pierre stood in the doorway, evidently having entered just as her supper went out the window, and his eyes were extremely angry. "You have little respect for the way of things," he went on as he came further into the room and the girl shrank away. "You have a debt to pay to me, yet you would rather starve yourself than pay it. Tell me, is it really worth it?" Fiona wondered fleetingly if he had read her thoughts. "You English are a proud people indeed. Oh yes, I know where you are from. And that is the very reason why you should be grateful to me; I do not ask why you are here, nor where you were going, nor do I hand you in as a spy; I merely ask for three years' servitude from you, and then you may go free. Is that so very much to ask?"

"I do not want to serve you," Fiona found herself saying, though her voice was little more than a whisper.

"Ah, so you have a tongue in that tight mouth of yours! So then, you do not wish to serve me; very well. Then you will serve my wife, for she needs a maid badly. And there will be an end to this waste of food, yes?"

"I do not want to serve the French," she repeated doggedly.

Pierre flung back his head and laughed, a clear, ringing, but utterly mirthless laugh. "My wife has less French blood in her than do you, O Norman-born. She is of Germanic descent, and by serving her you will be breaking no ties of allegiance. You see? I am not so cruel as one might think. Serve her for three years and you go free; if you do not—well, death surely is freedom, but not the kind of freedom you wish, I think."

This was so. Fiona did not care for the dark void that lay beyond this life, and Pierre's firm words only enhanced this feeling. She thought of Leah, with her silence and her otherworldly beauty; perhaps it would not be such a burden to serve her. "You swear I will go free in three years?" she asked hesitantly.

"If both us are still alive, I swear you will go free," he affirmed. "It is settled?"

"It is settled," Fiona repeated bleakly.

"Good. Now, come to the hall and eat; you look like a stray cat, the way all your bones stick out." He held the door for her and led her to the dining hall, saying as they went, "As Leah's personal maid, you will eat with us in the evenings and your chamber will be just across from hers. And," he suddenly swung about and frowned at her, "I expect there to be nothing lacking in your service. Understood?"

He seemed to have a habit of asking forceful questions for which there could only be one answer, and Fiona nodded silently. His treatment of his wife puzzled her all through supper, which would have been them alone save for Fiona's presence and that of a favourite hound's, for though when she was not present Pierre seemed somewhat concerned for her welfare, yet his manner toward her face-to-face was frigid. Once, though, she caught him watching his wife out of the corner of his eye with something like confusion in his expression, and it was in that moment that it struck her that he was hardly more than a boy, really. The way he dressed and spoke made him appear much older, and yet in that moment Fiona realized that the lord of Gallandon was not only hardly beyond boyhood but was younger than his wife.

Their story went this way, as Fiona later learned from an over-talkative kitchen servant. Pierre was the eldest son of the powerful

Jean, Duke of Alençon, born to him probably (or so the servant suggested) by a maid in his father's house while the duke was still only in his early teenage years. It was not unheard of and did not raise much scandal, but being an illegitimate child put Pierre out of the lineage to inherit the dukedom. That honour had recently gone to his younger, legitimate brother, also by the name of Jean, when their father fell at the Battle of Agincourt. Either to reward Pierre for his part in the battle or to pacify him—for there was a great deal of friction between himself and his brother, arising from the elder's jealousy—the Court had granted him the swampy land of Gallandon to be lord over.

Now, Pierre was not and never had been pleased with this turn of events, knowing that if the English continued to push, his lands would fall into their hands at any rate, and he determined that the best way to elevate himself was by a successful marriage. Through events that the servant did not care to elaborate on—Fiona was not sure if this delicacy arose from ignorance or fear—the young lord had but a few months ago been tricked into marrying Leah, who had nothing to her name save a substantial amount of money left to her by her merchant father.

The servant at this point in the tale took care to stress that Leah herself had been innocent of any conniving and that the blame lay on her brother. Still, Pierre was more than a little bitter over this turn of events; the whole story had only come out some days after the wedding when Leah's brother was far out of the way, and the lord was man enough not to seek a divorce—though the servant seemed to think that he would not have had such scruples had his wife been less pretty. That was how things lay now, the servant concluded with an evident note of satisfaction.

With this in mind, Fiona observed the lord and lady of Gallandon even more closely. Leah, she thought, was ashamed of the means by which they were united and often blushed and looked away when Pierre glanced in her direction. She spent her days sewing in her chamber, her slender fingers flying across the cloth, or taking turns about her bare little garden, laying out crumbs of stale bread for the animals to eat; but in all that she did she kept clear of her husband unless it was necessary to do otherwise. She was not the sort to enjoy being alone, however; her sensitive soul longed for company, and she took an immediate liking to her new maid. As for Fiona, after the passing of several weeks, the feeling became mutual.

It was difficult for the two to communicate, for Leah's primary mode of translation was through the written word, and the symbols meant nothing to Fiona's untrained eye. Yet it was imperative that they learn to do so; when guests dined with them in the banquet hall, Pierre was visibly ashamed of the muteness of his lady. Twice now he had stopped the new maid in the hallway and asked harshly, "Do you understand her?" And Fiona could only reply that she was learning to.

One afternoon as they were walking together in Leah's garden, which was her supreme delight, Fiona said aloud, "I would like to learn how to read."

The other glanced up from where she was spreading seed across the white ground, her dark eyes glittering. Then she turned back to her task and watched the robins dropping from their perches, placing shallow marks on the pure, unblemished bank of snow, cheeping softly and cocking their heads to look up at her. She went back inside, her step quickened with purpose, and Fiona followed curiously. Leah got ahead of her and the English girl came around a corner in time to see her mistress backing away after having collided with her husband. The two retreated, both looking embarrassed, and Pierre remarked roughly as he brushed himself off, "Your cheeks are red—you've been out in the cold too long. The weather is much too harsh for you to be taking walks out of doors. Where were you?" He turned to Fiona.

"Out in her garden, my lord," she replied; after hearing his story, she did not feel so afraid of her master. "Just a bit of land over on the south side of the manor; it's her favourite place to go."

"Is it?" Pierre glanced at his wife, perhaps trying to catch a glimpse of her downcast eyes. Leah nodded, shrinking back and seeming to hide behind her maid. "Ah. Well, perhaps we may plant some roses there this spring; do you like roses?"

Leah nodded again, raising a hand either to brush back the bit of hair that had escaped her net or to hide her face still further. Fiona watched as Pierre's eyes flicked over his wife's face a moment, and then he jerked quickly to one side and walked off down the corridor without another word. The lady raised her head and glanced after him then took her maid's hand in her own—Fiona noted how cold her fingers were—and pulled her along as she made her way to her chambers.

Once there, Leah took the leather-bound tome down from its perch on a shelf near the bed and laid it on the floor before the fire. She sat, beckoning Fiona to do so as well, and flipped to the closest picture. The maid started: it was a picture like the statuette she had seen so many times in chapel, an engraving of a man hanging on a cross, his head bowed—as before with the shadows in the sanctuary, the positioning left his face in darkness—and blood on his hands and feet.

"Why this one?" she asked. "Why not the one of the beautiful garden at the beginning?"

Leah's lips curled up into a smile and she tapped the cross with a finger, then, taking a quill and ink, wrote some symbols on a bit of parchment. Again she pointed to the picture and then to the symbols. Fiona looked at the latter, peering closely at them, and said at last, "Is that *cross*?"

The lady's whole face brightened immediately; she nodded, pointing to each single mark in turn and then underlining the entire thing with her finger. In this manner she would point to a part of the picture, write some more symbols, and Fiona would say what she guessed the symbols to mean. It was slow and difficult, but Leah was by no means a bad teacher and Fiona began to learn by the recurring patterns what each of the marks meant of themselves. Her eyes soon grew weary of searching out the arrangement, though, and at last she sat back and shook her head. "I can't think anymore," she protested, and Leah wisely set the lesson aside for the time being.

They continued to sit before the fire for awhile, both idle, and Fiona stared into the leaping flames and thought in silence. She was unsure as to whether she should speak her thoughts, but at last she said aloud, "I think he wants to please you."

There could be no doubt as to whom she spoke of, and she saw Leah stiffen slightly. Then the lady's thin shoulders moved in something like a shrug, though it was too quick to denote indifference. Fiona had no more to say but subsided and wondered what effect her words might have. In a detached sort of way she felt sorry for them, feeling something only a little stronger than a stranger's pity; she did not wish to grow too close to the family, for it was French even if Leah herself was not.

It occurred to her that Leah was once more opening the book and searching as though for a specific passage, and Fiona turned from her scrutiny of the deep flames to look at the picture that her mistress was pointing to. It was of a woman holding a baby in her arms and weeping what appeared to be tears of joy, and Leah was pointing as silently as ever to the newborn.

Fiona glanced at her companion's face, and the expression there filled in all that was missing. "You—you think he would love you if you gave him a son?" she asked carefully.

Again the slight shrug and inclination of the chin that Fiona took to be an assent. She had nothing to say to that; she had never considered marriage or love very closely before and she could not even fully understand Leah's unhappiness with her match. After all, many women had far less than she did; there was not much love involved, but at least Pierre was faithful and not a cruel man. And Leah's material gains were considerable as well: simply by giving her acquiescence at the altar, she had traded a hard life in an out-of-the-way, unheard-of town for life as the lady of a manor. Fiona could not see anything so very undesirable in that.

There were several guests at supper that night, as was usual in Gallandon. None of those present were very high ranking nobles, but none of them were merchants, either, and most were either at or a little below Pierre's own status. A few were his friends; most were merely his acquaintances. As Gallandon lay on the very border of French dominion, some of the noblemen were closer to Leah in frame and complexion than to Pierre, who was purely French. One thing had they in common, however: all present supported Charles VI in his claim to the throne, even if he was—as was common knowledge—insane. This characteristic made the group rather an oddity, for the Burgundian faction was prevalent in the close-lying region of Luxembourg to the east and many of the French people were nowadays siding with Henry in his claim.

As the evening wore on and the wine did its work, the talk became looser about the table. The topic took a swerve from a discussion of politics, which Fiona no longer cared to listen to, to Pierre's new bride, whom most of the men present had not yet seen. "Well, my lord," one man grinned through his beard, "you may have done better with fortune, but her looks are certainly well enough."

Anger flitted across Pierre's face, but the man was much older than he and so he kept his mouth shut, merely nodding briefly.

"That may be," another man spoke up, "but money and title surely are the best motives for marriage; after all, beauty is handy enough in maids."

"It is not a subject I wish to discuss at my table, gentlemen," Pierre interjected before the conversation could get off to a rolling start. He began a new topic and made sure that none drifted back to the former, but Fiona knew that for Leah the evening had been spoiled. She glanced over at her mistress; Leah's face was whiter than ever and her eyes were focused on the hands lying idle in her lap, the blood pounding visibly in her bare neck and behind her jaws. Fiona was accustomed to men's rude talk, but it was clear that the little lady, only recently introduced to the larger world, was not. On impulse she reached over and squeezed Leah's hand in her own; her mistress smiled faintly in reply.

That evening after Fiona had readied herself for bed, she stepped out of her room and went to cross the hall and see if Leah needed anything more before she went to sleep. The lady's door was open slightly, and through the space she saw Pierre and his wife standing before the fire talking—that is, Pierre was talking. Fiona pricked up her ears and listened.

"So … you like your new maid, then?" Pierre was saying brusquely.

Leah nodded, barely raising her head as she did so.

"She serves you well? You need nothing?"

Leah shook her head.

"Then you are happy here?"

Leah at last raised her head and looked the man in the face, began to nod her head, then shook it slowly. Fiona thought she saw tears glimmering in those huge, doe-like eyes, and then the maid drew back and shut the door gently before her with a slight smile, though she was unsure just why she felt pleased. Everything would be well for Leah now, she thought, and she was glad for her mistress.

As she lay in bed late into the night, however, her thoughts were not concerned with Leah. She was thinking of Giovanni and wondering who he might have married had he lived on; how strange it was to think of herself being an aunt. Or a mother—who might Giovanni have married her off to? It was yet stranger to consider that somewhere in England there was a man whose wife she would have been, but for the Battle of Agincourt.

"One little event can change so much," she whispered aloud, rolling over and looking out the dark window. "I suppose those things are unimportant in the eyes of Heaven, though; if God above is so mighty and infinite, he cannot care much for us mortals. So we have bishops and priests to keep us in line." She sighed, a part of her wondering what it would be like to serve God Himself and not the nearest cleric. Then she shivered: God cared about heresy; that much she knew.

She closed her eyes and saw again the picture from Leah's book of the bleeding body on the cross. If that tree-like figure was used to kill men on, why had Giovanni worn it around his neck? Was that not a rather morbid thing to do? And the carving in the chapel—surely such a worldly, violent depiction as the crucifix should not be presented to people at Mass. She opened her eyes again. "How is there peace to be found in that?" she asked the darkness. "I shall never understand."

THE NEXT DAY THINGS seemed the same as before between Pierre and Leah, but Fiona noticed that the latter blushed when the maid tactfully mentioned the lord's name. Fiona smiled and was silent on the subject then, and Leah's smile was grateful.

They spent the morning at study, this time using the picture of the place the older girl called *Eden*. This was Fiona's favourite of all the engravings, for it was done in colour and she liked to look at the vibrant greens and blues and reds, the garden all painted in shimmering, crystal-clear hues like a spring landscape. The artist had made everything as fresh and clean as it had been at the dawn of time; the sun seemed almost too bright to look at, the sky was deep as the ocean, and the dangling fruits looked as though they would taste like Beauty itself. Only the red, thick-bodied snake sunning itself on one branch seemed curiously out of place, and Fiona said so. As with the picture of the cross, Leah could only smile and keep on with her instructions.

At midday there was a knock at the door, and when summoned, Pierre showed himself. He hardly glanced at Fiona but swung out one arm toward his wife to show her the cloak of some soft animal's fur that draped it. "You need something more to keep you warm if you're going to be walking in the snow," he explained distantly, not sounding at all as Fiona imagined a passionate lover should.

A smile shot across Leah's face for an instant as she scrambled up from the floor, but she constrained herself and accepted the gift with a quaint little curtsy and with her eyes cast down as usual.

"Her ladyship is pleased with the gift, my lord," Fiona said, in case Pierre could not see that for himself.

He shot her a surprised glance as though he had forgotten her presence then headed for the door. He paused a moment before leaving to swing back and add, "I will be going hunting for awhile; you should not walk far from the house." Once again his words were directed at Leah, but Fiona assured him that they would not. He grunted and left them, and once more Leah's face blossomed in a smile she could not contain. Fiona also smiled, but it was only partially a happy one; what would she give to be as happy as her mistress!

Neither could focus on the lesson anymore, and so they went out into the garden—Leah with her new cloak flung across her shoulders, oddly thick and heavy on her slender frame—and stood looking out to the woods on the western slope. The manor sheltered them from the blast of the stormy north wind, but Fiona still shivered in the winter air and glanced at her mistress to see how she fared. Leah's face was calm again, but the laughter remained in her eyes and in the flush of her cheeks.

"You are happy, aren't you?" Fiona asked suddenly, startling herself by speaking.

The other turned from her perusal of the horizon, her lips turned out in surprise. She nodded but continued to look grave and did not smile.

"Why?" Fiona knew it was a silly thing to ask; Leah could not answer, at any rate.

But in this she was mistaken, for Leah answered by taking from under the cover of her dress a gold necklace, obviously several generations old at least, and held out the ornament that hung from it. The maid started forward slightly, then fell back; it was a cross, yes, but not Giovanni's: this one was made of tarnished gold and had tiny red gems like rubies encrusted down its length. It was small, and yet it seemed to glow with more life than Leah possessed of herself.

"My brother wore a cross like that," Fiona said after a moment. "He told me it could bring me peace, but I have not found it yet." She was unsure whether she meant that she had not found peace or that she had not found the cross, and it occurred to her that it was not just for Giovanni's spilled blood that she sought the heirloom, but out of her own selfish motives as well. She wanted to know that same restful assurance that had shone in her brother's eyes, even when times were bad; surely he had been far from perfect, and yet Fiona could think only of how joyful he had always been, how he had always seemed to rest in something greater than himself. A pang like a knife-thrust struck her heart, and she missed him terribly.

Leah's hand brushed her arm and she came out of her reverie sharply, shaking her head. The ache remained, but she ignored it. "The cross makes you happy?" she asked.

A frown knit the other's brows, as though she was not quite sure how to reply, and she shook her head slowly. There was a hint of frustration in her eyes, for she could not speak and explain the things as she wished to. She spread her hands helplessly.

"Never mind," Fiona quickly reassured her. "Come, we had best go inside; there's no point in your taking ill by being out in the snow too long." Leah agreed reluctantly and they retired indoors, Fiona changing the subject and speaking of all the different flowers they would plant in the garden come spring. Though she generally loved to hear her maid talk about the garden, which was indeed the place where she was happiest, it was obvious that the lady was not paying much attention to Fiona's words; she sat with the needle idle in her hand, gazing through the fire without blinking.

Suddenly she rose, sending her handiwork spilling across the floor, and crossed the room to where she had laid the book on a low table. Fiona glanced after her in surprise as she knelt to gather up the unspindled thread, but Leah found the picture she wanted and then eagerly beckoned Fiona to come and look at it. The latter obeyed, finding the engraving once again to be that of the man on the cross.

Leah once again held out her own ornament and shook her head, then pointed with one long, slender white finger to the marred body in the picture. She repeated the motion, her eyes begging Fiona to understand.

"It is not the cross that makes you happy," Fiona translated slowly; "it is the man on the cross?"

The radiant, dawn-like smile adorned her mistress' face again as she nodded her head.

"Well, I still don't understand how his death makes you happy," Fiona sighed, turning away. "Shall we work on my lessons again?"

The celebration of Christmas was fast approaching. It was not to be a grand one, for the state of France at this time forbid an excess of meat and drink, but there were Masses to attend all the week to celebrate the Nativity and there was to be a banquet at Gallandon on the eve. Fiona's lessons were put aside for awhile, as she was busy translating Leah's orders to the servants as the manor was decorated for the festivities. She was once more set in the role of mistress of the house, for she was Leah's mouthpiece and thus was allowed almost complete sovereignty over the household.

Holly boughs were secured across the entrances, their bright berries twinkling; the dining table was draped with the freshest cloth; candles glimmered throughout the hall; spices filled the air along with the crisp scent of new snow and the aroma of the logs snapping in the hearth. The mistral winds howled outside, but within all was warm and cosy. Even Pierre was cheerful in his own way, impatiently waiting for the first guests from his seat at the head of the table. His nostrils twitched, taking in the smells like an eager hound. "You've done well," he commented to his wife as she passed, exciting a blush. Then he added, "Have you been wasting the grain on the birds again? They'll grow fat and lazy and you shall catch cold."

That was the way it went between them, Fiona noted. He would compliment Leah on one point and then take her to task half-heartedly on another, apparently afraid that he might spoil his pretty, silent wife with too much favour as one spoils a small child with too many treats. She did not seem to mind, and Fiona watched their exchanges with a dry kind of amusement.

The first two coaches pulled up side by side before the stables, and Leah flew to finish those last little preparations that no one would notice one way or the other. The servants disappeared into the background to be silent and invisible assistants, and all the hounds save Nicé, Pierre's powerful, muscled black hunting hound who lay by his feet, were sent to their kennels. At last Leah stood still in the entryway, shaking all over and her lower lip quivering, for this was to be her first time hosting a great banquet. Even Fiona, who felt that the dinner was as much hers as it was that of her mistress, was nervous as she stood by Leah's shoulder to act as interpreter. A thousand questions flitted across her mind: Would the pheasant be too dry? Would the roasted apples be too runny? Would the seating be acceptable? There were too many possibilities; surely something must go wrong.

But nothing did, or at least nothing noticeable. Perhaps Lady Marguerite was not satisfied with being seated lower than Lady Marie and her husband, and the pudding could have been a little less gelatinous, but these things, major in and of themselves, were lost in the overwhelming success of the rest. Leah beamed like an angel from the foot of the table and Fiona, who was developing a headache from the hubbub and stress, managed to gather herself together and smile and nod and join in when the conversation was lagging. Her task as Leah's interpreter was much easier than she had expected, for it was enough for the guests to look at the lady of the manor: her words, if she had had any, could only have been second rate to her face.

When the dinner was over and the talk became sluggish, guests beginning to leave, Leah drew her maid into a dark corner apart from the rest. Her eyes shot pointedly to her husband and she mouthed a word, laying a hand on her flat stomach. Fiona stood uncomprehending. "Are you sick?" she suggested.

Leah shook her head, merriment dancing in her eyes even as her brows pulled down in frustration. Again she repeated the action, tapping Fiona on the chest and gesturing toward Pierre. Her lips moved again.

And like a sputtering candle, the light dawned. "A baby?" she gasped. Leah nodded violently, her hairnet bobbing wildly against her neck as her teeth showed in a smile. "Well, that's wonderful, but surely you don't want me to tell him? Me, of all people? Why, you made *me* understand—why can you not tell him?"

Leah's glance was reproachful. It was clear that she did not want the joyful message ruined by her own fumbling gesticulations, and so Fiona was to be thrown before the proverbial lion in her stead. She found it hard to be glad for her mistress, dreading her task as she did. She could only hope as she watched Pierre carefully that the wine would have the proper mellowing effect on his mood.

Too soon the guests had all gone and, Leah having retired, Pierre was the only one left in the hall, slouched to one side of his chair, his chin in his hand. She came up to him slowly and waited until he acknowledged her presence by sitting upright before beginning. "My lord?"

She was immediately interrupted by the speedy entrance of the household steward, who seemed to appear by Pierre's other side out of thin air. "Eh, what?" Pierre snapped at him impatiently, and the man proceeded to spill out his worries about something—a silver platter lost, or some such. His monologue took much longer than it should have, and the lord seemed irritated by it, waving away the servant with a vague, "All right, all right, speak to my wife about it tomorrow. There's no need to be stretching your jaw over it; get off with you."

The steward scurried away again, obviously relieved to have his task over with. Fiona could only wish she might feel the same.

"Well, what were you saying?" Pierre asked, rising so as not to have to look up at her.

The courage she had had at the start had waned into nothing through the steward's speech, and she barely found the strength to say, "My lady wished me to tell you something."

Something like worry flickered in his eyes a moment and he turned sharply on his heel, walking toward his own chambers with Fiona trailing along behind. "So? Out with it," he demanded.

She searched madly for the words she had prepared beforehand, but they were gone. "She said—she wanted me to tell you—," she tripped and stumbled over the words, fumbling far worse than Leah could ever have done.

Pierre whirled back in the hallway, crying, "Good heavens above, are you as mute as she? Wind up your tongue and speak coherently now."

"She wanted me to tell you that she is going to have a baby," Fiona blurted and the next instant wished her voice had not come out quite so loud.

It took a moment for the words to sink in, and then Pierre was standing open-mouthed like a fool, his face wiped clean of every expression save shock. A few unintelligent words dribbled from his mouth, and his first comprehensible sentence turned out to be not so very clever either: "Is it a boy or a girl?"

Fiona only looked at him long and hard.

In a moment he realized his mistake and tried to redeem himself, stammering, "Oh-oh, right, of course, you don't know yet. Eh … well, that is—yes. Thank you for telling me." And he turned and hurried off, hands clasped at his back, leaving Fiona wondering whether to laugh or cry. In the end she decided that her head hurt much too badly to do either, and she went slowly back to her chamber and crawled into bed without even taking the time to tell Leah about it.

The next morning when Fiona woke her mistress and calmly went about laying out her clothes for her, Leah sat up, flinging off her sleep, and looked eagerly at the younger girl. Her expression could not be misunderstood. Still, Fiona finished her task with painstaking care before replying, "Yes, I spoke to him."

Leah's eyes were half fearful as she tried to see what the other was leaving unsaid. She caught Fiona's wrist in her hand and tugged it insistently.

Fiona sighed. For some reason she was reluctant to tell Leah all; she was reluctant to make the other even happier. Though she had adjusted to life here as a servant, she had not forgotten the aching pit inside herself. Time only seemed to widen the gap and deepen it so that she now believed nothing, not even the cross, could fill it. It did not seem fair that others should have such a perfect life when she had nothing.

At last she did speak, though. "He was pleased, I think, albeit somewhat confused."

The fear faded from Leah's eyes and she retracted her hand. She did not smile as usual but only looked content. She did not ask and Fiona offered no more, so the subject was dropped and not taken up all that morning. They returned to Fiona's studies, but she found it hard to concentrate on what she was doing. Her headache from last night had carried over into the day, the pictures did not seem beautiful to her, and her mistress' sketchy symbols made no sense.

"Oh, what good is it?" Fiona cried, shoving the book almost into the ashes. "What does it matter whether I can read or not? I am tired of it all; I'm tired of crosses and pictures and emptiness—always emptiness! I want to go back to the way things were before—before the battles." And Fiona dropped her head into her hands and began to cry, unable to stop the flow of tears. It seemed like years since she had cried; it felt good to have the dam broken again.

Leah drew Fiona's head into her lap as a mother would and stroked her hair, humming softly the one noise she could form. The younger girl did not want to be comforted—it was enjoyable simply to revel in her own misery for awhile—but in time she could not help herself. Her sobs quieted into occasional sniffles and she asked brokenly after a moment, "Do you love Pierre?"

The hand on her head paused and she felt Leah nod.

"Do you think he loves you?"

There was a longer gap this time before a slower, more hesitant nod came.

"I would like to be married," Fiona sighed. It was the first time the thought had occurred to her plainly, but it was true. How wise Giovanni had been; she wished now that he had chosen a husband for her, for then she would not be here: she would be safe in her own home, comforted from her grief and far from the cares of the distant world.

There was probably much that Leah wanted to say, but none of it could be spoken in words; that was the worst of her muteness. Her thoughts were as intact as Fiona's, and yet the separation between them was greater than a difference in languages; languages could be learnt, but Leah could not learn to speak. A heavy sigh whistled through her nose.

That afternoon, when Fiona's emotions had been carefully put back together and the two, after taking their daily walk and their domestic rounds of the manor, were sitting by the fire warming their chilled hands and faces, Pierre blundered into the room like a whirlwind without stopping to knock. Both ladies started and Fiona wondered fleetingly where he had been during the morning—perhaps out hunting to relieve his feelings.

He ignored the maid's presence; indeed, he did not seem to realize she was there at all. He moved straight across the room to stand before Leah, who had risen to greet him, and said eagerly, "It is true, then? You are quite sure?"

Leah nodded and Fiona saw that she was trembling; the light of fear had been rekindled in her eyes. But a smile lit up Pierre's face, again making him appear boyish and somewhat the fool. "A son to bear my name," he said proudly, then added, "though I would not mind a girl-child. What? Why do you hide your face?" His smile changed to a frown and he glanced bewilderedly at Fiona, who could only suggest,

"It is not modest to discuss such things, my lord."

"Modest? Nonsense. What is wrong with talking about our child? Come, don't be blushing—you blush far too much as it is. Look at me. No? You will not? Well, then, I'll leave you womenfolk alone and cease to embarrass you further." He dropped Leah's hands, but not angrily. He was too proud and filled to the bursting with excitement to be angry. He remembered something as he reached the hallway, however, and came hurrying back. "Leah?"

His wife jumped and even Fiona was startled to hear him say her name; it sounded strange coming from his mouth.

"Leah, I wanted to tell you—" he paused uncomfortably, "I wanted to tell you there is no other. I am faithful to you, and I will stay so. I thought you might like to know." And then he was gone again without waiting for a look in reply.

"You are fortunate in your husband," Fiona commented as the door thudded shut at Pierre's back.

Leah smiled demurely and buried herself in her perusal of the household accounts.

†

In the months that followed, maid and mistress set themselves to the task of sewing clothes for the baby. Winter turned into spring; the farmers under Pierre's lordship sheered their sheep and a portion of the fleece went to him, and the women used them to sew the child's winter clothing. Leah got her roses and waited eagerly for them to bloom, sitting under a tree in the garden, her hands sewing and her eyes watching the healthy young bushes. She no longer set out food for the animals, for it was warm enough for them to find their own, but it seemed to Fiona that the birds still sang more cheerfully when the lady was among them than when she was absent.

As for Fiona, she often daydreamt of spring back home and missed the great green slopes and the freshness of the leaves and the sight of the sun sinking west of the towering mountains of Wales. At such times her needle would fall idle in her hand and she would stare straight before her with a longing that, unbeknownst to her, made Leah's heart ache for her. Spring had always been her favourite season; she had loved the way the whole earth seemed to break forth from the shackles of winter and rejoice at its newfound freedom. She remembered once saying to Giovanni that she thought there was nothing that spring could not thaw. She found now that she was wrong: the warmth could not thaw the bitterness inside her heart. It only made the cold cling more tenaciously, thickening and hardening like a scab over her soul.

She did not think much about the cross these days, though. She was too busy with household affairs during the day—helping Leah to keep the servants in check during the long weeks when Pierre had to be away on business—and during the night she had scarcely a moment to think clearly before she slept. Her lessons continued and she made a great deal of progress, now being able to read short, clear sentences, but they did not use the picture of the dying man anymore and it was not the kind of thing that Fiona liked to dwell on. Occasionally Leah would have her try to read passages from the book, but it was difficult and the words rarely made sense.

As the season progressed, it became harder and harder to fit her reading into the course of the day. At the first of spring Pierre had set the progress of the manor in motion, for he had not forgotten his desire to make something of a name for himself. There was little that could be done to the east, where the marsh lay, but the forests to the northwest were rich in those trees most needed by craftsmen, and the southward slopes were easily ploughed. The household grew as he brought in more men to work the fields, and the money increased as he charged for the felling of the trees; Leah was, as ever, in charge of the accounts, while Fiona had been set under the head steward to keep the household servants in check. It was not hard work, but it kept one busy and her studies lagged.

Outside the world of Gallandon, little was happening as far as Fiona knew and cared. From bits and pieces of conversations gathered at dinners, she understood that King Henry was still in England but that things had not been satisfactorily concluded between the two nations; it was likely, or so Pierre seemed to think, that another campaign would soon be launched against France. No one seemed to have great faith in the power of the French armies, and yet she could not feel proud or pleased. What, she asked herself again, was France or England to her?

She was at times appalled by the way her zeal for her nation had thus begun to slip away; she no longer thought of herself first and foremost as English but simply as Fiona. If anyone had asked her, "What are you?" she would have replied without blinking, "I am Fiona." It was an odd feeling for her, raised as she was to respect and love and defend England's honour with her life blood. But now she only thought, *What is England to me? She took my brother from me. What is England to me?*

This is not to say that she felt any growing attachment to France as a nation. The two powers meant equally little to her, for both had played their role in Giovanni's destruction. To her, England had decided his fate; France had merely been the executioner. She hated both.

Pierre and Leah, however, she could not hate so easily. Though Pierre had fought and been wounded in the Battle of Agincourt, bearing the marks still to prove it, she no longer felt the passionate loathing toward him that she had upon first coming here. She respected him for his ability to love Leah and remain faithful to her in a world that laughed at such morals, and at the same time a part of her excused him for his part in the battle because of his youth; she half wondered if he had even known what it was to fight and kill before that time.

And Leah? Fiona found it impossible to conceive of anyone not liking the sweet, charming little lady, with her charitable spirit and her white beauty. The two were more like sisters than mistress and servant, though there were many things about her that Fiona could not understand—the cross most of all. Leah had tried many times to explain its purpose, but she was forced to write longer words than her maid could understand, and it always ended in even more confusion than had been there at the outset.

SPRING BECAME SUMMER, A warm, generous summer as the land rested from war. Leah's belly began to round out and she and Fiona sewed faster, arranging the child's room and preparing for the birthing during those times of the day when Leah was not troubled by sickness. Neither expressed the fear that surrounded that mysterious date in the future, almost overpowering the joy; neither made mention of that horrible, enigmatic question: would the child live? So many babies did not, and Leah herself was not a strong woman by nature. Fiona feared for them both.

She thought at first that the possibility had not occurred to Pierre, but one hot day as the end of summer approached he called her to him. He was standing in an empty stall in the stables, seemingly watching the chestnut gelding stabled in the space next to him, and his face was hidden in shadow as he asked harshly, "Is the baby healthy?"

Fiona was taken aback. "I believe so," she supplied tentatively, and then, guessing by the way her master shifted that this was not a good answer, she added, "The doctor seems to think so."

He grunted. "And my wife?"

"She is as well as one might expect. She still has her morning sickness—"

"Yes, I know of that. But tell me, Fiona," he glanced about and gestured her nearer, "tell me, is she *well*? Do you think…? Bah!" He swung away, one fist planted on his hip. For a moment he breathed hard, and then he turned back and began afresh. "I know as well as you do—perhaps better—the dangers of childbearing. I want to know, do you think she will be well enough to … to bear the child without complications?" His eyes flickered back and forth between Fiona's, but because of the dark she could not see the expression in them.

"I do not know, my lord," she answered truthfully. There was nothing encouraging to add; that was where things lay for the present.

"No," he sighed, "I suppose you don't. God knows, and He alone." His voice shook slightly as he said the last, and he waved Fiona away fiercely as though he did not wish her to see his fear.

The conversation explained to her why Pierre went nearly every day to the chapel and why as the months passed his face became tighter and more pinched. He feared for his wife more than Fiona had thought at first, and she was unsure whether to respect him further for it or to laugh at him. As it happened, she did neither; she was too busy at her own worries.

Leah entered into her confinement sometime toward the latter end of August and the air about Gallandon grew tenser. Pierre went hunting more often; so often, in fact, that his favourite horse grew lame from overuse. Leah stayed in her bed for the most part, her legs weak from the weight above them, and Fiona stayed with her and haltingly read bits and pieces out of one of the lord's books. Her performance was quite poor, but her mistress never seemed to mind; she smiled, though her eyes were tired, and nodded encouragement.

Fiona glanced up from the book, wiping a hand across her wet, sticky forehead. The fire was blazing even though outside the earth was scorched brown by the pounding summer sun, for Francis, the physician, had ordered that it be kept so for the benefit of the pregnant woman. Leah did not look particularly benefited, however; her own face was beaded with sweat and she shifted miserably beneath the heavy covers.

"How are you?" Fiona asked wearily, adjusting the pillows at her mistress' back.

Leah forced a smile to her lips, which were starkly red against the ashen hue of her cheeks. She nodded her head slightly to indicate that she was well, but her complexion did not back up her words. She indicated for Fiona to keep reading and turned her head to watch the door; she was waiting, the maid knew, for her husband's daily entrance.

Hours more seemed to pass. The curtains were drawn to keep the glare from wounding Leah's weak eyes, as they had been for Fiona's father, and the air was close and as sultry as ever an August day could be. The water began to drip off the end of her nose and splash on the thin, aged pages; she wiped the spots away with a stifled sigh.

At last the door opened and Pierre thrust his head in to assure himself that his wife was awake, and as he stepped in his expression changed. "Saints alive! Is she to be broiled alive in her bed? Fiona, bank that fire! No excuses, you sorry wench! Saints!" he muttered furiously beneath his breath, himself stripping the excess blankets of Leah's swollen form. He felt her face, ignoring the noises of protest, and cursed again. "Fiona, get some cold water and rags."

Fiona scuttled off, wondering if doing the obvious really would be a help; it did not seem logical that making Leah comfortable would kill her in the long run.

Things go slowest when one is in a hurry, and Fiona's task seemed to take her forever. When at last she returned, breathing hard and ready to collapse, Pierre was standing by the bed with his hands flung up, glancing about him bewilderedly. He looked up when she came in, his eyes blank. "She says her water has broken," he said with a helpless gesture.

Fiona stood still a second, trying to recall something, anything that she might have learned about midwifing. She had never expected to be doing it herself, though, and she was nearly as lost as Pierre. "Get those sheets off," she ordered, drawing herself together and affecting an attitude of certainty. "And—wipe her forehead." She shoved the pitcher and rags into Pierre's hands and flew out the door, shrieking the physician's name long before he could possibly have heard her from where his cottage stood near to the chapel.

She collided with him just as he was coming out his door, apparently preparing to visit Leah, and Fiona did not even need to speak; the absurdly calm, knowledgeable look showed itself immediately in his dreamily blinking eyes and kind smile, and he toddled back inside to gather his kit together.

"Must you take so long?" Fiona burst out impatiently, standing at the doorway and hopping back and forth between feet. She jerked her head toward the manor as though to hurry him along, but Francis was not to be hurried. He hmmed and hahed carefully over each thing that he tucked into his bag, not even bothering to offer reassurance to the anxious maid. At last he had all that he needed, and Fiona grabbed his arm and hauled him off after her.

She would gladly have run back, but the physician had no intention of setting his appearance in disarray by running all that distance under the sweltering August sky. He walked, and Fiona felt compelled to walk as well. Yet the thought of strolling casually down the dirt path while Leah was giving birth with no one but Pierre to help her was ludicrous; she broke into a jog then fell back into step with Francis.

"Now, now, don't be anxious," he admonished her as they at last gained the manor. "To be anxious is certainly the worst thing for her—she must see you as quite calm. Compose yourself."

"Oh yes," Fiona grated. "I will indeed—I shall compose myself, if only you will move a little faster!"

Francis sighed but did not comply, only continuing to amble down the corridor at his own steady pace. Fiona announced their presence by flinging open the door and rushing to Pierre's side, for she did not care to let him know that they had walked the whole way back. "How is she?" she gasped.

Pierre glanced up, clearly thanking God that they had finally appeared, for he looked to be at his wit's end already. He did cast the doctor a murderous glare, however, showing that he had not forgotten that this man had tried to boil his wife alive; but he let the subject lie. He gave a partial shrug in reply to Fiona's question; "I don't know, really. She keeps saying she wants to get up."

"Get up?" Francis looked scandalized. "No, no, no—do you want to drop the child on the floor? No, no. Now you—" he pointed a long, accusing finger at Fiona "—why have you let the fire die? Stoke it right away."

"Why, do you wish her to die of the heat?" Pierre roared at last, his hand gripping Fiona's sleeve to keep her from obeying the doctor's orders. "Warmth, my foot. If my wife dies under your hands, I swear I will see you run out of France like a vagabond!"

Francis did not seem outwardly affected, but he grunted and turned back to the task at hand without pressing the matter.

Leah's contractions were not yet close enough together, and so came the waiting. Pierre sat by her head and spoke encouragements in her ear while Fiona paced and the physician sat with his feet up, looking as calm as could be. They were the only three in the chamber, for those servants who knew of the matter wisely kept away until they were needed; Leah's hoarse breathing filled the room.

And then the time came. Leah stiffened and her breath came quicker, her whole body quivering with fear and pain. Francis unfolded himself carefully from his seat and came over, pronouncing cheerfully, "Yes, here it comes. My lord, I think that you should—"

"I'll stay where I am," Pierre growled.

The doctor shrugged. "As you like it. Ah, girl, come over here now."

Poor Leah could not scream or cry out but simply writhed and moaned as much as she could. Fiona's stomach flip-flopped sickeningly and her mind cried before she could check it, *"Oh God, take care of her!"*

The temperature of the room seemed to rise by the minute. Once again the sweat was running down Fiona's arms and drenching her hair, and Pierre stripped off his heavy doublet and pushed the long, white sleeves of his shirt up his arms. The blood was gone from his face. Only the physician was still composed, even pausing to remark, "Ah, 'tis nearly chilly in here." Pierre and Fiona could only glance up and wonder fleetingly if he had lost his mind.

At last the baby's head became visible, and Francis said that it was turned the right way. Leah was heaving like a spent mare now, her tangled, wet locks spilling across the pillows and her hands clutching at the bed covers until her knuckles turned white. Suddenly she reached out and blindly grabbed at the neck of Pierre's tunic, tearing at it so as to burst several of the buttons. Her mouth formed the word *baby* repeatedly; he tried to reassure her as he disentangled her hand. "'Tis all right," he said encouragingly, squeezing her hand.

Fiona saw his own hands shaking as they helped to coax the child free, and she glanced up briefly to see how he fared. He was pale and his half-parted lips were wet with the saliva that he had not had time to swallow, but the look in his eyes was firm and tense. He paused a moment to shake the sweat from his eyes, and the motion set something swinging at his neck—a bit of silver falling from the cover of his shirt.

It dangled hardly an inch before her eyes, mocking her impishly: the figure of a cross. It was no beauty, though it probably had been in its time. The silver was not tarnished with age, but one arm had been bent and then hammered back into place. She could see all the fine details: she could even see the dark bits of mud engrained in the ornament.

Her mouth was dry. She thought back to her dream and sought to recall the images, now hazy in her mind, of the two soldiers, but she could not say whether the one was Pierre. And yet there was no mistaking it: the cross was Giovanni's, her brother's, her dearest brother's.

All this took less than a second of time. Her hands left their task—she raised a finger and pointed at him—she tried to speak, but nothing came out. Her body shook and all became dark except the swaying cross, all silent except the rhythmic pounding of her heart in her ears.

THE WORLD BEGAN TO clear above her and she wondered how it had come to be so distorted in the first place. When at last everything had settled like dust into its proper place, she turned her head and found that she was lying, as she had fallen, on the hard wooden floor; it seemed that Francis and Pierre had merely pushed her limp form out of the way and continued with the birthing. She sat up dazedly, clutching her head, and looked around.

It was strangely quiet—the sort of quiet that was never welcome. Her thoughts skipped hastily from the cross and she remembered Leah and the baby, and she knew what the silence meant. The thudding in her chest stopped; she got slowly to her feet and came toward the bed. *Oh God, oh God, I am cursed! Dead, everyone is dead. Oh God, oh God …*

"Well, you might have told me you so disliked the sight of blood," a harsh voice spoke in her ear.

She turned as if in a dream and saw Pierre, still in his torn shirt and with a bit of smeared blood on his face and hands, cradling a newborn in his arms. She opened her mouth to exclaim, but he replied, "Hsst! We only just got him to sleep. And let her alone," he nodded toward the still form on the bed; "she sleeps as well, no thanks to you. The physician says she did far better than he had expected and we have no need to worry for her," he added with the smallest hint of pride.

"And the child?" Fiona heard herself asking, trying to catch a glimpse of the infant.

"He is healthy enough, or so Francis says, but … you know how children are. There is always the possibility." He did not seem as worried as he had before, though; something in the child's rosy, healthy face and delicate body could ease anyone's fears.

"I *am* sorry I fainted," Fiona said at length, her eye catching sight of the cross lying on Pierre's chest even as she spoke.

He nodded somewhat curtly. "Well, I suppose I should not have expected so much of you."

Fiona was not sure what to say to that, so she held out her arms instead and offered, "Shall I take the child for you?"

Pierre looked loath to give up his son, obviously not seeing how ridiculous he looked coddling a baby, but at last he gave the child up. "He will be hungry when he wakes," he commented. "I will arrange a wet-nurse for him."

There came a moan from the bed at their backs and they turned. Leah was pulling herself up slightly against the headboard, shaking her head as vehemently as she could make her light, dizzy head move. She held out her arms for the baby and Fiona lowered him into them carefully. The new mother tucked the body close to her own and rocked him, her lips forming a silent word: *mine*.

It was clear that she wanted to nurse him herself, and Pierre did not raise the objections that Fiona expected. He only frowned a little and said, "I don't want you to weary yourself, my love. Perhaps for the first few weeks we should have a nurse, hmm?"

But Leah shook her head again and looked so pleadingly at her husband that he merely shrugged, a smile beginning to twitch at his lips. Fiona was shocked that he would let his wife degrade herself so; a noblewoman, even a noblewoman by marriage, should not have to take on the task of caring for her infants. Was it not bad enough that she had to bear the child? Fiona watched with a look akin to resentment as Pierre gathered up his discarded doublet and left, all the hatred she had ever felt for the French coursing anew through her veins. If he had stood before her with his hands literally covered in Giovanni's blood, she could not have despised him more.

"Come, you ought to rest," she said in a grating voice, snatching the baby from its mother's arms before Leah could raise a protest. "He can sleep in the crib here, and when he wakes I will tell you."

Her mistress was reassured by this promise, but no sooner had she drifted off to sleep than Fiona was hurrying from the apartment, her head in a whirl. She ran to the garden, where she was sure of being left alone, and flung herself down under the shade of an elm tree with her head laid against the bark. Her temples throbbed; the ground seemed to shift beneath her.

At long last she had fulfilled the first part of her mission: she had discovered the cross. She could hardly believe that after nearly a year of being without it, a year of missing the one thing that recalled an image of Giovanni's face to her mind, it had hung barely a hand's length away from her. It had been within such an easy distance—as good as hers. She had lost that chance, but she knew that it would not be very hard to take it from him; she had only to slip into his chambers one night and take it from his neck, and then she could be off, heading back for England and home.

A part of her was taut and shivering with the urgency of it all, but another part of her—her conscience or her common sense, she knew not which—spoke out to check the other. Summer was fast drawing to a close, autumn would soon be upon them, and the mistrals would come quicker than she could reach the coast and be back in her homeland. No, she must bide her time here until spring came again; then would be the best time.

She shut her eyes fiercely and gripped the old tree as if to strangle it. She hardly knew how she would survive so long in continued dependence on her brother's killer—how she *had* survived so long, without some instinct telling her who it was she was living with; the thought was like bile in her throat that would not be swallowed. "But if it must be so, it must be so," she murmured, loosening her handle on the elm. She almost offered up a prayer to the Virgin Mother, but her thoughts went back to the other times she had requested anything of Mary; under the sight of Heaven, it seemed that Fiona was abhorred.

The wrestling of her mind took longer than she thought, and when she raised her head she spotted Francis walking toward her as leisurely as ever. He came right up to her before saying, his voice completely lacking in the worry that the words bespoke of, "You should not leave your mistress alone. She will need constant attention for many weeks, you know, as will the babe. And of course, there will be the christening. You will hold the child for that, I think; I doubt that the lady will be well enough. You shall not neglect your duties, will you?"

"No, sir," Fiona replied mechanically, her eyes fixed on a point somewhere above Francis' left shoulder.

"Good, good," the physician beamed. He looked as though he had just returned from a refreshing dip in a river or a bracing walk but not at all like a doctor who had just delivered a baby. His expression never seemed to change, for it was always cheerful, calm, and a little blank; Fiona never could decide whether to like him or be disgusted by him. His message given, he ambled off again in the direction of his house.

Inside, she found the baby, whose name was not to be spoken before his christening, just beginning to awake in his crib. He stirred and stretched his quaint little fists above his head, his toothless mouth opening in a yawn. Dazed, he blinked at the unfocused world around him before he realized the emptiness in his belly and discovered his lungs. His weary cry pierced the quiet like an arrow and all Fiona's cradling and rocking and soothing words would not lull him into serenity again.

There was no need for Fiona to wake the mother, for Leah started into consciousness at the first scream. Though she looked fit to die from exhaustion, she reached for her child and Fiona had no choice but to reluctantly hand the babe over. "You must not tax yourself," she admonished, frowning.

Leah merely smiled wearily and nursed the baby until he was quiet then handed him back to her maid. She reached for a scrap of parchment—the back of one of Pierre's maps—and wrote in a sloping, weak hand, *Is he not handsome?*

Fiona had had enough teaching that she understood the meaning of the words; she cast about her nervously. "You must not be too proud of him," she whispered. "The Devil—" she crossed herself "—is sure to steal him away if you do."

Leah's lips opened in a soundless laugh and she shook her head pityingly. She shifted so as to have a better view of her son, but soon sleep was again clouding her gold-flecked eyes; just before she succumbed to it, she took a firmer grip on the quill and scrawled, *A son to bear his father's name.* She was asleep before Fiona could reply.

The days and weeks that followed the birthing were strained. A child was at risk during any part of the year, but autumn and winter were certainly the worst times to give birth, and Fiona could only hold her breath and wait until that first tenuous month was over. The baby seemed to grow as it should have in the days leading up to the christening, but Fiona knew nothing of the matter herself. Every time the crib was still, every time she lost the sound of the child's soft, steady breathing, her heart leapt into her throat and that inexpressible fear sent a shiver down her spine.

Leah seemed to feel none of this. She was, Fiona thought, inordinately proud of her son and expressed not the slightest bit of doubt that he would grow and mature as he ought, and her complacency only made Fiona even more alarmed; it could only be asking for demons to snatch the baby's soul away. Though not religious, Fiona was as superstitious as ever an Englishman or a Welshman could be and she believed in spirits to the same degree that she did not believe in the effectiveness of prayer. She worried that a draft of cold air would steal away the child's breath or that if a window or door was left cracked a faerie (if they had faeries in this stark land) would slip in and abscond with him. And yet Leah only laughed at her fears.

On the eighth day after the birth, though the weather had unmistakeably shifted straight from the seasonable warmth of summer to the blasting, shuddering winds of winter with only a few days' pause for the harvest, the baby was to be christened. As expected, Leah was not yet well enough to carry the child to the chapel herself, and so Fiona took her place. Under the mother's instructions she painstakingly bundled the baby up until it cried from the heat and its face turned pink then cradled it in her arms and stepped out into the cold.

The household walked to the chapel in a long procession with Pierre leading, a lantern in hand, Fiona following with the child tucked close to her chest, and the servants ending the train with their own lanterns. There was as yet no snow on the ground, but the dry, crackling, brown leaves swirled and tumbled along the path at their feet like eastern dancers and the gusting wind tried to tear off their cloaks. Pierre and Fiona were all too glad to at last reach the shelter of the church, but the servants were consigned to remain out of doors until the end of the service.

Inside, the candles on the altar burned bright and their waxy scent wafted down the aisle and filled the sanctuary. The stone walls captured the heat and left the room with a familiar warmth, but not a friendliness, for the figurines and the murals seemed to look down on all who entered with a kind of arrogant scorn that made one feel guilty of one knew not what. A basin lay on the middle of the white cloth covering the altar and the priest stood ready beside it.

The babe in Fiona's arms took a bleary look around it and immediately let loose a shrill wail, which she vainly tried to stifle. Pierre glanced at her, and she could not tell if he was angry or surprised; those of the church did not seem to notice the child's noise. By some unseen signal the ceremony began, and surrounded by Latin chants from the choir, Pierre and Fiona brought the baby slowly down the aisle and handed him over to an attendant of the priest. The latter dipped his fingers into the scented water, made the sign of the cross over the baby by touching its forehead, mid-torso, and shoulders, and then with an incomprehensible benediction sprinkled its forehead and gave it its name: Pierre Jean Charles.

Fiona released a hollow breath, realizing that up till now she had been holding it as she watched the proceedings. The first part of the ceremony was over without any mishap, though young Pierre continued to scrunch up his eyes and cry through it all; a few other rites were to be performed for the child's entrance into the Holy Church, and then they had only to get him back through the cold and safely home again. Her female mind objected to the idea of bringing the newborn out into cold with the sole purpose of sprinkling it with water, then bundling it back out into the cold so that it (more than likely) would catch a fever and die. She crushed such thoughts, however, and hoped with a shiver that they would be overlooked.

The ritual, all in all, took a little more than half an hour and when they returned they found Leah sitting up in bed and vexed over all the things she imagined to be happening to her young son. She was glad to be able to cradle the warm little body in her arms and nurse it, and she demanded a full account of the events. Fiona found that she could call no more to mind than that the chapel had been hot and the air close, but Pierre remembered more and was willing to sit and recount it for his wife.

Leah's eyes smiled as her husband spoke, but Fiona noticed the little lines at the corners of her mouth that told that she was in pain. The maid soon got Pierre from the room and convinced Leah to give up the baby so as to put him to sleep, remarking as she laid the sleepy form into its crib, "You should rest as well, my lady; you look tired."

Leah sighed and shifted, for this enforced rest was the one thing in which she showed an uncooperative spirit. Fiona caught the movement and continued sombrely, "The more you rest, the sooner you will be up again. Now *do* be good and sleep a little." She helped her mistress to lie down and settled her in then left the room—not to sleep, but to grab this precious little bit of private time with her thoughts.

IT DID NOT LAST long. She heard a disturbance in another part of the house but did not pay attention to it until Pierre himself, re-attired in his best clothes and wearing a sword at his waist, came to her door and knocked. She came out, frowning.

"Fiona," Pierre began urgently, "there is a guest newly arrived, and as my wife is unwell, you must fill her place in greeting him—the guest."

Fiona's frown deepened. Many guests came to Gallandon, but there were none among Pierre's acquaintances as far as she knew to make his knuckles turn white and anxiety show in his eyes. She opened her mouth to protest, but he cut her off with, "Nay, no questions; come along. And keep quiet," he added as he hurried down the corridor; "I do not wish him to know how ill bred you are."

Fiona's curiosity was too piqued for her to be hurt by Pierre's words; she followed him closely and wondered if her clothing and appearance were acceptable. At the entrance her master halted suddenly and began to glance over his own clothing, adjusting his sword nervously and swiping at his doublet. He shot Fiona a critical glance as well and nodded with a slight grunt to tell her that she looked well enough. Then she saw him take a deep breath, shut and open his eyes, and raise his head high as he went out to greet the newcomer. Fiona followed at a respectful distance, keeping in the background as a woman was to do on such occasions.

The man stood in the courtyard by his tall, black devil of a horse which had not the slightest appearance of having carried its master any distance at all; it stood flicking its tail lazily and looking about while the man did the same, though, having no tail, he twitched his fingers idly back and forth instead. The newcomer had his back to them at first and when he turned Pierre's body stood between himself and Fiona so that she could not see his face, but when he spoke the voice rang in her head like a church's warning bell.

"Ah, brother, I have come to visit you for a time and to—but why so harsh an expression, friend?"

Pierre shifted and the man came into view. The first thing Fiona saw was his eyes, his bright blue eyes that looked like bits of rock in their sockets, and that and his voice were all she needed to take her back to the night in the St. Pol tavern; a cold feeling came to rest in her belly, unaffected by the air around her.

For the moment the man had not noticed her. Pierre took a moment to draw a breath and cool his temper before replying with a care that belied his anger, "I have no reason to welcome you."

The other did not seem in the least affected by this greeting; surely he had been expecting it. "You still hold that grudge, brother? Surely time and my pretty sister have thawed it for me."

"Brother!" Pierre scoffed. "What right have you to call me *brother*? You are my wife's brother, but not my own. Now get off my land."

"Would you turn a man out with neither food for the travel nor lodgings to go to, and with the winter hard upon us already? You are a harsh man, but I think you will honour the ties of family."

Fiona could not see Pierre's face, but she guessed by the lengthy silence that he was struggling to contain himself. When he spoke again, the strain of his tone proved her right. "You play me by that part of my nature you know," he grated; "and your tune is not a pretty one to my ear. Family! You speak of family! If I were to turn you out like a rabid hound, I would be doing no less than what I know you would do yourself. Family! You sold your own sister for the dowry price, and you speak of honouring family ties.

"I will open my house to you, then," he continued to Fiona's surprise, "if only to show that I am not such a man as you. You may stay for the winter months, but on the first warm day of spring you will be gone from my house and I will give you neither bread nor ale to take with you."

An expression that was either a smile or merely a curl of the lip showed on the man's face, but he only gave a mockingly low bow and said, "Ever a fountain of goodwill, my lord."

Pierre turned back toward Fiona and she saw his eyes flashing as he replied coldly, "Stable your own horse; my servants have better tasks to hand."

In all this Fiona had said nothing and had not once been noticed, but she was not sorry. She only wished she could hide herself forever from those eyes, and her sinking heart clung to the hope that he would not remember her. As she hurried after Pierre, close enough to tread on his heels, she recalled the feel of the man's powerful hand on her wrist; her arm even began to tingle and she wondered that there were not still marks upon it.

"Christopher is my wife's brother," Pierre said suddenly, so suddenly that it made Fiona jump. They stood in the great hall, though her feet did not recall bringing her there, and Pierre was fondling Nicé's slender, pointed head in both hands. "Some time before you came, he tricked me into an alliance with his sister, Leah, and the deal sits badly with me still. I assume you were wondering who he is."

Fiona recalled her talk with the loose-mouthed servant, but she only nodded slightly. "It … was kind of you to let him stay," she remarked tentatively.

"Kind?" Pierre jerked his head sharply. "Kind, perhaps, but I think it was foolhardy. Ah, well, I cannot go back on it now." He frowned savagely and slapped the dog's rump, shoving it away. "Tell Leah nothing of it yet; I will in time."

In time did not come for several more days, and in the meanwhile Fiona was able to avoid Christopher admirably. She was not called to dine with them but ate her meals with Leah in her mistress' apartments and thus was not a witness to the tension that hung between Pierre and his brother-in-law. Suppers, she heard the servants gossiping to one another, were like a bit of Hell. The maids hardly dared enter to change the courses, for they said they feared being in the room when the verbal explosion came. Everyone in the household, even Leah, felt the hostility in the air; she wrote a note to Fiona asking if something was wrong, and Fiona, her heart skipping a beat, smiled as best she could and replied, "No, nothing is wrong. Would you like me to read to you some more?"

During this time, Fiona's thoughts were more occupied with the problem of Christopher than with the cross, but she had not forgotten the latter altogether. She still recalled it in her sleep and would wake with a start to find herself in a sweat, heart pounding, her mind racing with guilt. That feeling—guilt—had been growing in her since the baby's birth, for even though she knew that Pierre was the one who had killed her brother, she found it harder and harder to hate Pierre or his family. Often she found herself forgetting about the cross altogether, and when the memory returned to pounce on her, the thought of vengeance was no longer sweet in her mind. Every day that she stayed strengthened the feeling, and the thought of leaving her little haven here at Gallandon tore her apart.

The day that Leah was able to get up and walk around the room a little bit was the one which Pierre, whether by accident or design, chose to tell his wife about the unwelcome guest. He came in just as Fiona was helping her mistress to sit down in a chair by the crib, and he wasted no time in getting to the point. "We have a guest among us, my love," he announced.

Leah glanced up, smilingly oblivious, and looked at her husband expectantly.

"Not a particularly welcome one," Pierre added. "Your brother decided to pay us a visit several days ago and asked if he might stay for the winter."

His wife's face paled instantly and Fiona, her dread aroused again by his words, shuddered and turned away to play with little Pierre again. She tried to shut her mind to what her master was saying, but the words still drifted into her hearing.

"I have granted him his request," Pierre continued with a grimace. "I think he will do us no harm."

Fiona shot a quick glance at Leah, but her mistress' expression said that she was not so sure. Leah reached out a hand for her husband and Pierre crossed the room and accepted it, leaning down to kiss her cheek briefly; Fiona politely dropped her eyes.

"It's only for a few months," he continued, almost cajolingly. "You have no need to fear him under my roof."

Fiona hoped that was true, for both herself and for Leah.

†

On the first of October, after a full month spent in her chambers, Leah was allowed by the physician to come to the dining hall for supper. She needed no one to lean on, but her steps were like a baby's: small and shaky. Fiona kept close and sometimes caught her arm to steady her, but though Leah's face was paler than ever when they reached the great room, there were no accidents along the way as Fiona had feared.

They found Pierre and Christopher already seated, but the latter jumped up as the ladies entered and flashed his brilliant smile; Fiona thought briefly that she had never seen such perfectly white teeth in her life, nor ones so dagger-sharp. She dropped her head in the hopes that he would not recognize her, but his eyes were only on Leah. "Well, sister!" he cried, coming to them. "What? Have you no greeting for me?"

A tremor ran through Leah's body as he bent and kissed both her cheeks; she pulled away as quickly as possible. Seated as she was at the foot of the table, so far from her lord Pierre, she looked no more at ease and it grew all the clearer to Fiona that her mistress, like herself, was terrified of Christopher. Even Leah's crimson lips were pale.

At the start the meal proceeded in silence, but Fiona knew it could not last. Too soon, far too soon, Christopher was breaking the silence with, "So, does your wife please you at all, brother?" His voice echoed to the very rafters and all the kitchen servants could hear it.

Pierre glanced up from handing a titbit to Nicé, a thundercloud on his brow. "We get on," he replied laconically, for Christopher was not to be ignored.

"Well, that is at least an improvement. I hear you even have a child."

Even Fiona's face blazed scarlet at that, and Leah dropped her knife to the stone flags with a clatter. Pierre snapped back, "And who told you that?"

Christopher shrugged. "I hear things. Your brat screams at night, anyway."

Pierre's lips curled back, but he said nothing; Fiona swallowed hard and turned a little sideways, nominally to indicate for her mistress to continue eating, but in reality only to hide her face. Leah bravely picked at her food, but she shook so badly that her brother questioned demurely, "Are you cold, sister?"

If the meal had taken five minutes, it would still have seemed like an eternity; by necessity it lasted for over twenty, and Fiona's limbs had turned to jelly by the time she was allowed to accompany Leah back to her apartments. Christopher had not spoken to her, but twice she had seen or imagined him casting curious glances at her from over his flagon. She shivered and Leah, whose arm she was holding, looked over at her with a sympathetic glance.

Fiona had never been more thankful to be able to cloister herself away in young Pierre's nursery and spend the day playing with his fat, roly-poly little form. At one month old he moved very little and his body was still tender, but he had learned to giggle a little. Even his father would occasionally come and sit in the room to relax, listening with a smile to his son's childish laughter; it gave him, Fiona guessed, a sanctuary to flee to when his brother-in-law became too much for him, for Christopher despised the child and never came to the nursery.

"Do you have family?" Pierre asked unexpectedly one such frosty morning when Leah had not yet risen.

Fiona glanced up, the baby in her arms. "Not anymore," she said, trying to keep her expression smooth and cold and finding it very difficult.

"No father, no mother? Not even a brother?"

Fiona felt a stab of pain like a knife-thrust in her heart at that last. "No," she whispered, tucking the little body even closer to her own, "not even a brother."

"Perhaps that is better than having one like *that*," Pierre mused, nodding toward the door to indicate Christopher. Then he added, as though only just taking in the full import of Fiona's words, "I'm sorry."

She nodded briefly.

"Where will you go when your three years of servitude are up? Will you stay with us?"

"No," Fiona replied sharply, then swiftly amended, "but I do not know where I will go." She thought of the big manor under the Welsh mountains, of the branching apple tree with its white blossoms and sweet fruit, of the fields that glowed in the summer sunlight and the meadows that glistened with dew on spring mornings, and it hurt to think that she could no longer call it home. It belonged to another, bore the mark of another family. She would no longer find her father's and grandfather's and great-grandfather's crest over the mantel in the great room, and if she returned she would be greeted as a stranger.

"Are you crying?" Pierre asked, leaning forward in his seat.

Fiona came to herself and found that a tear had indeed escaped from her eye and dropped down her cheek, and she could not strike it away for the baby in her arms. "No, no, I am not crying," she said even as Pierre pushed a handkerchief into her face. She laid the baby down and swiped the trail away then shoved the handkerchief back and said shakily, "Little Pierre needs to go down for a nap now."

Pierre rose and bowed slightly as though in apology then left with the air of one who did not at all want to return to face the problems of the world. Fiona watched him until the door shut at his back and felt her heart sink; she knew now that her feelings for him were almost as she had felt for Giovanni, and it disgusted her to think that she should have liked to call the man *brother* who had killed her blood sibling. Some parts of his personality reminded her keenly of Giovanni, and when they came to light in him she felt the renewed twinge at her breast as of an old scar never fully healed.

She sighed and bounced young Pierre in her arms, for he did not need to go down for a nap at all, but she could not feel happy in his toothless smile. She looked hard into the baby's bright blue eyes and thought of her master's words, which she had taken to be an invitation: "Will you stay with us?"

"Oh, saints," she murmured, partially in prayer, "how I would like to stay!" And though she focused her mind on the memory of the cross swinging from Pierre's neck, the longing would not leave her alone.

LEAH CAME IN NOT long after her husband had gone, walking on steadier legs now. Her face was still worn, but Fiona guessed it was as much because of Christopher's presence as it was the baby's birth; she knew that her mistress was worried over it, but she was not sure why.

"How did you sleep?" she asked as she handed over the child.

Leah frowned and shook her head slightly to indicate that she had not slept well, and not merely on account of her son. She glanced questioningly at the door.

"Yes, your husband was here a few minutes ago; he didn't stay long. Perhaps he will spend some time hunting today." The season was unfavourable for the sport, but still Pierre seemed to find a vent for his emotions in falconry and often went out in the early morning, returning an hour or so after the sun had risen. Fiona concluded from something she had overheard him saying to his wife that he disliked leaving the womenfolk alone with Christopher for long, and she certainly could not blame him.

Glancing pensively out the window, Leah made a slight humming noise in vague assent. She looked very frail and ghostly in her simple white dress with her hair done up out of the way, the baby on her hip almost too large for her to carry, and her skin seemed thinner and more transparent than ever from the months spent indoors; her hands shook when they were not firmly clasped around something.

"I think we should take a walk around the garden," Fiona announced positively.

The idea did not seem to sit well with her mistress, but Fiona was firm. Little Pierre was to stay indoors and his mother laid him in the crib to sleep before they went out, leaving him playing happily enough with the horses fashioned for him out of wood and corn husks. He was not hard to keep occupied and he rarely cried, so that he did not burden his mother over-much and Fiona's worries on that score were relieved; still, she reflected as she and Leah walked down the corridor, it remained strange for her to see the little lady take on her child's needs herself.

Outside, the land was covered with the first snow of the season even though many leaves continued to cling tenaciously to their branches. The harvest had been gathered in several months before and the fields were now barren strips of stubby brown stalks and frosty earth; the marsh's stench was dulled by the needle-sharp cold, though it remained an ugly bit of black and brown earth that lay like a boil on the face of the estate; the forest, though the trees had shed most of their foliage, remained a proud dark line to the north, standing like a line of soldiers against the sombre grey sky. Fiona raised her head and sniffed the air, curious to see if the scent of Christmastide was in the wind yet.

"We still have a while to wait," she commented, coming back to Leah. "This will be Pierre's first Christmas."

Leah smiled, but the expression was tired; Fiona dusted off a stone bench for her and she sat down heavily. She waved a hand off Fiona's concern, though, saying through her motions that she would be well soon. She gestured for her maid to continue walking.

"Are you sure? If you are really too tired, we can go back inside."

But Leah was insistent, so Fiona, after one or two worried glances over her shoulder, kept on her rounds through the rose garden and turned out of sight around the corner of the manor house. Here she found a bit of bryony growing up the stones and, with no one to watch her or call her a fool, she made herself a belt and a crown of the scarlet-splashed vine. When she completed the work she laughed at what she could see of herself, throwing aside the crown.

"Oh, why not keep it? 'Tis a pretty addition."

Fiona whirled, clutching her cloak tighter to her. Christopher, leading his horse and apparently newly returned from a ride, stood some paces away and regarded her with amusement in his shadow-darkened eyes. He was not blocking her from getting back to the garden, but when she moved for it he intercepted her with ease.

"You always run when I want to talk to you," he commented with a melodramatic frown; "just like at the tavern." He touched the corner of his eye as though recalling the feel of Fiona's knife on his skin, and his movement into the filtered sunlight and her proximity to him allowed her to catch a glimpse of the thin, pale scar that could barely be seen on his forehead and cheek. He took a step away, glancing over her to see if she carried a weapon on her this time.

"Not one for conversation, are you?" he continued, but still watching her hands.

"Not your kind," she gasped back. She also watched the other's hands, waiting tensely for the moment when he would reach for her, and so they stood a moment—wavering, taut, waiting for the other to make the first move.

It was Christopher's horse, that great, arrogant creature with hate in his red-veined eyes, who broke the stalemate. It started at a wind that hit it the wrong way and shied, bringing one hoof clanging down on a rock so that both Fiona and Christopher jumped and turned to look at it. By a stroke of luck she recovered herself first and scrambled for the corner; she felt him grip her cloak near the shoulder, felt the pull on her throat, and then the mantle fell from her shoulders as the cross-piece of the brooch snapped. She dove away from him and gained the corner of the building, and once past that and in view of the garden she breathed easy.

Leah was still sitting on the bench and glanced up as Fiona came closer, noticing her uneven breathing and flushed cheeks. She rose, catching hold of her maid's arm to steady her, and her eyes demanded to know what had happened.

Fiona shook her head breathlessly, looking back over her shoulder; Christopher had not come out yet. "No, no," she shook her head. "Come, we should go in." She in her turn caught Leah's wrist and pulled her along beside her, all the while continuing to cast tremulous glances at the corner of the house. Just before the two women moved out of sight Christopher made his appearance, rounding the corner with his horse's reins clenched in one fist; there was a thundercloud on his face.

Leah also looked back and saw him and immediately jerked back to Fiona with huge eyes. Again the maid shook her head at the question she saw there, quickening her steps.

It was not until they reached the refuge of the nursery where little Pierre lay asleep in his bed that Fiona told her mistress in a shaky voice what had happened. She was not as afraid as the time at the tavern and her heart was not beating out of rhythm as it had then, but she still could not control the quivering of her body as the adrenaline flooded through her. She finished with, "We shouldn't speak of it to anyone—it would only make your brother angrier. We'll just keep to the house for now."

Leah looked as though she wanted to tell Pierre, but as it happened she did not need to. Over dinner the atmosphere was staler and more brittle than before; everyone eyed Christopher with distrust and dislike, and he returned the favour so that from every part of the table fire-lit eyes gleamed over the rims of goblets and candles as they shifted from person to person. Everyone's nerves were rubbed raw; the sound of doors opening made them jump or grit their teeth, Pierre kicked Nicé when the hound yawned too loudly, and the sharp little noises of knives and spoons scratching on silver made Fiona's head hurt.

Christopher looked at her so intently that Fiona expected every minute that he would speak, but he did not. No one did. The voicelessness almost made it worse, for she felt that if only someone would say something the dam would be broken and this horrible, screaming silence would be gone. But still it continued, and up until the very end no one spoke. Pierre shoved back his chair (even Leah winced visibly at the noise of the wood squealing across the stone) and rose but did not leave immediately. He stood stone-faced at the back of his chair until Leah and Fiona slipped like thieves from the room, blushing though they had done nothing.

As soon as the door shut behind them, it was as though there was an explosion in the room. A voice echoed at their backs, undoubtedly Pierre's, and had they wished they could have heard all that he said through the solid wood of the door. But they did not wish; they only looked at each other nervously and crept to Leah's chamber, where they waited for the storm to pass.

It must have been hours later when Pierre came in at last, his face saying nothing of the argument; his expression was impassive once more. He held a dark form draped over one arm and when he tossed it at Fiona's feet she saw that it was her cloak, the bent pin still jabbed into the cloth. "This is yours, I think?" he asked, and his voice was not unkind.

Fiona said nothing and Leah did not move. They sat and stared at him, tight-lipped and uneasy, and Fiona wondered whether or not she should speak.

Pierre came forward and crouched down in front of her chair, arms crossed on his knees, and looked seriously into her face. As she looked back timidly like a naughty child, it occurred to her almost absurdly that the rough stubble lining both his cheeks made him look a good deal older than before. She was a little afraid of him again.

"Has Christopher been bothering you?" he asked gently.

After several swallows she managed to find her voice, albeit it was a little off key. "He stopped me when we went out to the garden today, my lord," she whispered, no longer able to hold Pierre's gaze.

"I know of that—" Pierre shoved at the heap of cloth "—but have there been other times?"

Fiona nodded slowly and said in what was almost a whimper, "He stopped me at an inn a little while before I came here."

Pierre seemed to be waiting for more, his brown eyes calmly searching her own in the meanwhile, and after a moment she found herself spilling out the whole story to him, cursing herself all the while for talking to a French soldier so. He listened gravely until the end then rose and moved to the window. He looked out into the snow-scented darkness and presently pronounced sentence. "Christopher will leave. I have already told him so."

A wave of relief swept over Fiona, leaving tears stinging her eyes. She crumpled into a little heap in her seat and dropped her head in her hands, keenly aware of her own exhaustion from the building paranoia and feeling like a small child lost in the world. Her head ached and she wondered why she was in this position; why was she, with so little beauty, the object of prey to such a devil of a man? Who was it who pulled the strings and played her like a puppet, writing her fate on the wall of time? It was so hard. She could see the cog that was out of place and saw how she could fix it, but she was separated from it by a gulf called the Past; if only she could fix that one part, her life would run smoothly!

She opened her eyes for a moment with a choked sob and found the world dark and spinning, the pounding in her head increasing and a sound like the ocean roaring in her ears. She wanted to sit down and cry, but the utter hopelessness of the knowledge that it would do no good only made the tears bitter. Forgetting about Pierre and Leah, she gave in and sank lower than ever into her misery.

FIONA HAD WHAT THE doctor called a breakdown, and she was obliged to stay in bed for a day and rest. The time was not restful; for awhile she thought she was going insane, and then, when she had determined that this was not the case, she wondered fitfully what was going on outside her doors. She never heard Christopher's voice, but a part of her was unwilling to accept the joyful possibility that he was gone—it was too good to be true.

Sometime late on the second day, when she was still in bed but allowed to sit up, Pierre came in. Nominally the visit was to see how she fared, but he did not seem very interested in her reply. When she concluded, he grunted, as was his custom, and said bluntly, "Christopher left yesterday morning for Reims."

Fiona was not sure what to feel at that. She was glad, but her worries about herself trumped the feeling; she merely nodded and murmured, "Thank you."

He blew a sharp breath through his nose. "Thank you for providing me with an excuse. It was not a hard decision to come to. He took something when he left, though—" Pierre frowned, rubbing his neck again. "'Twas a little trinket I gained at Agincourt, a silver cross. You have not seen it, have you?"

Fiona was so surprised by this that her negative response, spoken as it was after several seconds of gaping and blushing and soundless movement of her lips, was hardly credible. "What would he want with it?" she questioned as he nodded and rose to leave.

Pierre shrugged a shoulder. "Probably he only wished to take something from me, or perhaps," he frowned, a new thought occurring to him, "or perhaps he will present it the Court as his spoils of war in hopes of a title." The thought did not seem to please him at all, but he continued mechanically, "I had it two nights ago when I went to sleep, and it was gone the morning after. It is no great loss—not enough to pursue him for. Will you be up soon?" he added, changing the topic sharply.

"I—yes, sir. I'm doing better now."

He bowed ever so slightly and left, pulling the door shut with a bang behind him. Fiona sat for some time, her hands limp on the covers and her eyes staring sightlessly before her, listening to the ring of boots on stone and processing what he had said. The fever of mind did not return, but her thoughts were still agitated, as water is when a pebble is dropped into it.

"Gone?" she whispered, forcing herself to believe it. There had been something restful in the knowledge that the cross was nearby, even when it was not in her possession, and that peace had been for a second time cruelly stripped away. Part of her felt like an old, old wall whose last firm stone has been pulled out, leaving it to crumble away; but a larger part was only angry. And the longer she sat and thought, the more her anger grew. By nightfall the fury had taken over and she fairly shook with it, and she hated Christopher with more passion than she had felt in a long time; and yet her fear of him was not gone but merely masked under her rage.

Leah came in to say goodnight, but Fiona pretended to be asleep and the lady left on tiptoe. Fiona waited long after the door had shut, her breathing the only sound in the heavy silence. Occasionally a wind would stir the limbs outside the window and they would scratch against the wall, but other than that there was perfect stillness in the room. She took to shifting her position merely to hear the sound of her own body moving across the blankets, but she fancied the sound did not come from herself but from someone else lurking in the unknown; after a moment she lay still, shivering.

She thought it was around midnight when she finally rose and carefully put her legs over the edge of the bed, dropping them into the emptiness below her and feeling for the floor. She dressed in the cold, trying to recognize her clothes by touch, and then fumbled until she finally located the door and was able to step out into the somewhat greyer corridor. By the differing shades she could see that Leah's door was shut, and she crept on down the hallway with her shoes clenched in one hand.

She stood still in the entrance to the great hall, wondering if Pierre's hunting dogs still lay by the hearth and dreading the first step into that expanse of darkness. She could vaguely see the gleam of light on the high, arched windows and there were a few familiar shapes in the room, but while her chamber lay in a part of the house that was sheltered from the wind, this section lay open to it and its hollow noise drowned out any other sounds. How black and empty the space looked! It called to mind images of a tomb scarred into the side of a hill, like those she had seen in the British knolls.

She shuddered and carefully stretched out one leg, bringing her bare foot to rest on one of the stone flags. No change in the atmosphere greeted her movement; she put out the other foot and was fully within the room. She could not hear any hounds stirring or whining in their sleep, so she crept on toward the kitchens. It seemed an interminable distance from one end of the hall to the other and the dark never seemed to change, so that she seemed to be walking around and around in a circle and never getting closer to her destination. Just as she decided that this was the case, she found herself facing the short, wide hall that led to the kitchen and the back entry that the servants used, and then, after she had stolen a little distance down that, she was at the exit.

For a moment after lacing her boots she stood there and debated whether to continue on, but a sound like a footstep sounded behind her and she cast a wide-eyed glance over her shoulder as she hastily shoved the door open. A blast of air met her and rushed in to fill the void at her back; the wind screamed and howled like wild cats or witches. All Hell seemed unleashed on the night, and it was all she could do to press on, drawing the door shut at her back and making her way to the stables by feeling along the wall of the building until she reached it. The cold stung her cheeks and hands as she fumbled with the stable door, but at least there was no snow tonight.

The door creaked and groaned as she struggled to pull it open and the horses stirred within; one snorted and whinnied softly, shuffling the straw with its hoof. Fiona left a gap at the entry, for inside all was as black as her own apartments and there were twice as many things to catch one's self on. She tried to hear a sound that might tell her where the stable hands were sleeping, but the wind and the horses' movements drowned out the noise of human breathing. She crept on, her numb fingers seeking contact with the wood of a stall.

She had no time to saddle her horse, for the beast's snuffling and whinnying was sure to wake the hands if it kept it up much longer. She drew it out of the stall by its mane and managed to entice it out into the night. She felt like a thief as she scrambled up onto the horse's back and drove her heels into its flanks—she *was* a thief—but she rudely shoved away the knowledge and urged the creature on.

She did not intend to go far tonight, for the blackness could succeed in making the most knowledgeable person lose their way. She knew enough of French geography now to know that Reims was southwest of her current position, and for more direct instructions she would appeal to the folk in the surrounding villages; for now she moved toward the woods, where she meant to lie out the night and leave before daybreak.

Under the trees, she and her horse were a little more sheltered from the hellish wind, and the equine was not as inclined to spook or shy but followed her willingly enough as she dismounted and pressed deeper into the cover of the forest. Fiona found it encouraging to have another living creature beside her in the dark, to be able to hear its inquisitive snuffling and feel its warm breath on the back of her neck. She swore to herself as she gripped its mane tightly that she would never again hate a horse; perhaps they were smelly creatures, but they were companionable on a night like this.

She went on for a long time before feeling secure that Pierre would not easily find her in the morning, which was but a few hours away, and then she was faced with the problem of what to do with her steed. She had no rope with which to hobble it, and more than likely it would simply trot back to its warm stable the moment she shut her eyes. Fiona regarded it with a frown, and the beast regarded her back for a moment before demurely dropping its head and searching for a bit of grass to eat.

"You won't go anywhere, will you?" she asked it.

The horse snorted and she saw the form of its tail flicking irritably.

Fiona sighed. It was unwise to sleep anyhow, lest the cold freeze her limbs and she stay asleep forever, so she let the horse graze fruitlessly and paced about the little clearing to wait for the first paling of the sky. And she waited indeed. And waited, and waited, while the dark canvas above the fierce, jagged branches never seemed to change its shade and the mistrals continued to scream.

In time the wind dropped to a whine, like that of a spoiled child, and a little while after she detected a lightening of the clouds. She wakened the horse, which had fallen asleep when the search for food became too depressing, and changed direction so that they were now heading in a more southerly direction where they had been moving northwest. It was still dark and she lost her footing several times, slipping on the wet leaves left over from autumn, and briars clung to her dress and scraped her hands until they were smeared with blood.

When the sun came up behind the grey shroud of mist, Fiona had an unpleasant revelation. The horse whom she was leading was not one of the work horses or little brown mares, as she had hoped, but it was Pierre's own wide-chested, powerful grey gelding that was his favourite for hunting. She had thought the beast seemed larger than it ought. Her thievery sat harder in her belly now, for in her mind it was one thing to steal a shaggy little creature and another thing entirely to take the choicest that the stables had to offer.

Césaire looked at her with something like cheer in his big, liquid eyes, the delicate eyelids dropping and rising happily. He was willing to serve and seemed not to care that the girl who was leading him was also cursing him viciously; she had forgotten her oath to never hate a horse. Since she did not seem to be moving, he went back to searching the ground.

"Oh, come along!" Fiona fumed, jerking the horse's mane. She knew that where Pierre might have overlooked her escape, he would not let his favourite steed go so easily. While she tried to find Christopher, which was searching for a needle in a haystack of itself, she had also to be constantly looking back to see if her own pursuer had gained on her.

"Well," she said aloud, sidestepping a rabbit hole, "at least I have this morning to get a head start."

Césaire snorted and picked up his heels.

Mid morning the two of them came out of the woodlands and stepped into the open again. Meadows, dotted occasionally by trees or lakes, stretched out before them to the west and south and a little creek ran quite near them. It was frozen, and Fiona could see two forms on the ice. She mounted Césaire and urged him closer to find that it was a girl and a boy crouching over a carefully hacked out hole, their bodies tense and their faces pale with either apprehension or cold. Their features said that they were siblings; the girl was no more than ten, Fiona guessed as she came closer to the bank, and the boy was a few years older.

"Excuse me," she called, "can you tell me the way to Reims?"

The girl's head came up sharply and her cheeks flushed an indignant shade of red. "You made us lose the fish!" she said crossly, getting to her feet. Her brother also straightened with a sigh, slapping his hands on his breeches and blowing on them while regarding the intruder critically.

"Oh, I'm terribly sorry," Fiona said, not feeling particularly sorry at all, but rather piqued herself from cold and lack of sleep. "It's only that I'm trying to get to Reims. I was part of a hunting party and I lost them."

The girl looked as though she considered it Fiona's fault to have gotten lost in the first place and thus thought that Fiona ought to get out of the scrape herself, but at a glance at the style of clothing the lady wore and the handsome creature she rode, she kept her tongue behind her teeth. Her brother pointed a finger southwest, a little more south than west, and directed laconically, "'s thatta way. Don't ride your beast across the ice, neither; walk him, 'nless you want a bath." He said no more, asked her none of her business, and did not comment on her stupidity of getting lost, for he was not a lad given to much talking.

Fiona thanked them and dismounted, stepping down from the bank and drawing Césaire, who put his ears back and wanted to lock his legs in place, onto the ice with her. She felt the girl and boy watching her with amused interest and the heat rose in her face as she clumsily jerked the horse to make it take another step further. The surface beneath her groaned at the weight; her belly turned queasy.

"Oh, will you not *come on?*" she demanded through clenched teeth, wishing she had a halter with which to lead the uncooperative creature. She pulled and her feet slipped; Césaire pulled back, the iron on his hooves scratching marks on the ice. The horse's eyes were nearly rolled back in his head, his ears were flat back on his skull, and his thick lips were pulled back to show his yellow, jagged teeth and dark gums.

"You might want to make him move a little faster," the girl quipped from her seat on the frosty ground. "He may wear a hole in the ice doing that."

Pride, still a dominant characteristic of her British nature, kept her from asking the children for their help. She set her face and strained until the muscles bulged in her neck and her jaw was thrust out at an odd angle, practically dragging Césaire by his mane and gaining but little ground. The sweat was breaking out on her forehead when she at last reached the middle of the creek and by the time she at last got the horse safe on firm ground again the bodice of her dress had dark, wet patches across it.

On the opposite bank the boy and girl clapped and laughed at her achievement, their black eyes dancing with mischief, and then scampered off. Fiona sat down heavily on a bit of earth that had less snow than the rest of the ground and watched the children until they were out of sight, her hands balled into fists. It was not until she rose that she realized the main reason for their merriment, for she saw around the bend of the stream what she could not have on the other side: a little wooden bridge spanning the river. It was not large, but it was wide enough for her to lead Césaire across.

"The Devil take you!" she cried after the children, her voice echoing in the stillness.

Césaire, calm by this time, twitched and eyed her reproachfully as she swung up onto his back. She drove her heels sharply into his sides and his nostrils flared, his body straining as he trudged up the slope. "Can you not move a little faster?" she demanded as they topped the hill, but he seemed in no hurry to comply. He would move up to a trot for a second, but he sensed that his rider was not the experienced and demanding master he was used to, and he was quick to drop back to a leisurely walk.

As she rode, Fiona often twisted and scanned the horizon behind her worriedly, waiting for the time when she would look and see the black form of Pierre on horseback pursuing her. The more she did so the more it seemed that her own horse was moving at a snail's pace. Would the landscape never change? She did not like the way the sun was moving across the sky, reaching its zenith and then descending too quickly, while they, on the other hand, seemed not to move across the earth. She shivered and Césaire felt it, whinnying sharply as though to encourage her, and broke into a steady trot.

Streams were plentiful in this region of the country, and she sometimes found free-running rivulets at which to stop and drink to quench the hunger in her belly. She had thought of taking food from the store before leaving, but somehow that seemed like stealing from Leah; taking from Pierre was bad enough, but the idea of taking from her mistress was like stealing from a family member. Now, jolted about on the horse's back with her empty, cramped belly growling ravenously, she did not think very much of her conscience-driven decision. Food, however it was acquired, was all she wanted just now.

Her steed was probably not pleased with his own enforced fast, but he did not complain as she did. He flicked his tail and regarded his next step gravely, concentrating on putting one hoof after the other, until Fiona became aware of his patience and felt a twinge of shame that even a dumb beast was more tolerant than she. It was no wonder, she thought to herself, that women were meant to stay at home and not go gallivanting about like men; if she could not keep the bitterness out of her tongue after but half a day without food, she could never survive a soldier's march as Giovanni had. The bleak thought curbed her words, if not her wandering thoughts.

With the days still waning on their way to the winter solstice, dusk came far too soon. Farmhouses dotted the countryside, each set a good ways from the other, and the smoke curling up from the roofs was tempting and inviting, but Fiona was not willing to beg lodging at their doors. Instead she drew Césaire around to the back of the one of the stables when the twilight had deepened so that they were sheltered from the wind and the horse was able to feed at a heap of mouldy straw. He was content with that and Fiona did not think he would leave, so she found the most protected spot she could and slept.

On the morrow she woke and found Césaire still asleep on his feet nearby and the sun not yet up. Those of the farm would soon be stirring and coming out to milk the cows, and she hoped to find something in the stables to eat before they did. She left her horse as he was and crept around to the front of the building. Inside she found several fat and healthy cows, prospering after a good summer, and up in the loft she could see herbs hanging from the rafters. She got up the ladder, wincing at each creak of the wood under her feet, and stole on hands and knees across the hay-strewn upper floor; chickens stirred on their nests and raised their feathery heads to regard her with sleepily surprised, beady eyes. They were offended when she reached underneath one and drew out an egg, and they all clucked at her and jabbed their tiny grey beaks in her direction as she ducked away.

There was not much to be found here in the loft save for drying plants and those few eggs that she could discover, but she took the latter and hurried from the building as quickly as she could. Again came the twinge of guilt at her robbery as she mounted Césaire and drove him on, cradling the eggs before her.

Fiona stopped once out of sight of the farm and dismounted to find a way to eat her unconventional breakfast. She thought at first that she should make a fire and cook them but then realized that she had no frying pan. She thought of trying to roast them by setting them in the warm ashes of a fire, but was too afraid of being spotted. She was about to give up and throw the eggs away or take them back when her stomach roared out and pangs spread across her abdomen; she had to eat, and she knew it. She cut a hole in the shell of one egg with her fingernail, raised it to her mouth with a grimace, and sucked out the contents. It was smooth and slimy the whole way down and though it did not taste like much, it was the most atrocious thing Fiona had ever had in her life.

She could not bring herself to eat the rest of her eggs, at least not at the moment. Her face screwing up as though she were going to be sick, she dragged herself back onto Césaire's back and went in search of a creek where she might wash her mouth out. The cold, clear water could not take away the taste at the back of her throat, though, and the flavour of egg stayed with her all morning.

Every few hours Fiona would spur her horse to a canter or gallop before letting him drop to a walk again when his breath began to come too hard. In this way she hoped to put more distance between herself and Pierre, whom she had no doubt was not more than a morning's ride behind her; she did not really expect to catch up to Christopher before reaching Reims. And when—or if—she did, she was not sure how she would reclaim the cross; it was not as if she could simply walk up to him and ask him for it nicely. The thought of trying to steal it from him petrified her, for she could only imagine what he would do if he discovered her, and her imagination was vivid enough.

Her mind was kept occupied over these questions for most of the long, tedious ride, her thoughts swaying with Césaire, but she came up with no answers. She was driven by an almost animal need that would not be controlled by the reasoning of her head, a need for the peace that she believed lay in the little silver trinket. To hold it in her grasp again was the pinnacle of her desire; she wanted to be able to rest, to have the assurance given by something stable in the midst of an ever moving world, and whenever she thought of that her hands would shake and she would drive her heels into the horse's sides.

By late afternoon of the next day she came within sight of the great city of Reims. The town was an ancient one, dating back to the time of the Romans, and had been prominent in Gaul long before Paris was more than a backwater village—but Fiona knew none of that. It was large, perhaps one of the largest in France, and while Fiona wondered how she was to find Christopher amid the crowd, she also hoped that she would blend in well.

She soon reached a slope that proved difficult both to get around and to descend, being both rocky and ever-changing in its topography. The hill lay some distance from the city, and at its base stretched the chalk plain for which Reims was famed. It was this feature that had prompted the Romans to build a city there, along with the fact that Reims lay on the trade route between Rome and Britannia; those minerals in the plain provided the source for a great many weapons and tools. The sight was a pretty one as she stood about a mile from the city at the top of the rise, the snowy, grey-white earth glistening dully and reminding her of the downs back home in the countryside of England.

After a few minutes of gazing, Fiona took a firmer grip on Césaire's mane and began to lead him down the steep, overgrown slope, hooves and feet slipping on the lingering snow and wet grass. She dared not ride him, lest he slip on a loose stone and send them both rolling down to break their bones at the bottom; the thought sent a shiver up her spine and she breathed hard with each shaky step they took. She considered it a miracle that they reached level ground with all their bones intact, and the great sigh that Césaire heaved could easily have been taken as a prayer of thanksgiving. His nostrils were edged with red and spots of foam speckled his hide, his legs shuddering slightly from the weight they had had to sustain. Fiona let him rest awhile before leading him on toward the border of Reims.

They had not walked far when a black object like a boulder lying under a mass of bushes caught her eye, and she moved toward it cautiously. Césaire shied as they came up to it, the form of a black horse in the shadows. It had evidently been dead some days, but there were few flies because of the cold and the creature was well preserved, even so that Fiona could see the place where its right foreleg was turned at an unnatural angle. She shivered, drawing back; though there were no markings on the flank turned toward her and the harness in the beast's mouth was only the most common variety, there was little doubt in her mind but that the horse was Christopher's. She had never seen a more massive, coal-black, powerful equine than his, and this horse was its equal in all.

Césaire seemed eager to be away from his dead companion, disliking the glaze over the open eyes, and Fiona brought him away. She shook her mind to be rid of the image, but it stayed with her; she shuddered again.

Reims was a city of political importance, and its gateways were patrolled and those who wished to come in were to show identity of some kind. Fiona knew as much from conversations around the table in Gallandon, and as she drew nearer the town she felt her heart drop into her belly; her false French accent would be seen through in a moment if the soldiers knew their job. She had no money, not even the shilling of Porte Dubris, no jewels, no finery at all that might bribe a corrupt man, only her own person, and *that* she was determined not to sell at any price.

As she considered she continued to walk, and she was within a stone's throw of the entrance—she could see the forms of men standing by the gates and pacing the perimeters—when her horse's snuffling at her neck struck an idea in her head. It was not a nice idea, for Pierre, she knew, would be out of his mind with rage if ever he learned of it, and she did not relish the idea of walking any long distance again, but so it was: Césaire had to go. He seemed to sense his mistress' intentions, for he was not eager to get to the gate and set his body stubbornly.

"I can't help it," Fiona growled as she dragged him along. "Must you be such a bear? Come along now."

When she came up to the entrance, a man unfolded himself from his position against the wall and intoned, "Papers, miss?" He was a middle-aged fellow with a sallow complexion and a bored, tired face, as though he could think of a great many things he would rather be doing than this. His companions were the same, and most sat playing at dice in the dirt instead of patrolling.

Summoning her courage, Fiona replied clearly, "I do not have any papers." It appeared from the way all the men looked at her in surprise that honesty was not the way to go, so she hastily added, "I lost them along the way. It was a very nasty ride."

That put the soldiers at ease, and the first man even nodded sympathetically. "We get many like that. 'Tis a pity, but I cannot let you in without the proper papers." His eye searched Fiona's hand eagerly, though, looking for a fat purse.

Fiona saw the gaze and she led Césaire into clearer view. "I only have my horse left, a very noble creature and worth a fair amount. Will you take him?"

This time none of the younger men looked up from their game but religiously ignored the conversation going on over their heads. Their superior cast about him nervously then came forward and inspected Césaire to see what kind of beast he was. In time, through which Fiona held her breath painfully, he nodded in satisfaction. "All right, all right, get on in with you," he ordered, opening the gate for her and taking hold of the horse's mane. As she ducked inside, she heard him say to one of the soldiers, "Ai, you there! Get this horse away, would you?"

Fiona smiled a little as she took her first step inside the city of Reims and the gate shut behind her, for the affair had gone better than she had expected. If the rest of her mission was to be fulfilled in the same manner, she had little to worry about. The thought cheered her and she picked up her step.

The most prominent feature of Reims, though grand in many other ways as well, was the cathedral that rose up from the square in the town's midst. This chapel had long been the site of the French kings' coronations, the extensive sanctuary, with its high, stained glass windows and its murals and its chanting priests, having heard generation after generation of kingly vows. Fiona stood in the cathedral's shadow and stared up at the towering steeples and massive architecture, craning her head back as far as it would go to see where the bell tower ended. The natives moved past her, jostling her with their shoulders and not once stopping to marvel at the cathedral that they had seen all their lives, but Fiona stood rooted to the spot and stared with her mouth open. It reminded her of her first sight of the Tower of London or Westminster Abbey, when she had hardly been able to believe that mankind was capable of such grand works of art. She did not know, but it would not have surprised her to learn that a century and more had been spent on the recovery of this chapel since its destruction by fire in the year 1210.

She would have liked to have gone in, to pass the carved statues and walk in under the towering, arched doorways, but something in her feared to do so. It was not fear of discovery but rather a fear of the eyes that looked down on her from the doors, which depicted scenes that for the most part she could not understand. They all seemed to be far and above her; the woman in white with the glow about her head, whom Fiona took to be the Virgin Mother, appeared enwrapped in a kind of trance that made Fiona feel very out of place and worldly, while the men on the right hand door looked sternly and unyieldingly upon her and the art of the left hand door showed horrific scenes of destruction that made her flesh crawl. She turned sharply away, colliding with a man so quickly that she nearly knocked him over with the shock of it.

Stumbling and then righting herself, Fiona backed off, raising a hand to shade her eyes against the sun and see his face. He, too, was recollecting himself after a startled exclamation; Fiona stood rooted to the spot before him, hesitating, unsure whether to run or stay and apologize. "I-I beg your pardon," she gasped, gathering her cloak nearer to herself as if to hide in the haven it created.

The man got his feet firmly underneath him and, before he raised his head, Fiona's heart gave a sickening bound and fell hard to the pit of her stomach. Like Christopher's voice, this man's twisted leg was unmistakeable to her. She gaped and said nothing.

"Ho!" exclaimed David, swinging so that he did not create a shadow on her face. "You!"

Fiona knew what he meant by that: he recognized her as she had recognized him. She dropped her gaze, too late, and blushed at the thought of his wondering how she had come to be in Reims—or France at all. "Yes," she faltered. "I beg your pardon. I never thought I would see you here." She was not sure if she were begging his forgiveness for tripping over him or for unwittingly coming to a city where he was; but it did not seem to matter either way.

"Did you think about it at all?" Then he went on, "I am a merchant; I get around. I find it more surprising that *you* are here. Was Dover not—what you expected?"

"No," she replied, more sharply now. "It was not. I came here on the same business."

If she had been looking she would have seen an expression of pity on David's face; but she was watching her own hands and did not see it. His voice was incapable of sinking into tangible gentleness, and when he spoke it was still rough, as if he did not care at all. "Ah. Are you staying here in Reims?"

"Only for tonight."

"Do you have money?"

The question was blunt—clearly he was thinking of London—and it sent a blush up Fiona's neck when she thought of the emptiness of the money pouch in her dress. She had not thought of taking any from Pierre and Leah, and even if she had, she did not think she could have brought herself to do it. "No. No money."

"I expected as much. Here now, it is growing dark and I doubt you can find an innkeeper willing to let you eat and sleep for nothing; you come with me and I will get you some lodging."

Again Fiona turned scarlet, but though she could have cried at the humiliation of it, she dared not resist when he took her arm and propelled her toward the nearest inn. She did not thank him; she was too mortified. *Why*, she wondered, *must this always be the way I meet people? Hungry and penniless and at the mercy of their charity. I, who was once a nobleman's daughter. You would not think it now.*

Yet David's presence calmed her trembling when, stepping inside the crowded tavern, she scanned faces for a sight of Christopher. She saw no one who even resembled him, but her disappointment was mingled with relief and she was grateful to sit at one of the tables without feeling his eyes on her. David watched her—she felt it as she ate—while he sat with his arms set on the table across from her, but his gaze only made her feel inferior, not terrified. He asked no questions until he had seen that she finished the last bits of her food. Then, and only then, he took a tell-tale breath; Fiona stiffened; but he only said, "You'll be tired."

She exhaled. "Yes."

"You go and ask one of the maids to take you to your room, then. Tomorrow we will talk again and see what this business is that you are on, and I'll help you as best I can."

So the questions were only to wait until morning, not be done away with altogether. But she was too tired and groggy from the warm food and ale to think deeply about it now, and when the maid showed her to her narrow tick, Fiona fell across it with a rush of thankfulness for its softness. Her last clear thought was that she would wake early and think about what was to be done—and then she was off into a heavy, dreamless sleep.

EXHAUSTED THOUGH SHE WAS, Fiona still woke at least two hours before sunrise. For a little while she remained as she was, her face pressed into the loosely-covered straw, and then slowly she began to stir. At last she sat up, blinking and looking about her like an owl wakened in daylight as she tried to get her bearings and remember where she was and how she had come to be there. Now she remembered: David had brought her here and was going to talk to her this morning. She felt again the panicked flutter in her stomach and she rolled off the tick, standing still in the room to listen to any noises around her. All was perfectly still, as if not even the innkeeper had roused yet, and the place was chill from the lack of a fire in the main room. How long it would be until the inhabitants were stirring, Fiona did not know, but she could not wait until then and risk meeting David; she crept out of her little room and down the stairs.

The ashes in the hearth were cold and the room empty as she came into it, the floor and tables still littered, here and there, with an odd scrap of food that had not been eaten. There was a wasted dog lying in the dirt, but it was deaf and did not stir a limb at Fiona's approach. She turned aside from the creature and found her way to the storeroom behind the innkeeper's long, high wooden counter, her hunger overpowering her guilt for the time being; David would pay for what she took, no doubt, but that was no comfort.

The door groaned as she pushed on it. It was black as a cave within, the smell of spices wafting out to her. Her breath sounded unnatural in the silence, her footsteps seeming to echo. She felt along the shelves until her hand came into contact with a crusty loaf of bread—it even *felt* delicious on her fingertips—and wrapped it into her handkerchief, beginning the search anew for some meat or cheese.

What she found next was neither. Her fingers touched something cold and metallic, and as she moved her hand down its length she found that it was a butcher's knife. She picked it up and tried to see it through the blackness, catching only an indistinct glimmer of steel, and then felt her hair with her other hand. The thought was impulsive and she did not stop to consider but took a firmer grip on her mane, raised the knife, and hacked off a length and let it float to the ground between her feet. Her hair, she knew, was her most distinctive feature, and with it gone there was a chance that Christopher and Pierre might not recognize her.

She set her teeth and kept slashing at her hair. It hurt almost physically to feel her head becoming lighter and lighter, the weight of her cherished locks diminishing with each cut, and when she finished it felt as though she had struck off her own arm. The knife became still and she raised a hand to her head, feeling the uneven hair and wincing. The effect was ghastly, and had she been able to see it she would have been horrified at how monstrous she looked; she had tried to cut it evenly, but it had only made her hair shorter and shorter, until it barely covered her head.

Leaving the knife and clutching the bread to her chest, Fiona slipped out into the pre-dawn and scurried from the inn. She drew the hood of her cloak over her head but could not resist reaching up occasionally to feel her mutilated hair again; it was horribly fascinating to her.

When she reached it the square was empty, the black form of the cathedral looming up across the way. The stars were disappearing one by one overhead as the eastern sky lightened and she was able to find her way to the southern gate without difficulty. The soldiers gave her no trouble, for while they were careful—nominally, at least—as to who came into the city, they cared little who came out; they even nodded respectfully at her with weary smiles as she went past, her head down.

It was Fiona's design to reach Paris, where she hoped to discover Christopher. She did not delude herself with thoughts of meeting up with him before that time; though this was the commonest road to Paris, he could easily have gone a roundabout route in the hopes of losing any follower. And, indeed, if he thought Pierre were tracking him, it was likely that he would do so. Paris was a large city, but there was a chance that she would find him, especially if he was, as Pierre had proposed, attempting to persuade the Crown to grant him a title. Her mission did not seem so hopeless in that light, and she occupied herself with thoughts like these to keep her mind off the walking.

By early morning carts and riders were passing her going in both directions. Peasants mainly occupied the former, while nobles of one degree or another rode by on horseback with feathers quivering in their caps and their gaudy clothes standing out against the greys and browns of the farmers'. There were a few men on foot as well, but most of these seemed to be jongleurs of disreputable appearance and Fiona kept clear of them. No one stopped to talk to her or offer her a ride, but at the same time no one seemed particularly interested in her; the sight of a girl walking alone was not an uncommon sight outside the major cities and did not excite much curiosity.

This stage of the journey was perhaps the most tedious yet. Nothing happened. Wild animals did not bother her at night as she slept by the wayside; she ate her bread and had no need to steal more supplies; there was no one to talk to and the road continued to stretch on before her. It was the kind of trip whose details fade away so swiftly that one wonders if they occurred at all. She crossed a bridge early on the first day, but after that the landscape remained very much the same until, after dark on the second day, she reached the banks of the Marne river.

Against the inky blackness Fiona glimpsed clear, bright yellow candlelight glimmering from inside a farmhouse. She moved toward it, thinking of how good it would be to sleep safe behind solid doors for a night instead of out in the open, where she woke every hour or so with a start and had to reassure herself that everything was as it should be about her. Soon she was rapping on the wood and a lanky youth, who appeared to have more joints than was physically possible, opened it to look out at her suspiciously.

"Good evening," Fiona began, trying to peer around the young man to see who occupied the room behind him; from the noises issuing from the house, it seemed that the boy was not the sole resident. "I was wondering if I might ask the master of the household for a room to stay in for the night."

From within, a woman's harsh voice resounded, "Philippe, who is that? Shut the door; there's a draft!"

The boy sniffed, his long nose wrinkling up like a cat's or a dog's, and opened the door for Fiona without a word. She stepped inside and looked about her. The room was common and not much to look at, everything being crafted from bare, unadorned planks and lit only by a small fire, and even the smell of supper was not the hearty, appetizing scent Fiona was used to. A man sat at the end of the table, his grey hair the most conspicuous thing in the room, and regarded her expressionlessly; beside him a tow-headed youth sat swinging his legs and chirruping like a lark; and over on the other side of the room by the hearth stood a gaunt, middle-aged woman who looked a great deal like the youth who had let Fiona in.

"Well, what is it?" she asked crossly, straightening from her pot. "You'll be wanting a room, I suppose? Well, well, as you like it. Can you pay?" she added, her eyes narrowing into slits.

Fiona worked her jaw for a moment before stumbling, "Well, ma'am ..."

"She can't pay! They never can pay! Always asking for charity. Huh! As if we don't have barely enough to feed ourselves these days."

"Woman!" boomed the man who had thus far kept silent. "Cease this babbling and finish my supper! A guest will never be unwelcome at my table, so not another word of complaint from you. Philippe, don't stand there gawking—pull up a chair for the lady."

And before she knew what was up and what was down, Fiona found herself seated next to the younger lad at the table awaiting the meal with the rest of them. She cleared her throat and observed her gratitude to the party, but the patriarch only grunted and fell back into his reverie as if nothing had happened. The whole position would have been uncomfortable indeed had not the tow-head turned about on the bench and given her a bold, mischievous wink designed to set her at ease; she smiled slightly in reply.

In a moment the woman came and dropped the food—what exactly the food *was*, Fiona did not care to guess from its colour or texture—onto the table with a half-snarled, "Here." Everyone became seated and the man's conversation became livelier, for he turned to the newcomer and asked her pleasantly, "What's your name, miss?"

Fiona, grateful for the chance to delay her first bite, replied. He smiled as if that was the grandest thing he had ever heard and began to point out the names of those in his own household, saying, "That is my wife, Louisa, and that is my eldest son, Philippe, and this young rascal—" he ruffled the younger boy's hair "—is Robin. Oh, and I am also Philippe."

Seeing as the silence asked for a reply, Fiona remarked politely, "You must be very grateful to have two sons to help on the farm."

From her place Louisa growled, "We had a boy between them, but we lost him at birth." She spoke as though she thought this reason enough not to be grateful for the other two, but her elder son did not look at all sorrowful and Robin even chuckled outright. What the joke was Fiona did not understand, but she respectfully murmured that she was very sorry.

Robin piped up from around a mouthful of the edible concoction, "Mama will go on about poor Louis so. Hardly a day goes by she doesn't mention him."

Louisa continued to glower, but something like amusement flickered across her husband's face, and Fiona realised that the male part of the family coped with her by never taking her seriously. Throughout the meal she continued to throw in dampening words—"Well, the crop *would* have been better, if you would have just worked a little harder;" or, "Beggars are always stopping at our door to beg a crust of bread;" or, "Robin! Must you slurp so? Manners!"—but the conversation went on without a pause. At first Fiona thought this rather unfeeling of her family, but before supper was over she realised by the straining of her own nerves how wise they were. Louisa's constant talk was a trial that they could not put a stop to, and so rather than be worn down by it, they chose to take it as a grand joke.

As the dishes were being cleared away and Louisa was just beginning to bank the fire, another knock came from the door. The woman sighed and stormed over to it as though to devour the poor unfortunate who stood outside, but before she could turn the person away her husband cried, "A traveller? Let him come in, let him come in! Robin, get some food for the fellow, would you?"

There was a general bustle as the stranger was brought in and supper was broken out again. The room was even darker than before, and again it was his voice rather than his face whereby Fiona recognized him: the clear, sharp way he pronounced each word, almost as if they pained him, sent a chill to her bones. She shrank away and got a good look at him from underneath the hood she continued to wear, finding her fears confirmed.

"Thank you, ma'am," Christopher grinned, sliding onto the bench that was much too low for him; his knees nearly touched his chin. "Nasty weather out; winter is hardly the time to go travelling."

"I should say so," Louisa snapped in a way that clearly said, "Why then are you doing it?"

Christopher glanced up and scanned the room, his eyes pausing for a moment on the shadow that was Fiona. She felt her heart drop and her skin grow cold, but he moved on again without a change of expression. "I am on my way to Paris," he said by way of an explanation.

"Ah, Paris!" The elder Philippe looked pleased at this, hoping to hear news of the outside world from this traveller. "Have you been there before?"

The other smiled the condescending smile that Fiona recognized. "Many times."

"Business occasionally takes me there, but I prefer to stay here on this side of the river for the most part; Paris is too large for me. Is it your birthplace?"

"No, not my birthplace."

The conversation continued, at least on Philippe's part, but Christopher's expression soon became bored and his smile disdainful as his gaze continued to drift. Fiona froze every time he looked in her direction, but he did not appear to recognize her or even take much notice of her until he suddenly broke off his host with, "Is this another guest?"

Philippe looked over at her as though he had forgotten her presence then smiled. "Yes, she came a little while before you."

"Oh, is it a she?" the other raised a brow sardonically. "It's hard to tell under that hood. Why do you skulk away in the corner like that? Come join us!"

Fiona crept forward, wishing with all her heart that she had not told the farmer her true name. If he heard it, Christopher would not doubt her identity for long; she felt sick at the thought.

It was Robin who saved her, appearing at her side like a sprite and throwing aside all rules of etiquette to demand that she play a game of rocks and twigs with him. With this excuse she could sit on the floor away from the table and keep her head down, praying over and over in her head that someone in heaven would think of her and make Christopher blind.

She was not sure how late it was when she realized that the discussion around the table was lagging as Philippe's tongue grew weary, but soon Louisa was calling Robin off to bed and Fiona lost that protection. She set forward the excuse of being exhausted and the housewife led her—grudgingly, as always—to a room in the loft. It was little more than a partitioned corner of the main loft and spartanly furnished, with only a blanket laid across the floorboards to serve as a bed and a basin beside it to wash one's face with, but Fiona's pride had been taxed by her trials and this was enough for her.

For a long time she lay in the darkness, shivering as the cold seeped into her body. Even had she wanted to, she was sure she could not have slept: her eyes were wide open, peering into the blackness all around as she strained her ears to catch the noises of dialogue going on beneath her. Every time she thought the voices had stopped, they would pick up again and the partial words would filter up through the ceiling and the floor until she wondered what more they could have to talk about. Her body became cramped and itchy from its forced immobility.

At last came the distinctive sounds of footsteps down below as the party broke up and the men went to their separate chambers. For another hour or so she remained as she was, hoping Christopher would soon fall asleep, and then she got up, her shoes once again in hand so that her footsteps would be silent, and stole across to the door. She stepped out into the main loft.

A HUGE, BLACK CREATURE met her, towering up in front of her like a monster from a fairytale. She dropped a shoe with a clatter and shrank back, but the thing did not move. She stepped forward; she reached across the distance, hand shaking, and touched the form. With a gasping sigh of relief and a rush of heat to her face she realized that this bogeyman was no more than the frame to Robin's room, creating a shadow-filled hollow in the wall. Fiona knelt to gather up her boot, eyes darting up and down the length of the cramped little loft in the hopes that no one had been alarmed by what had seemed to her like a catastrophic crash.

From her right something moved and a hand shot out to seize her arm, another moving to cover her mouth before Fiona could cry out. Eyes and teeth flashed, white against the blackness, in what she guessed was meant to be a smile. "Afraid of your shadow?" a voice hissed, its breath warm and sweetly sickening as it touched her face.

She whimpered in reply, and Christopher snapped, "Hush! Do you want your neck broken?" He pushed her back into the room and shoved the thin door shut with his foot, cutting off the bit of light that the crack had provided. Fiona was in darkness again.

Christopher spoke again from directly in front of her. He held both her skinny arms and twisted them and pressed them against the wall, keeping his other hand closed over her mouth. "I'm going to take my hand away. If you scream or make any noise at all—well, you remember what I told you all those months ago." He squeezed her wrists to emphasize his words then slowly eased off her lips. "Hsst!" he repeated, almost daring her to say anything. She did not. She waited, shaking from tip to toe.

"You have been following me," he remarked presently. "What do you want? Did—," He broke off, calculating.

Fiona felt cold metal bumping against her jaw, no doubt the cross he was wearing around his neck. "I was not following you," she gasped, speaking the first thing that came to her mind, though it was foolish.

He cursed at her. "I'm in no mood to play at word games. That you follow me is obvious: why? I think it is clear enough you care nothing for me personally." His teeth flashed again, a stray piece of light glinting off them.

"No, no, I wasn't. I only want to get to Paris, to get away from Pierre and Leah. I was not following you—truly."

She felt him check a moment, his grasp loosening for just an instant before tightening like a vice once more. "Liar," he said, but his tone was not as assured as before. She shook her head but said nothing, waiting. There came a stretch of silence in which she felt his eyes roving over her face and wondered if he could see her any more clearly than she could see him, and then he moved away. "Stay," he ordered when she made to follow him. "I have not finished with you yet."

After a moment Fiona realized that the room was empty—there were no other sounds of breathing than her own, no movements around her—but when she began to stir there was a flash of light in the doorway and Christopher stood there, holding a lit candle in one hand. She thought his face looked as thin and wicked as ever with the flame casting its weird shadows against it, and—yes—there lay the cross on his breast, odd and out of place.

He set the candleholder down on the floor and shut the door, easing it into its slot without a sound. "Here we are," he announced, crossing the room. His tone spoke of a thousand other things, however, and Fiona shied away like a spooked horse. He caught her by the throat with both hands and though she tore at him with her stubby fingernails, trying to pry his grip loose, he held her firmly in place and bent low so that he was speaking directly into her ear. "You are not pretty," he told her bluntly, shaking her like a ragdoll. "But as you keep turning up, I feel obliged—"

There came a pounding on the door downstairs. Christopher started and let her go, turning toward the door; Fiona stumbled away, gasping for a clean breath of air. "Hsst!" he snarled at her again, jerking his head at her; "keep quiet, you hear me?"

She wanted to run away, to slip past him and get down the stairs, safe in the company of her host and hostess, but she was terrified of him. She obeyed and held her breath, listening to the sounds renewed beneath her; her head ached and the coursing of her own blood through her veins nearly drowned out the conversation, but this much she caught:

"Come in! … Bad night … take a room…." The farmer's voice was broken and distorted so that she could only catch the highlights of what he said, but presently another voice, the newcomer's, spoke up, firm and young.

"Of course, monsieur. No, no need to trouble yourself: I've eaten my supper already. If you would just be so kind as to show me to a room, I will not burden you with anything more." Muddled noises followed for a little while, and then she could hear footfalls on the creaking ladder rungs coming up the loft. Christopher swore softly and she saw him glance at the candle, which sat blazing and dripping puddles of wax halfway across the room.

The second voice continued, softer this time, just outside the door. "I was wondering, monsieur, if any other travellers had passed this way recently: particularly a blonde man and a young woman, about this tall—not together. Have you happened to see either of them?"

The farmer's reply was lost, and all that could be distinguished came at the very end: "And you may share my youngest son's room, if it is no trouble to you, so as not to wake our other guests."

Thanks were given and received; the voices faded; the door across the way shut; footsteps receded from the loft; all was as it had been. "Well, this is a pretty kettle of fish," Christopher growled as he snatched up the candle and put it in a darker corner of the room, where it was not so easily seen. "The three of us together under the same roof—faugh! I knew I should not have taken the main road."

The door creaked on its hinges for what seemed to be the hundredth time that night and Christopher and Fiona tensed as the figure stepped in. Pierre glanced between them then jerked his head toward the other bedroom. "He sleeps soundly; I don't think we will disturb him."

Christopher straightened, trying to put a careless smile on his lips again. "Fancy meeting you here. Is it her that you want?" he gestured toward Fiona.

"Partially. But what is that around your neck, brother?" Pierre's lips curled back and up as he tipped his head, regarding the silver necklace. "Where did you get it? Perhaps it was a present."

The other laughed softly, moving closer to Fiona. "It was a present, from *her*. We are good friends, you see."

A little less frightened now that Pierre was there, she cried, "It's not true! You stole it, not me!"

"Shush!" Pierre waved impatiently at both of them as though they were children squabbling. "That is mine, Christopher; I want it back." He held out a hand expectantly.

Time stood still. They all listened to the quiet sizzling of the candle, of the *plop, plop* of the wax splashing on the floor, and each waited to see what the other would do. Slowly, slowly, Christopher at last reached up and pulled the chain over his head; he held it out toward Pierre, and for a minute it hung there, so close that Fiona could almost feel it on her skin. It was going away, leaving her—once again it would be in someone else's possession, not her own.

She did not even cry out, only lunged forward and tried to snatch it away from both men. Everything happened at once, then: Pierre made some kind of angry, disgusted noise and his hand jerked back as a reflex; something flashed in Christopher's left hand and Fiona felt a stabbing pain in her shoulder as she fell to the floor, clutching the cross. She rolled over again in a flash, crawling backwards to press herself into a dark corner and watch what happened with large, frightened eyes, her fingers still gripping their prize.

Fiona's movement had signalled the time for both men to fight, and, both afraid that the other would move first, each lunged forward and barrelled into the other. Pierre's handle on Christopher's wrist sent the knife cartwheeling away into the shadows so that they were both reduced to their own bodies as weapons; they battered against one another recklessly so that Fiona was not sure if either had any clear idea what he was doing or what his goal was.

And then, as though by an unheard signal, both backed off at the same moment and began to regroup. There was no sign of surrender in either pair of eyes, only hate and anger and a kind of savage joy in the scent of the blood. They did not look at Fiona: she was forgotten. It occurred to her that it was not simply for the cross that they were fighting but for the anger that Christopher had so unwisely provoked in his foul dealings with Pierre.

Pierre flung himself forward and ploughed into Christopher's belly, sending the latter doubling over. Fiona winced as some distinctly feminine part of her nature cried out against the idea of one man hurting another, but the larger part wanted to see Christopher pounded to the floor. She did not like it when he drew himself up and landed a blow with a resounding *crack* on Pierre's jaw; she did not like the way the lord stumbled to one side as a dumb animal does when it is kicked. But neither did she care for the sudden gleam in the latter's eye as he gathered himself up again and faced Christopher, and it appeared the latter did not either: he scrambled away on hands and knees, the fear in his face almost comic, and groped hastily for his knife.

Fiona was scared to watch the rest. She read the ending in Pierre's eyes, but all the same she could not force her own to close. She gaped as he—coming upon Christopher just as the latter reclaimed his knife and was about to spin around—brought his knee down in the hollow of his enemy's back, sending him sprawling. She heard a scream coming from her own mouth as the one man hoisted the other up and flung him across the room as though he had been no more than a child. There came a hideous sound of cracking bone and Christopher's body sagged against the wall.

She screamed again. She did not know what possessed her to do it; the man was no friend of hers and she had never considered herself weak when it came to blood, and yet her whole being revolted at the thought of two men fighting like wild animals to the death.

In a second Pierre was kneeling beside her, pressing his hand across her mouth. "Hush, girl; if we did not wake them already, you shall have the family down on our heads! What? Why do you stare at him so?" He released her mouth but continued to hold her chin between his thumb and index finger, shaking it roughly. "You should be grateful: do you think he would not have taken you for himself if I had not killed him?" Suddenly he sighed, drawing his hand away. "No, but I suppose it is no sight for a lady." He stood and readjusted his clothes as though what he had just done was nothing then reached down to help her up. "Come along, we should be going before they get up here and brand me a murderer. Hand me the cross."

"No, I won't!" she threw back, her voice louder than she had expected it to be. His hand was too close to her cross; she leaned over and bit it as hard as she could, until she felt blood.

Pierre jerked his hand away, smacking her hard across the cheek with the back of his left hand before he recovered himself. "Wench!" he cried as he glanced down at the blood-streaked skin. "I have half a mind to deal you the same fate as *him*. Thief! You have taken yourself, my horse, and my cross: hand over my property, you sorry girl!"

"No, I won't, I shan't!" she repeated, huddling over the cross as the pain began in her shoulder. "It's mine; it's not yours: you have no right to it! It was my brother's and you stole it from him! It is mine, I tell you: mine!"

Pierre had not time to reply, for from other parts of the house sounds of doors opening and feet pattering across wood came up to them. His nostrils extended a moment and he set his teeth, drawing back. "Very well, then. I will explain how the matter lay between you two, and then you may go. You will soon starve out in the winter cold, at any rate, but it is no concern of mine now. Get up now and do not scrabble on the floor like a hound—up!"

She was just getting to her feet when there came a knock on the door and, at Pierre's voice, the host and hostess came in. Louisa looked less irritable and more frightened now, strange black circles around her eyes as she peered about her nervously, but her husband was the picture of calm and composure. "What is this?" he demanded, sweeping the room. "Have I housed a murderer?"

"A murderer! Oh, we never should have opened our doors to him!" exclaimed Louisa, giving Pierre a horrified glance.

"Not at all, monsieur, I can explain. I found that man there attempting to force himself on this girl—" he shoved Fiona with his foot. "I interfered, and such was the result. I am most sorry to have wakened you."

"A pretty story!" Louisa scoffed, though Philippe seemed pacified by the explanation.

"Indeed," Pierre smiled. Something of a warning note began to creep into his tone as he continued, "A pretty story, and a true one, too. Also, madame, I bear a title. It would be unwise of you to try to question my word."

His meaning was clear. Fiona watched the interchange drearily and the words did not really register in her mind until Pierre concluded abruptly with, "I will take him away in the morning; nothing can be done tonight. Good evening."

Philippe and Louisa withdrew; Robin, ironically enough, had slept through the night's escapades despite his proximity to the room and Fiona did not once hear a stirring from his chambers. They were alone in the room once more, the candle continuing to sputter and accentuating the eeriness of the scene, and Fiona glanced again at the body across the room.

"You were leaving?" Pierre grated, turning toward her.

"It's still night out," she protested weakly, dreading the cold and the darkness and the wind stinging her face. If either of them was to leave, it ought to have been Pierre: it was he who brought this whole thing to pass, after all, and Fiona was not in the mood to be grateful.

"Morning is not more than a few hours away. Besides, do you care to sleep in a room with *him*, dead or alive?"

She shivered. No, she did not like the idea, but was freezing to death truly worth it? She glanced at the blood on Pierre's hand and wished she had not been so hasty. So it was to be; in what seemed like no time at all she was left standing outside the farm, shivering now with physical cold as the wind pounced on her and tore at her clothing and stung the bare wound on her back. Tears rose in her eyes at the sharp pain and she huddled in the lee of the building, taking what refuge she could find until morning came and took the bite off the air.

Fiona did not sleep anymore. She crouched and waited, half fearing to close her eyes in case her spirit left her, and the morning never seemed so far away. Rocking back and forth, humming sporadically to reassure herself of the presence of her own body, she watched that part of the eastern horizon she could see and hoped to and imagined that she did see a lightening of the clouds. At last it came, but the day that appeared was not a pretty one: the thick, woolly grey clouds remained and hung low in the sky, and the sunlight was filtered and stale. The wind continued and blew into Fiona's face as she rose and trudged off along the riverbank, heading south.

HERE FIONA CAME BACK to herself as she lay on the bench in the chapel of the Couvent de Sainte Marthe, wiping her eyes with a sigh. She was not sure whether she had slept and dreamt or only been thinking, but she sat up and found the room more grey and less black as dawn approached. Soon the nuns would be waking and coming to morning services, and she did not care to be found there; it was no crime, perhaps, but she would be questioned. She hurried from the chapel and back through the maze, losing her way twice and having to double back before she found her own bedchamber again. It was nearly light when she did, and her room was a milky colour from the half light coming through the glass. She got back into bed, still dressed, and pulled the bedclothes up to her neck; she only meant to pretend she had been there all night, but she fell asleep again waiting for Annette to come.

The sound of someone rustling in the room woke her next. She lay still for a moment and processed the full light all around her then rolled over gingerly and looked over the edge of her blanket. Annette was bustling here and there, laying out fresh clothes like her own at the foot of Fiona's bed, and she began talking about nothing in particular when she saw the guest was awake. Fiona listened with only mild interest, concentrating instead on the way the cross in her hand shimmered coldly in the morning sunlight, its metallic face turned yellow. For awhile she let it swing then fastened it about her throat and turned her attention to what Annette was saying.

"After your bath, I will take you to see the Mother Superior. Are you hungry?"

Fiona nodded, pulling back her blanket. "What time is it?"

The other gave a half laugh, laying out a fresh pair of clothes for her guest. "A little past noon; you slept well enough, I suppose. But then, you must have been tired after all that walking." She went into the adjacent room, emerging after a moment and jerking her head back sharply. "The water's ready, if you would like to bathe now. If you need anything, you can call; I won't be too far away."

She left and Fiona got out of bed, scowling against the light. She had a dull headache and would have preferred to stay in bed until it passed and she could think clearly again, but a residual curiosity to know what the Mother Superior was going to do with her gave her body the fuel it needed and she gamely struggled into the bathroom. A wave of steam, clean and stinging, smacked her in the face as she went in; it curled in heavy strands over the edge of the tub and rose to fill the room, reminding Fiona of the cold outside and the snow on the ground and the grey skies above. She shivered, dreading a thorough wash, but she was sure that was what Annette had in mind for her to do. Looking at her own arms and legs, covered in scratches and dirt, she could not see how anything but complete submersion in that water would make her clean again.

Pulling off her nightgown and feeling the bandage that had been placed over her wound to be sure that it was secure, she hesitated at the edge of the tub, half fearing that the water and the cold air would make her sick. But then with another shudder she slipped into the water and, drawing a deep breath as the heat stung her for a moment, tried to relax against the edge of the tub. When she stirred herself to begin washing, she was horrified at how quickly the water turned from pure to a pale, strained shade of brown; in the polished copper of the tub's sides, she could see a patch of red on the cloth across her back that psychologically made the gash begin to throb anew. She tried not to think of Christopher and Pierre, of that momentary gleam of metal before the fire started in her back, of the terror she had felt when she heard that horrid cracking noise and saw Christopher dead. But still they came to mind, making every bit of comfort stale and deepening the pit in her soul.

When she had scraped off all the dirt that she could from her body, she got out of the water and hastily dried herself off on the rough, thick towels Annette had left for her. It felt strange to be clean and drenched all over and then to put on the sombre black and white garments like the nuns wore; they made her feel hypocritical: outwardly starched and prim, inwardly empty and black as pitch.

Before calling for Annette, Fiona went and stood by the window in her bedroom and looked out. Below her lay a garden, walled in like the rest of the convent's grounds, thick with greenery despite the lateness of the year. Ivy climbed the stone walls even up to the height of her window; holly bushes speckled the area, ripe with berries; and amid the glossy, deep green foliage she could see birds hopping on the branches, picking off the fruit with their beaks. The wind kicked up the sheltered snow and sent it whirling about like tiny stars, and Fiona thought of Christmas and wondered if it was approaching or long past—no, it must not have come yet.

"Ah, ready to see the Mother Superior now?"

Fiona started, turning from the window with a sudden flush to her cheeks as though she had been caught in some crime. "Yes, please," she said.

Annette nodded and led her from the room, taking her through the convent (Fiona recognized nothing from her own wanderings during the night, for every wall and hallway appeared the same) until at last they passed through a large room and came to a simple, narrow door. The nun knocked and the Mother Superior's voice called for them to come in.

"Will she ask many questions, do you think?" Fiona asked on impulse as Annette reached for the door handle.

"It is not our business to pry into the affairs of strangers and guests," the other replied comfortably. "I think a few will be asked, but if you are an honest girl, what do you have to hide?"

As she was shown in, Fiona thought back over everything that had happened to her in the last two years and wondered if she could still be called *honest*. Her memory could no longer keep track of all the lies she had told during that time; facing the head of the holy sisters, a woman cut off from the world and consecrated to God Himself, she quailed.

The woman was sitting in a chair stitching at a bit of fabric, peering closely at the cloth to be sure that the needle was doing what it ought, and it struck Fiona as an odd picture. It had never occurred to her that nuns and monks had to do such simple tasks as eating and drinking and making clothes for themselves to wear, just as ordinary men and women did; she had assumed that they spent all their days in prayer or in perusal of that great and mysterious Book or in chanting eerie hymns in Latin, always with a fixed look of piety. But far from making her feel more comfortable, Fiona only felt her world gone more awry.

The Mother Superior glanced up, gesturing for Fiona to sit near her. "So, you are finally awake," she said with an indulgent smile. "I hope you are not very used to rising this late in the day."

Fiona blushed hotly and felt a spring of irrational anger well up within her at the words. "I was very tired, ma'am," she said, grinding the words.

"I should think so. This weather is not the sort for travelling in; saps the strength right out of a body. Where were you heading, my dear?"

"Nowhere in particular. I don't have anywhere to go." It hurt her pride to admit it, but she did so out of the hope that if she gained the Mother Superior's pity, she would be given a shelter at least until the winter passed.

Once more the nun looked up from her sewing, giving Fiona a very long and searching gaze. Presently she dropped her eyes again and asked, "Are you an orphan?"

Fiona thought of her mother, whom she scarcely remembered, and her poor, weak father and his forgetful mind. She thought of Giovanni, who would have been a better father to her than Sir Madoc, and how white he had looked lying in the straw on the back of that cart. So far as she knew, she had no relations in the world worthy of mention. "Yes," she said after a moment, not looking at the Mother Superior, but rather staring into the fire. "Yes, I am an orphan."

"Our Father in Heaven instructs us to care for the widows and the orphans. You may stay here as long as you will, my daughter, and perhaps in time you yourself will take a vow. There will be work for you to do while you stay here but nothing exceedingly taxing; we are here to worship and to serve, and we must not allow ourselves to be distracted by an excess of anything—even work. Does that suit you?"

Fiona was not sure what suited her and what did not, so she merely nodded. The Mother Superior, however, had not finished. For awhile she stitched in silence, but just when her guest was becoming uncomfortable and wondering if she should ask if she might leave the room, the nun spoke. "You are, of course, a member of the Church, are you not?"

Nervous as she was, Fiona jumped for the second time that day at the suddenness of the other's words. "I—yes, madame, I was baptized as a newborn."

"And your attendance at chapel? Is it regular?"

Here Fiona was standing on shaky ground, and she wriggled in her chair as though somehow she might thus worm her way out of the question. She groped for a suitable excuse or half-truth, for she did not care to tell plain lies before the Mother Superior, and at last hit upon, "I go as often as I can, madame." It was true enough: she had gone regularly while with Pierre and Leah. She did not add that it was difficult to attend Mass while tracking one man and being chased by another, but the thought passed briefly through her head.

The other nodded, apparently pleased with the answer. "That is well. God does not demand a perfect role of attendance, after all, and here you will be fully able to attend every day. Can you speak or read Latin, by any chance?"

"No, ma'am, I can barely write in French."

"Such is the case with most men and women. Well, should you choose to remain with us and take the cowl, you may be trained in that language for your spiritual benefit. It is not a common thing to do, but we here at the Couvent de Sainte Marthe believe that those set apart to worship God ought to know His words. As it is, I think the best task that we have for you is the care of the herb garden. Do you know anything of plants? A little? That will suffice: knowledge comes with practice. We have been without a gardener for several years now, since dear Sister Marie died, and I am sure that the women working in the kitchens will be glad to be able to use spices again."

A little something in Fiona's heart stirred at the proposal. She loved gardens: she loved the way they smelled in summer, all golden brown and warm; she loved listening to the rustling of leaves over pathways in autumn; she loved picking berries in winter and cutting holly branches to hang over the doorways at Christmastide; and best of all, she loved the sight of the pale green shoots reaching out of the rich earth in spring, full of hope and happiness at the sight of the sun after so many months of black and grey. A garden of her own—that was something to bring a spark of life into her again.

"I would like that," she said slowly.

"Excellent. Now, I will call for Annette and ask her to show you around the convent: I know it is easy to get lost if one does not know every inch of the place." When the nun was called, the Mother Superior beckoned her into the room and said to Fiona, "You may go and wait in the room out there while I have a word with Sister Annette. She will be along shortly."

Fiona obediently went out and stood in the adjoining room, looking about her curiously. The chamber was big, with great, thick rafters stretching across from one wall to another overhead, but it was quite empty save for the table that stood in the middle of the floor. Arched windows lined the eastern wall and looked out to the crisp landscape, snow lying on the outer shelves at their bases; the sunlight, grey though it was, fell through the glass and made the room both bright and cold.

From Fiona's position, she could see that there were three doors that led out of the room: the first was the one she had just come out of, lying in the corner where the south and east walls met, quite hidden from the rest of the room by the jutting fireplace; the second was at the far end of the hall and Fiona thought that it was the one she and Annette had entered by (but it was so easy to get turned around with the monotony of that place that she could put no credence in the guess); and the third was on the west wall, where the room took a turn into a very short, fat corridor that sheltered this door, like the first, from plain sight. She thought it must lead through to the kitchens and that this room had in times long ago been a great dining hall.

While she was still thinking about this, the door shut behind her and Annette appeared at her side. "Would you like to have a look around the convent?" she asked cheerily.

"Yes, please," Fiona replied, trying to sound respectful; it was not a tone that she was accustomed to using. "What is this room?"

"Oh, it's nothing now. You see, the convent used to be a palace of sorts; not a very grand one, you understand, but they say that many years ago a young baron or a rich knight had it built for himself for when he came here to hunt. He died mysteriously—or so they say, at any rate, but you know how people are inclined to make up tragic stories about every sort of place. I like to think about it sometimes," she added confidingly, and then amended, "But it's far more likely that nothing of the sort ever happened." And she shook her head as though to fling off such childish fancies. Once more she was prim and proper, and the pose was strangely comforting to Fiona's tired mind. Annette took the newcomer's hand and began to lead her through the place.

It was no slight task, to be certain. The place was large and rambling, and Annette remarked that even she had some difficulty remembering every part of the place, but Fiona became acquainted with a few of the main rooms: the kitchens, the chapel, the set of main bedrooms, and the dining hall. "This is all you really need to know," Annette told her when the rounds were completed. "We hardly ever go into the other parts of the building. I would take you out to show you the garden—the Mother Superior says you are to be in charge of that—but the cold is terrible."

Fiona did not mind, not being in the mood to go out of doors at any rate. "Is there anything I can help with inside?" she asked. "I feel a little bit awkward; I don't want to be too much of a burden." This was not quite true, because in fact she would have had no qualms about being a burden if she had not felt so guilty watching the nuns bustle about, all with some light business to attend.

"Oh, you're no burden. You are to be my protégé, the Reverend Mother says, and I will look out for you and show you what it is we do here. Have you ever been to a convent before?"

"Once, a long time ago, but I was only a little girl and we did not stay long." Fiona thought back to the vague, black and white memories, adding wistfully, "Father was there to give a donation to the nuns. My brother and I sat in a big room—like this one—all by ourselves for a long time, and I remember everything was big and dark and gloomy, and the fire died down, but I wasn't afraid, because he was there…," her voice trailed off and she shook her head sharply, scolding herself for letting her mind wander away. "Strange things we remember," she said with a small, harsh laugh.

Annette kindly did not pursue the subject but went on, "Well, life is good here. Everything is peaceful and quiet, and there are hardly any obstacles to overcome or troubles that get in our way; we are at liberty to be ourselves and to worship God."

Fiona looked at her for a moment, her lips pursing slightly and her brows furrowing. "That sounds very nice," she said dubiously, "but what is life but trouble?"

The nun looked at her pityingly, as though she were looking at a very old, warped woman whose years had been filled with trials and chaos and whose heart was bitter and hard as stone. Fiona wondered with a pang if that was what she looked like; was there to be no redemption from the pain and the sorrow? Would she live out the rest of her days tormented by the past, grasping after a cure, only to find that it was nothing but a shadow that slipped away when she opened her fingers? When she tried to look forward, she saw nothing but a dense fog.

"You have questions," Annette said gently, taking her by the arm. "We have answers here. I am not very knowledgeable myself, but what I do not know you may take to the Mother Superior and ask her to help you with. Come along now and let us go to eat."

There was to be no time for questions that day, for after the meal Annette took Fiona to the kitchens and showed her how things were done—the latter was to help there until the harsh weather slackened enough for her to start planting in the garden—and the rest of the afternoon was a whirl as she tried to adjust to the nuns' pattern of daily life. It was not very complicated, only not what Fiona was used to: there were services to be attended in the mornings of weekdays and then again in the evenings, but the space between was filled with work, the kind of servant's work that Fiona had never done nor considered doing in her life. On Sundays, the services were longer and the nuns spent much of the time in the chapel, where the Mother Superior read in Latin from the Book and the sisters sang hymns. There was more involved, Annette said, but these were the basics, and they were all that Fiona wanted.

After the evening mass, Annette went with Fiona to her chambers to lay out the few changes of clothes that had been provided for the newcomer. "We must all attend to our own routine," the nun remarked as Fiona stood waiting to be helped out of her habit. "There are no servants here to help you."

A spark of colour came to Fiona's cheeks. She knew she could not expect the same luxuries here that she was used to, but it was difficult to break out of her paradigm; even at Gallandon, there had been a maid to help her with her toilet. "It's just that I'm not used to this," she said quietly.

Annette flashed a sympathetic smile and showed the younger girl how to take off and put on the clothing, saying, "I was the same way when I came here. I am the youngest of four daughters, and my father and mother were at a loss as to what to do with all of us, so I ended up here. It was not what I would have wanted then, but now—" she paused, looking at the latchet between her fingers "—now, I am glad I do not have to be out in the world."

"I understand that," Fiona returned bitterly.

Annette sighed, finishing her task. "Into bed with you now. Tomorrow, you will have to get ready by yourself; be sure not to be late for Matins, for the Mother Superior is not fond of tardiness. Goodnight."

Almost as soon as she got into bed and buried herself under the covers, Fiona felt a heavy drowsiness overcome her and she fell asleep. It did not last long, though; sometime late in the night she woke with a cry, ripping the sheets away and flying out of bed. She stood in her nightgown in the middle of the darkened room, breathing hard, feeling the sickening pounding of her heart in her breast as she strained her eyes to see through the darkness. Christopher's face was emblazoned in her memory, sharp and clear, with the blaze of fire in his eyes.

Slowly it came to her that she must have dreamt his presence in the room. She straightened a little and stopped shaking, adjusting her garment over her shoulders, but with the calming of her fear she became acutely aware of the cold under her bare feet and the noise of the wind outside and the impenetrable blackness all around her, and she could not bring herself to go back to bed. She moved carefully across the room, her child's fear of something pouncing on her from the shadows prominent in her mind, and felt for a candle. Kneeling by the hearth and pushing back the ashes to find a coal with a spark of life left in it, she coached it until it burned brighter and lit the candle with it.

The flare hardly seemed to touch the darkness at all. A branch scraped against the glass with a noise like a cat's shriek; Fiona shuddered and clenched the candle holder more tightly, curling into a tight ball beside the fireplace and rocking herself. Her mind went back to the convent's history, made all the more plausible by the night, and she wondered if the convent was haunted by the knight. The wind sounded like a voice crying.

Turning her mind a little away from the idea of ghosts, she thought about the knight himself, instead. She wondered more and more drowsily if he had had a wife and what had happened to her after he died. Had he had children? She thought he must have, for the convent was too large and empty for one man and his servants to live in. She imagined happy gatherings in the evening here when the building had been a place of careless laughter and cheer instead of a quiet, peaceful place of sanctuary for troubled souls. Outside the wind was dying down; Fiona set the candle down and ran a hand along the warm stones that surrounded the fireplace, laying her head against them.

When she awoke in the morning, she was lying on the hearth and the candle had burned down until it was no more. It was not yet light, but as she sat up and wiped her eyes she could hear the nuns stirring out in the corridor as they went to mass: the morning was getting away from her. She shivered in the cold as she pulled on her dress, her cold fingers clumsily dropping the latchets in the attempt to make them secure, and when she at last had all her clothing on properly she felt disordered and her nerves were worn to a thread. She knew that she was not pretty, with her shorn hair sticking up from her head in spikes in some places and hanging in short, wiry knots in others; her usually dark skin was pale as death against the black fabric she wore. Somehow the knowledge made her feel worse than ever.

She was a few minutes late to the chapel, but no one seemed to mind. She sat quietly in the background while the service was conducted and was swept once again into Annette's care as soon as it was over. "Did you sleep well?" the nun asked as they walked to the hall for breakfast. Then she continued, "I suppose the food will not be what you're used to, but it is filling and warm. This is the largest meal of the day, so take care to eat plenty."

Fiona glanced curiously up and down the table as she sat down. She was not sure what everything was, but she tried a little of everything and managed to find a few foods that were not so foreign as to be inedible to her. When the meal was over, she was immediately taken back to the Mother Superior's quarters. "She wants to talk to you again," Annette explained, almost apologetically. "About spiritual matters, I understand."

This was the last thing Fiona wanted to talk about at such an early hour—or at any hour—but arguing was out of the question, so with some misgivings she stepped into the room. Annette did not follow but withdrew and shut the door behind her: Fiona was alone with the Mother Superior, and she was not sure that she liked her situation.

"Did you rest well?" the nun asked, fingering the pages of the book in her lap.

"I think it will take me a while to adjust to the new place," Fiona answered honestly, stepping further into the room. It was chilly, the fire being all but banked, and the ivy covering the window made the chambers dark and musty; it was not unpleasant, but neither was it cosy or inviting. Fiona wondered how the Mother Superior could read in the dim.

"I hope you had everything you needed," the other went on. "Life is not meant to be luxurious here, but neither must it be uncomfortable. Come and sit down here, where it is warmer."

Fiona did so, cupping her hands as though to catch the warmth of the fire. "The days seem to be getting colder," she remarked conversationally after the silence had gone on for two or three minutes.

"We still have some time to wait before spring comes," the nun nodded, shutting her book with a heavy sigh. She shifted to face Fiona, her eyes stern and sombre, and said quietly, "Sister Annette tells me that you have questions."

"It seems my thoughts will not be my own while I am here," Fiona said bitterly before she considered her words. "I have had troubles; that is all."

"Annette cares for your welfare, as do I. If helping you means invading your sense of privacy somewhat—well, the eternal position of the soul is far more important. Would you be angry with one who seeks to help you?"

Fiona had no answer.

The Mother Superior leaned forward and took one of the girl's hands in her own, an encouraging smile stretching across her face. "What are your questions, child?"

A thousand and one raced through Fiona's mind, but she took the nearest and blurted, "I don't understand why all these bad things have happened to me. I have done everything properly all my life; I've gone to the masses and the services, and I haven't done anything very wicked, so why does Heaven shun me now? Why me? What have I done?"

The smile twitched. "Is it in your mind, then," the Mother Superior asked almost mirthfully, "that every man who attempts to live a halfway decent life has a clear path from cradle to grave?"

"But why me?" Fiona repeated piteously.

The nun's face hardened, the smile dropping away, and she spoke more harshly. "Do you know why anyone suffers? Is it within the bounds of your wisdom to tell why one man can sit in luxury and another man starve on the streets? Do you accuse God—" her voice dropped "—of injustice?"

This was a little farther than Fiona had wanted to go. She sat in silence, looking uncomfortably at her hands in her lap. When her companion did not say anything more but continued to wait for a reply, she at last muttered, "I only want to understand why."

"Many do, but I think you might find that the reason is not one you care to know. It may be that in the eyes of God you are not so honest and worthy as you think, and not one of the things that have happened to you was undeserved."

Her face going red, Fiona flung up her head and cried shrilly, "What right do you have to accuse me?"

"None whatsoever," the Mother Superior returned coolly. "Nor do I have any intention of doing so; it is for God to accuse and to judge. I merely seek to bring to light some possibilities."

"It was not my fault," the girl insisted. "All I want, all I have ever wanted, is a peaceful life. All I want is peace—how can that be wrong?"

"The only way you will ever find peace is to first accept that you do not deserve it. You ask 'What have I done?', so now I ask you the same: what *have* you done? Have you done anything in your life to make God count you worthy to receive any blessing whatsoever?"

Fiona reached out into her past and grasped at something—anything—that she could hold up as worthy of approval, but she found shockingly little. "I went to Mass," she offered weakly.

"Mass?" the nun smiled pityingly. "And with what spirit did you enter the chapel doors, daughter? With joy at the thought of worshipping God? I read the answer in your eyes. So, with your thoughts on earthly things and your mind distracted, you sat and listened with half-tuned ear to the priest's words; of what worth is that?"

Up until this moment, Fiona had thought it of great worth; now the nun's tone, the mixed scorn and compassion, took away the last shard of consolation she had. She felt naked and helpless beneath the gaze of Heaven. A tear trickled down her face and splashed on her hand.

"Your tears are of self-pity, I think," the Mother Superior commented quietly. "You are sorry that your guise has been stripped away but not sorry that you hid behind it in the first place. Ah, my daughter, you have a long and weary path before you yet."

Fiona whimpered and turned away. "Why can I not rest?" she demanded.

"In your present state, there is no rest. There is a source of it near at hand, but to reach it will be a hard task for you, I think. My dear, there is so much to explain to you that I hardly know where to start. Do you know anything of the teaching of Scripture?"

"I think it says something about how we ought to live good lives," Fiona replied, and it occurred to her that she really had not much of an idea at all of what the Book said. Her words sounded small and trite.

"Yes, that is a part of it but by no means its entirety. Have you not heard of Jesus Christ and His life and death and resurrection?" Her voice said that she was a little shocked and had begun to consider Fiona a complete heathen.

"I've heard of all that," Fiona admitted, "but I'm not quite sure ... what the point was."

The other sighed, shaking her head. "I see we shall have to start from the beginning. Well, at the dawn of time, when God first made the earth, Man and Woman—Adam and Eve, their names were—were perfect, and lived in a perfect garden that was called *Eden*."

Fiona thought of the beautiful illustration in Leah's book, with the pretty colours and the curious longing it stirred in her heart. That had been Eden. It was strange to try to imagine perfection; it stretched her mind.

"When He had created the world," the Mother Superior went on, "God made a tree grow in the middle of the garden where the Man and Woman were to live, the tree of the knowledge of good and evil. He told the Man and Woman—Adam and Eve, that is—that this was the one tree whose fruit they were not to eat and that if they did, they would die.

"Now into this garden came an angel—you know what an angel is, I hope? Good. Well, an angel in the form of a serpent came into the garden one day and spoke to the Woman and tempted her to eat the fruit, telling her that she and the Man would become like God Himself if they ate the fruit. Her pride and desire consumed her, and she took the fruit and ate it, and the Man did the same."

This much Fiona had an idea of, but she could not help voicing again what she had once said to Giovanni: "It seems a bit foolish of them, trusting a snake and doubting God Himself."

The nun looked at her very long and very hard, finally replying, "Have you never wanted something so much that you are willing to turn your back on your conscience to get it? You should not be so hasty to despise Adam and Eve; you commit the same sin every day of your life."

Overlooking the faint blush on Fiona's cheeks, the Mother Superior went on, "Paradise was broken. God cast Adam and Eve out of the garden for their sin and put on them the curse of Death; their lives and those of their descendants were from then on filled with toil, and at the end came the darkness of Death as a just reward for their sin."

Fiona thought to herself that this story was not a cheerful or encouraging one, but by now she knew better than to speak her thoughts aloud. "And that is where we are now?" she asked, her tone not without a hint of irritation.

"Almost. Listen on, but remember that what I am telling you is the short version of God's plan as it has thus far unfolded and as He has revealed that it will continue to unfold; to tell you the whole of the events leading up to each point in God's timeline, I would have to repeat the whole of His Word from beginning to end.

"Now, where were we? Cast out of the Garden, of course. Well, the ages unfolded, and God was never without a follower, though the world as a vast majority had turned their backs on God and continued the prideful sin of their first father and mother. And then, just about fourteen hundred years ago, something happened. A virgin gave birth to a baby boy and named him Yeshua—Jesus. And that child was the Son of God."

Fiona looked at her companion blearily. The Mother Superior looked back at her unblinkingly. The exchange continued for a second longer, and then the girl said tiredly, "I don't understand."

The other raised one thin eyebrow. "You have not heard the story of the Virgin birth?"

Fiona waved a hand as though to brush off the question, saying impatiently, "No, no, I've heard that, but all the same, I do not understand it. God is spirit; Man is a mortal—I know that. How is one to become the other? It makes no sense. You make no sense. God—" she paused, feeling her foot reaching out into the darkness of heresy. She withdrew it and fell grudgingly silent.

"I am the first to admit that it makes little sense," the other quipped. "But the very fact that Christianity is complicated points to the fact that it is Truth; could or would a mere man invent a myth that leaves him in hopeless darkness, or a story that condemns him to death and eternal torment?"

Fiona shook her head and groaned, placing her head in her hands. "If you would just tell me what I am to believe, I will believe it," she urged. "Just tell me what I need to do day-to-day."

"That is not enough. You must have a complete change of heart—no, you must have a new heart entirely. That is the key point of everything, the crux of the whole matter. That is why this Jesus, God and Man in one being, came to earth and died on the cross and rose from the tomb and went up to Heaven to be with the Father. Through the living out of His life and the spilling of His blood and His rising from the dead, our blessed Saviour turned back the clock; He went back to that day in the Garden and he withstood all temptations and broke that serpent. Ah, it is too much to be explained by me!" The nun flung up her hands and shook her head savagely. "But He is where you will find the rest and the peace you want, my dear. Those are things you will only find in Perfection, and that is what He is."

Fiona looked down at the cross dangling from her neck, watching the *t* shape swinging back and forth and thinking about the other picture in Leah's book, that horrid, bloody one of the man nailed to a construction of wood. Everything was still hazy and unclear, the mud seemingly only stirred up in the waters of her mind, but somehow even the brown shades were better than the still, dark stagnancy that had been there before. She did not say, "I do not understand"; she asked wearily, "What am I meant to do?"

The nun beamed. "Now *that*," she nodded, "is better. Do you believe what I have just told you?"

"I'm not sure," the other replied honestly.

The Mother Superior nodded again. "Well, think on it. If you would have your soul saved from Hell, and if you would truly have that rest that you want, you must believe on the Son of God, His work, and His person, and ask God in Heaven to forgive you all your sins and accept you into His Church. There is much that comes afterward, but that I will explain to you presently. Go and consider now, child; go and consider."

FIONA WENT, AND SHE did consider. She walked along the corridors and absently watched the nuns going here and there, all the while mulling over what the Mother Superior had told her and wondering what it all meant. Annette did not come to collect her, and she was glad; she wanted to be alone with her thoughts. She made her way back to her bedroom and shut the door, drawing a chair over to the window and sitting down where she could watch the landscape. It was not a windy day, so she cracked open one side of the window.

"I just wish," she whispered presently to the sparrow who hopped up on the ledge, "for it to be explained to me simply. Even Giovanni was always talking in riddles; why must they? How can I understand when it is all so convoluted, so tangled?"

The bird twisted its head around and gazed at her curiously from one black, shiny bead of an eye. His beak opened slowly as if in a yawn, and he shook out his feathers, nestling into them.

"Well, you aren't any help," Fiona exclaimed crossly. She sighed and set her elbows on the sill, resting her chin in her palm. Beneath her, deep, new banks of snow covered the garden like a fleece with hardly a thing left uncovered; their bodies shimmering iridescently against the sky, great, black crows sat in the trees and on the stone wall and hopped across the ground, their feathers ruffling in the breeze. The sparrow and Fiona both watched them, one warily, the other not really seeing them at all. Presently the latter remarked, "There may be something in her words, but I think I'm too simple to draw it out."

After dinner that day—which was, as Annette had warned her, a very light meal—Fiona went out into the garden to see what kind of place it was. Beneath the snow she found it ill attended and unkempt, its scraggly plants withered, having attempted to grow and push out of the earth and having found no encouragement to keep them going. It was a pitiful sight, but Fiona took delight in picturing how she would transform the plot of land come spring.

When this pastime was exhausted, she went for a walk around the convent. A small iron gate lead her out of the garden's allotted section and into a stretch of lawn, still within the confines of the wall, that stretched around to the back of the building. The ground was in shadow here, at all times blocked from the sunlight by the convent and the tangled knot of trees growing close by; the earth was coated in dead, wet leaves, and only tenacious ivy continued to grow there.

As Fiona walked and thought and looked about her, she caught sight of a form standing near a plot of land where the forest and a corner of the convent's wall touched. "Annette?" she called curiously.

The nun jumped and turned about quickly, her eyes startled and refocusing slowly as if she had been in a different world until the interruption. "I didn't expect you to come out here," the nun remarked, casting down her eyes.

Fiona came up to her and caught a glimpse of the holly twig that she held. "What are you doing?" she asked. "Are you waiting for someone?"

Annette shook her head, relaxing a little. "No, only thinking. It's so quiet back here, sometimes I come to think about things that—that do not seem good to think about inside. Home, mostly."

Fiona looked at her and caught a wistful expression on her face that was gone as soon as it was noticed, and she saw in it the truth that the young nun, however happy she was day-to-day, still longed sometimes for the outside world. The English girl wondered what it must be like to be always shut up behind gates and walls, to have no chance of escape or freedom; and she also followed Annette's gaze over the high wall.

The nun again shook her head and turned aside, drawing Fiona after her. "How was your talk with the Mother Superior?" she asked, eager to change the conversation. "I haven't seen you since then."

Fiona's mouth shrugged. "It went well enough, I suppose. She gave me many things to think about."

Annette laughed softly, nodding. "Yes, she will do that. When she talks to me, I get headaches; it is so hard to wrap one's mind around the things she says."

"You too?" Fiona glanced over at her companion in surprise. It was good to know that someone else faced the same struggles of the mind that she did and to know that not everyone's level of intelligence was as far beyond hers as the Mother Superior's. After a moment she confided, "I want to understand—truly I do—but it's so difficult to understand what everyone is talking of."

Frowning thoughtfully, Annette paused to inspect an icicle that hung from the low-hanging bough of a tree. Presently she said, with the same musing in her voice, "I suppose most people are simply told what they must believe from their childhood on, and then when another person tries to expand their scope, it hurts. I suppose it's like soldiers who are being trained: at first it hurts, what with all the new activities, but then gradually the pain dulls and they grow stronger, until they are ready to fight."

Fiona had started at the first part of Annette's speech, wondering if she had been eavesdropping on her conversation with the Mother Superior, but as the nun went on, the younger girl understood that she was only honestly laying out the way she saw things to be. "But is the pain really worth it?" she countered, out of temper with all this talk.

Annette raised and dropped one shoulder. "The soldiers think it is," she said, then added, "I think it is."

"It's different for you," her companion groused, digging the toe of her boot into a snow bank. "You've been raised here; of course it will be easier for you to understand."

"I never said it was easier," Annette returned with a laugh. "Only that I accept the difficulty of it because I know it leads to something greater than I can imagine.

"But now," she went on, shifting the topic before Fiona had a chance to respond, "how do you like the convent? I hear you are to be put in charge of the garden, come spring."

News travelled fast around the convent, apparently. "It's a very interesting place," Fiona said carefully, tipping back her head to scan the old, wind-worn stones of the convent walls. There was a bell-tower near the chapel, added on sometime after the construction of the rest of the place, and she could see bits and pieces of birds' nests thrusting out from it; the rustic nature of the scene added to the gothic, slightly eerie appeal of the place as a whole. "I think I will enjoy living here."

"It really is a beautiful place. The only times I dislike it are on those savage days in winter when the wind howls like dozens of wolves and the trees lash against the windows: then everything seems hostile and … and a little ghostly. But all other times, I think there must not be a prettier place in the entire world."

Fiona thought of the manor house again, of its shifting nature through the seasons, and of the White Cliffs shining in the sunlight. She remembered the look of the downlands in winter, of stark trees reaching out from under the snow, all scraggly against the sky, and of downy rabbits bounding across the open spaces. She thought of walks through the wheat fields in late summer, with the sheaves waving above her head. She thought of the breeze rustling through the leaves of the old apple tree and the sight of a ruddy fruit, freshly picked and tantalizing, lying in her hand.

"It may well be the prettiest site in France," Fiona murmured.

The nuns retired early in the evening, what with the early sinking of the sun and with candles being the precious commodities they were, and soon after supper Fiona was crawling under her blankets and laying her head on her pillow. She knew she ought to consider the Mother Superior's words before she slept, but words and thoughts tangled together in her mind and she found herself pondering unimportant things, such as why one post of her bed was taller than its companion. She recognized the tell-tale signs before it happened, but she could not help it; she fell asleep, glad to rest after last night's tiring vigil.

After she had slept for about four or five hours, her eyes suddenly flew open. Her whole body was tense, but not with a dream this time. She was suddenly very much aware of the Reverend Mother's words, every one of them, and she also remembered Giovanni's statement to her—words that had hurt bitterly at the time, though she had not admitted it. "You are worse than you know." The sentence sounded again in her head, and she suddenly realized that, painful as it was, it was true. Everything was clear, utterly and completely clear like smooth, polished glass, and her sleep could no longer contain it. "God," she whispered into the darkness. And then, as though that single word had taken all her energy, she dozed off again.

She had not had a vision, nor a dream, nor anything of the sort, and yet everything important that had lain in darkness for so long had come to light in one instant. It did not fade with her awakening, either; it remained sharp and distinct in the morning light. The Mother Superior's question—"Do you believe what I have just told you?"—rang in her ears, and every part of her strained to answer that yes, she did; she had been made aware by some force beyond herself of the incredible misery that lay inside her and the hopelessness of living as she was. "God," she said again when she woke, and a long string of other prayers, rambling and tearful and tight from having never been used, spilled out in her mind before at last she came to the thought that she had been trying to express: "God, forgive me."

She was tired and her head ached and there was too much relief welling up inside for her to be outwardly joyful and merry, but she lay staring out the window, fiddling with her cross for a long time as she mulled over her thoughts and feelings. Her heart still seemed to tremble and her mind raced over ideas too quickly, but she felt at last that she had grasped—something. Not everything, indeed, but something. And God, she had no doubt, could see the meaning and the heart that lay behind those last three words of hers.

She rolled over again and crawled from her bed decisively; she would go now and speak with the Mother Superior. Like a ghost she drifted out of the room and down the hall, glazed eyes fixed before her, and moved in the direction of the Mother Superior's chambers. When she reached them, the nun was not there; she took a seat by the cold ashes and waited.

Epochs seemed to pass before the door creaked open and the Mother Superior entered. Fiona leapt to her feet and faced her, her trembling renewed.

"Ah, there you are," the nun remarked, eyeing her with some slight annoyance. "You were not at Mass this morning."

"No, ma'am, I slept late and then I had things to think about," Fiona answered nervously. "And now I have things to talk to you about."

One thin eyebrow raised, the nun came over unhurriedly and sat down beside Fiona. She stoked the two or three living embers in the fire pit, careful to sweep off all the stray ashes from the hearth, and then smoothed her skirts with aggravating precision. "I assume you wish to talk about what I told you yesterday," she said; it was not a question.

"Yes, ma'am. I—"

"It would be best," the other interrupted with a kindly smile, "if you were to call me *Reverend Mother*; it sounds less as though you were a servant or a vassal here. But do go on."

"Reverend Mother," Fiona repeated dutifully. Then she continued, "You said yesterday that I should ask God to forgive me my sins, but you did not mention … if He would."

"If He would what?"

"If He would forgive me, were I to ask Him."

The Mother Superior looked at her unblinkingly for several long minutes and then asked in return, quite slowly and clearly, "Do you think that now He must by rights do so?"

"No." The earlier fear and terror was still fresh in Fiona's mind, and she had hardly to think before giving the sharp reply. But the hopelessness that that answer gave sent her heart sinking to the pit of her belly; her skin was cold.

"Then you should feel all the more the mercy He gives when He promises to do so. Yes, child, if you ask as sincerely as you may for the forgiveness of your sins, He will forgive you—but through no merit of your own, you must remember."

Fiona wilted back into her chair like a flower whom the frost has touched too heavily. "Then … I am free of it?" she breathed.

"'If the Son makes you free,'" the nun said quietly, reaching for her worn leather book, "'you are free indeed.' Now draw your chair closer; our talk yesterday was brief, and there is much more for you to understand."

And so Fiona spent that day, with hardly a pause for dinner, until the bell rang for supper and called her away. The next day was much the same, and the next, until a week had passed in which all but a few minutes of the daylight hours were spent in the tutorship of the Mother Superior. Fiona was by no means immune now to the longing for the daily comforts she was accustomed to; her belly growled for dinner when she knew she ought to have been listening to the nun and her limbs and eyelids grew heavy from the close air of the room, but she did her best to overcome them and apply herself to the best of her ability, feeling that she had much to atone for. There were times when she felt she could no longer understand what she had just learned, much less grasp new concepts; sometimes the Reverend Mother recognized this and would send her away for rest and a change of scenery, and sometimes it went unnoticed altogether.

The first week passed into the second, and in time a month had passed, and at last one morning Fiona looked out her window and saw the first pale shoots of the crocus, spring's herald, thrusting up from the ground. Winter had passed, and a new year was ushered in.

"WHAT YEAR IS IT, Reverend Mother?" she asked of the nun that day, calling to a halt the other's flow of speech.

"This one?" the Mother Superior asked in surprise, as if Fiona would be asking about any other. "The Year of Our Lord 1418. Why do you ask?"

Fiona smiled dismissively, returning to the perusal of the Latin words that she was just learning to understand. "It seems ages since I last kept a steady track of the days and months; it seemed unimportant for so long."

"Ah. Yes, there is little reason to record the date here, we hear so little of the happenings in the world. Do you miss it?"

By that Fiona knew she meant the larger world—the environment where things happened and there was change, both for the better and for the worse, and there was sorrow and laughter; the world where Life was truly lived, in all its differing hues of scarlet and azure and black and white. Fiona frowned at the palm of her hand, clenching and unclenching her fingers before replying slowly, "I don't know."

"I think you will not stay here," the nun said quietly. "But then, we shall see." There was silence after that for some time, and both women stared into the slate-grey ashes heaped in the fire pit for some time before the elder stirred and set aside the book, remarking, "Well, I see spring is upon us once more; it is time for you to start your work in the garden. Your days must not all be spent idly. Go along then and see what you can do out of doors, my child, and call Annette to help you."

The sunlight glittering on the remaining snow nearly blinded Fiona as she and Annette stepped outside. She had grown accustomed to the gloom of the shut-up convent during the dark days of winter; the change was as sharp as though she had stepped from one dimension into another. "I can't remember a time when the sunshine was so bright," she breathed.

Annette gave a sharp nod, herself blinking rapidly. "This is what makes winter worth going through," she remarked confidentially. Then she added suddenly, turning to Fiona, "Do you know what I like about you? You're the kind of person that one can talk to. I try not to be silly, but sometimes I just have to talk and tell someone my feelings." A smile lit up her face and she concluded, "I'm glad we're friends."

Like a fire flaring on a cold night, Fiona felt her whole soul warm with Annette's words. She felt honestly surprised that any of the nuns would be willing to call her their friend. Even with Annette, who was near her own age, she was as immature as a young chick beside a full grown eagle; she knew herself to be slow to grasp the concepts that the Mother Superior patiently explained to her, and she felt both silly and stupid alongside the other nuns when dealing with spiritual matters. To know that someone enjoyed her company and was pleased to address her as a friend brightened her heart. She made no reply, however, only took Annette's arm and walked with her around the perimeter.

A week later, Fiona and Annette, helped by several of the older nuns, set to work tilling and weeding the land to be used as the garden. It was both strange and pleasant for Fiona to be able to command others as she used to do, ordering them to turn up *this* patch of earth and not *that* patch, to leave one plant and pull up another, to set the first group of herbs a hand's breadth apart and the second an arm's breadth. When she shut her eyes she could almost imagine herself back home with a flock of servants under her command, and when she came back to the present her heart sank a little; it was from this that she first knew that she did miss what she had left behind.

The earth was still cold and flecked with hoarfrost, the wooden spades bouncing back from it as from a rock, and it took a week and a half to get all the seeds into the ground; all that was left was to wait and see if the old, dry-looking kernels still had life in them. Every day for a month or more Fiona would come out and search the ground for a sign of the herbs coming up, and, at length, they did. It was an amazing thing to look down at the dirt where there had previously been nothing and see a tender, smooth head of a plant shivering in the breeze, rising up there; joy and pride coursed through her at the sight of something that she had helped to live.

The first plant was followed quickly by others until, when spring was well situated outside the convent, the garden was full of small, green herbs of different shapes, texture, tastes, and smells. "It's been a long time since it looked like this," the Mother Superior noted one morning on one of the rare occasions that she came out to see what Fiona and Annette had accomplished. "You have done well."

Fiona looked up from her weeding, scanning the scene. "It certainly has changed," she agreed, not replying to the nun's last words.

"So have you. I believe the air here has done wonders for you; no one would take you for the exhausted creature on our doorstep all those months ago."

"Was it months ago?" Fiona squinted up at the sun, as if directing her question at it. "It seems like years. I can hardly remember a time when I wasn't here."

Dusting the leaves and twigs off a low stone bench, the Mother Superior eased herself onto it with a groan and clasped her hands together as she did when she meant to have a serious talk with someone. "Do you think you will stay here, then?"

Fiona let the question hang, straining a handful of rich black soil through her fingers and watching it fall back to the earth again. She was torn between the choices, for though she longed to stay and be protected from the lions that prowled outside the convent's gates, she knew in her heart that this was not where she was meant to be. The thought of facing the world again, though, had her trembling like a reed in a storm. "Yes," she said quietly, though the larger part of her cried out against the word. "Yes, I will stay here."

The nun made no sign of pleasure at Fiona's decision; rather, had the girl been watching, she would have seen the Mother Superior's brows furrow deeply in a frown. For the time being, however, she only said, "Very well. I think perhaps, though, your initiation should be delayed, in case you should change your mind."

It was neither a question nor a suggestion, so Fiona only shook her head and replied, "I will not change my mind."

"Do not be so quick to say so," the nun said evenly, rising from her seat and returning to the building. She added over her shoulder, "Circumstances may change it for you."

Isolated though the convent of Sainte Marthe was, news of great import was sure to reach it at some point in time. Travellers might bring it, or merchants following the trade route, and it might be outdated by several months, but news reached the convent nonetheless. It was near the end of June that the nuns heard that Paris, that seat of French power, had fallen to the Duke of Burgundy and was now in English hands. The news surprised Fiona; ignorant now of almost all politics, she had assumed that Henry V's campaign of 1415 had signalled the end of the war with France. She ought to have known, of course, that England's war with her sworn enemy would never be completed.

"Peace cannot be far away," she tentatively remarked during supper one evening when the nuns, not wholly free from the interests of the world, were discussing this new information. "The French—that is, the king must see that to continue the war would be fruitless."

Her companions, though her elders in all other respects, knew even less about the state of affairs than did Fiona, and all seemed eager to agree with her. "But how long will it last?" Sister Marguerite, who sat across from Fiona, murmured beneath her breath.

"It does seem odd to think of France belonging to England," Annette remarked, pushing her spoon thoughtfully through her stew.

Strange indeed, Fiona thought grimly. *Strange to think that I may at this moment be sitting on English territory.* Aloud she only said, "Half of France was allied with Henry anyway; I suppose most will be pleased with the turn of events."

Sister Miriam looked up with a puzzled frown from her bread, her dark eyes narrowing. "How do you know all that?"

At this point the Mother Superior spread out her hands and said in rebuke, "Hush, sisters! Is this the kind of talk that a place of God houses? Finish with your supper, all of you, and not another word on the subject."

Everyone obeyed, and as she bowed her head to her bowl Fiona felt her heart pounding against the wooden edge of the table. It was not so much that she feared being taken for a spy; she knew that thought had never crossed Miriam's mind. It was rather that she knew from the nun's look that she was yet an outsider to them. She had lived too long outside the convent walls to be treated wholly as one of them. Inhaling deeply, she took a firmer grip on her spoon and shoved the thought away. Day to day they accepted her into their circle—she needed no more.

Later that evening, when Mass was over and the chapel was empty of all other souls, Fiona knelt before the altar and tried to pray in the solitude. The dying sunlight spilled through the western-facing windows and set the long, narrow room glowing burgundy as the highlights in the old floorboards came to the surface. The coloured panes in the windows shone green and gold, silver and crimson, sending sprites of differing hues dancing through the chapel. She could not focus on her own grave thoughts; at length she stopped trying and simply knelt and watched the sunset through the murals on the windows.

"Fiona?" It was Annette's voice advancing upon her down the length of the aisle. "What are you still doing here? Mass has long been over."

Fiona came out of her reverie with a sigh, brushing back her hair, which almost reached her shoulders now, as she shifted to face her friend. "I was praying," she explained simply.

"Oh, I'm sorry; should I go? I had not meant to disturb you."

Fiona shook her head, though she still did not rise from her position. "No, you are all right; I was distracted already."

By now all the light was gone save for the little provided by the candles burning on the altar and in the alcoves of the windows. The glass was dark and the sprites gone; serenity lay over the room, cool and restful, but still Fiona was not at peace within herself.

"Is something on your mind?" Annette enquired tentatively.

Fiona nodded but did not make any move to say what that was. Annette waited, and, at length, the younger girl stirred. "I'm not sure I am meant to be here," she said softly, running her hand across the floor as though to indicate the convent as a whole. "I do not feel like one of you."

"Oh, is that it?" Annette laughed then quickly shushed herself. "I thought the news about Paris upset you."

"Paris? No. It surprised me, yes, but it did not upset me; I am not much interested in what happens between England and France." And this was, for the most part, true; Fiona had abandoned her thirst for revenge, or, rather, it had been slowly leeched from her, first through trials and sorrows, then through the simplicity of a new life. When she thought of Leah or Pierre, her feelings of curiosity for their welfare were mixed with very few other emotions. More time was needed to deepen the pink scar on her heart into silver, but she hoped that she had, to the best of her abilities, forgiven Pierre for his part in Giovanni's death.

She jerked her head to throw off her contemplation and repeated, "I cannot feel like one of you."

Annette squeezed her friend's hand and replied encouragingly, "But you will! When you take the cowl and become a nun, you will be as at home and content here as the rest of us. It will be different then. Be patient, and you will see."

Fiona half smiled and rose, hoping that what the young nun said was true but doubting it greatly. "Dear Annette. You always try to cheer me." She patted the hand that covered her own. "Well, I will be off to bed now. Goodnight; God bless."

Annette returned the wish and they parted, each to their own chamber.

Lying in bed that night with sleep very far from her, Fiona played with the cross about her neck and let her mind wander into the past, into the time before the name of Agincourt meant anything to her ears. She realized with a twinge of guilt that she could no longer recall a clear image of her father's face to her mind; she heard his frail voice in her head and saw his study, with its scattered books and papers and spilled ink, but he himself was no longer stamped in her memory. There had once been a time, she knew, when he had been a true father to her, but that time was long ago and she only knew of it from things that Giovanni had told her.

Giovanni.... She rolled over with a sigh and looked at the figure in her hands. She did not miss him as savagely as she once had, knowing that had he not fallen, she would as yet be lost in her soul—whether that would have affected her daily life or not. But still she wondered where he was, and her heart sank at the thought of him passing through the refining fires of Purgatory.

That night she dreamt that the convent was destroyed by flames.

THE YEAR OF 1418 passed by, with its spring and summer, its autumn and winter, and 1419 was ushered in. Not many weeks after the first of the year, news of Rouen's surrender to England and the fall of Normandy trickled into the convent, and yet still there were no whispers of appeasement from the seat of King Charles. Treaties were haggled over obsessively and the royalty dragged their well-shod feet while France quivered with anticipation and waited for the inevitable.

As for Fiona's personal life, there was nothing worthy of note that occurred in 1419 save that she turned a year older in October. The Mother Superior still made no preparations for Fiona's initiation, and summer dragged into autumn with no change in her position. She was content, though, as she was; she had her garden, she had Annette and the Reverend Mother, and she had her faith, and the combination of these things was more than she had had for many years. Yes, she was content, but the nagging sense of a responsibility elsewhere stayed with her.

Five more years passed after this—five steady, serene years, each blending into the next as a creek into a larger river, one hardly distinguishable from the other. Each year Fiona became a year older, but that was the only change; she drew no closer to her initiation, her role never changed, and life remained as it had been during her first winter in the convent.

Outside, things happened: in the spring of 1420, France at last acknowledged, at least in word, Henry's right to the throne. Many bloody battles had been fought and many lives lost in Henry's zeal for the kingdom of France, and for the time being the bloodshed was to be concluded by the signing of the Treaty of Troyes—

a mere scrap of paper, no more—and the marriage of Henry to Charles's daughter, Catherine. King Harry's son, should he have one, was acknowledged as the heir to the throne of France, and a tenuous peace was reached between the two nations.

It was short-lived, as Fiona had expected when she gave the matter any serious thought. The succeeding year passed without incident, save that a son was born to Henry and Catherine, but in the latter months of 1422, without the sheltering walls of Sainte Marthe, all Hell broke loose once more. And the telling of it went this way.

It was mid September and the evenings were as yet still golden, shimmering harvest days with only the slightest hint of frost during the night, and Fiona and a few of the younger girls recently sent to the convent by their fathers were working to bring in the herbs for the winter. The clatter of horse's hooves on cobbles and the clamour of several voices speaking together interrupted their work, and all the girls pricked up their ears in the hopes that it was a member of their family come to see them—the poor things did not yet know that they had been abandoned there for life.

"Merchants, most likely," Fiona said aloud, crushing their hopes early. "Come along, girls; get these last bundles tied off before we lose the light."

The young fingers flew to draw the herbs tight into clumps and bind the coarse rope, each and every one of them disregarding Fiona's first words and still hoping against hope that it was a retainer sent from their family to collect them. Fiona pitied them, but she knew that in time they would grow used to their status here.

The task was quickly completed and the children sent inside with their burdens while Fiona went around to the courtyard to see the travellers and help the nuns supply them with food for the rest of their journey. Men were not permitted to enter the convent itself, but many stopped en route to one of the larger cities to take provisions before continuing on their way. The merchant's horses were unburdened for a short space of time and allowed to rest while bread was doled out to their masters, a portion to every man, and the women were paid for their trouble by the news that the strangers brought. Indeed, it was not the pretty, worldly baubles that the equines carried that tempted the nuns, but rather it was that that the traders themselves bore: the fleeting glimpse of the things that were taking place beyond the iron gates that separated the convent from the rest of humanity.

Almost as soon as Fiona was in sight, Annette was flying to her side and whispering urgently to her, "The merchants carry such news! Why, it seems that the English king is dead—quite dead! Why, it seems like just yesterday that he became the heir of France."

"Henry V is dead?" Fiona repeated stupidly. "He was still so young; was he murdered?"

"I don't know myself, but perhaps you can find out if you listen to the merchants. It does seem very strange, though—" this as both girls moved closer to the group standing in the middle of the courtyard. "His whole reign was caught up in war, and just as he grasps at peace, the angel of death sweeps him away."

Fiona's lip twitched. "It may well have been his just recompense for all the lives he threw away," she replied, half to herself.

The news was soon followed by yet another death: that of Charles VI of France, the Mad King who had acknowledged Henry to be his heir, and hardly had his soul left this world than war once again broke out. The Burgundians in Paris claimed the throne for the infant king of England, child of the alliance between Henry V and Catherine of Valois, while the French in Bourges declared Charles VI's son, the Dauphin, king of France.

The short peace was over.

One June day in the year of 1423, when Fiona and Annette were sitting in the garden enjoying the warmth after a short cold spell, the latter mused aloud, "I used to think it a kind of punishment to be locked away behind the convent walls; now I know better. I'm glad I don't know everything that goes on out in the world, all the people who die and all the battles that are fought. To think, that if I were not here I might have a husband, and then he would be called away to war and I would be left waiting for him.... And then he might die ... and I would be left all alone...." She shuddered.

Fiona also felt her skin crawl as she thought of Giovanni and the match he had never arranged for her and of David when he had said she needed a man to look after her; but she managed a forced laugh and reproached her friend. "Such sombre thoughts hardly become you, Annette. Where did that come from?"

Annette also laughed, shaking her head and throwing away the sprig of thyme she had been playing with. "This talk of war is affecting me, I suppose." She was quiet for a little while, but she could not keep silent for long. Soon she asked, "What was your life like before you came here?"

"Nothing to speak of," Fiona returned sharply. Then she amended her tone and added more gently, "At least nothing that I want to speak of. There was much happiness, but there was more sorrow."

"You must be glad to stay here, then," Annette said sympathetically.

"I am leaving."

The second after the words had left her mouth, Fiona wondered what had possessed her tongue to form those syllables. They were true: she knew that now. She had to leave, even though the world outside the convent was torn by war again—and, after all, it was her own fault, for if she had left when she knew she ought to she would be safe in Gallandon at this very hour. This was the very reason she had not taken the vows that would bind her to the convent.

For one long, dreadful moment Annette simply sat there, staring at Fiona with huge, incredulous eyes. Then her lips formed one word: "Why?"

Fiona sighed, looking down at the pendant lying on her chest. "I have business that has not been completed. Besides, Annette, my place is not here. I tell you, I am not one of you; the world may tear me apart, but I cannot lock myself away from it for the rest of my days. Dear, *dear* friend, if I take the cowl, I know I would be doing wrong."

"Is it wrong to consecrate yourself to God?" Annette cried.

"Can a person not be consecrated to God and still live in the world? The most famous saints were not monks or nuns: they lived among their fellow men and did God's work there. Is that wrong?" Lowering her voice, Fiona urged, "You must understand, Annette."

Again Annette was quiet. At last she drew the back of her hand across her eyes and nodded sharply; her face was white but dry. "You have been the best friend I have ever had. Will I see you again?"

Fiona took the nun's hand in her own and pressed it. "I don't know, Annette, but … I do not think so."

"And when will you leave?"

"As soon as I may."

Annette drew a shuddering breath and rose from the bench, shaking her head incredulously as she breathed, "I can hardly believe this. This is so sudden; have you stopped to think about it, to really consider what this means? Does the Reverend Mother know?"

"I have thought about it, I assure you. I have wrestled with this since I first came here; this is only the conclusion. And no, I haven't told her yet. I will go do that now. Please don't cry."

The young nun made no reply, only led the way to the Mother Superior's room as she had six years ago and stood outside as Fiona passed inside. As the door shut, the old woman turned from her position by the window and her eyes bored into Fiona's, her face utterly devoid of expression; her eyes showed assurance, and that was all. "Have you come to say what I think you have?" she asked bluntly—she was becoming even brusquer with age.

THE DAY PROMISED RAIN. When the sun came up, late to rise, it could barely force its rays through the deep black storm clouds that hung suspended over the treetops, and the fog stayed until late in the morning, when the weak light at last chased it away. It was cold as winter again, and Fiona held her cloak tightly over her shoulders as she hurried through a stand of trees toward the main road, which, the Reverend Mother had told her, would lead her north to Reims once more. She met no one, for the day was not a promising one for travellers.

And yet, despite the weather, which continued bad for all but a day of her pilgrimage, Fiona's journey was far more pleasant than any of hers had been heretofore. The solitude was no longer lonely but only peaceful; thrushes and sparrows sang in the thicket along the roadside and her ears were open to hear them, and as she walked the rhythmic thumping of the cross against her breastbone kept time to her footsteps. She was a traveller going home, and she was happy in the thought.

As she continued north, the way that she passed showed more and more the effects of marching troops. There were no graves on the banks, but the grass was flattened by the tread of many heavy boots, and once Fiona saw a wide, brown and black scar on the ground from a campfire. Whose soldiers had passed this way, there was nothing to tell, but as she walked she wondered how many of them would live to return home to their families. She wondered also where Pierre was and if he was safe in Gallandon or if he had been called away to battle. Dear Leah, left all alone! Annette's words rang in her ears.

There were inns to stay at along the way, and every night found her safe lodging and a substantial meal. She reached Reims at noon on the third day and did not stop there but passed by it and hoped to find a tavern along the way by evening; she was unsure if the city was still guarded, and, besides that, Reims did not hold good memories for her. She would have liked to go and return the bread she stole from the innkeeper, but she could not; perhaps one day she might. She went on, and every step seemed to take her miles nearer her destination.

The farm where she had taken refuge with Césaire—poor Césaire! Where was he now?— and stolen a breakfast of eggs was still standing, the wooden planks of the house only a little scorched as though a battalion had halted there some time ago. Fiona came upon it at early morning and stopped to look at it from a distance, remembering with a smile and a grimace the feel of raw, slippery fluid in her mouth; she wondered if the family had hurt for the loss of their daily allotment of eggs, and presently, as if just making up her mind, she moved toward the barn.

The grey hens, offspring of the ones that had provided Fiona with her breakfast years ago, were still settled in their positions in the loft, and the heady scent of spices continued to pervade the barn. The fowl glowered at Fiona with the same beady eyes of yore and still drove their beaks at her and clucked in an offended manner when she came among them. She displaced them from their nests and collected the eggs she found there into a basket that had sat at the base of the ladder below, carefully transporting them back to the barn floor. She set her burden down by the door and added to the eggs a slab of cheese she had brought with her from the convent, and with that peace offering she went cheerfully on her way again.

There was one last hill to top before Fiona would come within sight of Gallandon. She picked up her weary feet and pressed eagerly up the slope, her breath coming hard, her legs weak with anticipation. The rain that had been so long in coming began just before she reached the summit, falling like a veil to the earth and sweeping across the landscape to meet her where she stood. Through the silver sheets she saw the shape of the manor house looming up on the edge of the marsh, stolid and powerful as ever, appearing unchanged from the day she had left; candlelight glimmered in two of the southerly windows, warm and inviting.

Her skin feverishly warm and her heart pounding with anxiety and eagerness, Fiona slipped and stumbled down the opposite side of the hill to gain level ground again. Her skirts were sodden and cumbersome, herself wet through and chilled by the keen wind, but she thought of these only as hindrances to her progress: it seemed to take her ages to reach the gardens. The splashing of the rain on the stones dulled the noise she made as she pushed open the low gate—a new addition to Leah's little sanctuary—and stepped inside a maze of winter-worn rose bushes and low-growing evergreens. The course of many years had transformed the scraggly piece of land into the most beautiful garden Fiona had ever seen—and that in winter still. What it looked like in spring and summer, she could only imagine.

She passed through the labyrinth of greenery and came out of the garden by another gate at the southeastern corner of the building. A path led to the courtyard and she walked along it, her steps slower and more cautious now as the slight fear of how she would be received returned to her. The sound that first reached her ears as she drew nearer was that of a horse, its hooves clanging on the cobbles as it blew great breaths through its nose and stirred impatiently, evidently eager to be off somewhere, and the next moment Fiona came into sight of the courtyard, though she remained half hidden behind a shrub. She halted there; Pierre, whom she could hardly believe she had not seen in six years, stood there with his horse's reins in hand, and he was wearing armour.

Shifting so as to see better, Fiona caught sight of Leah standing near the doorway. Her hair was loose and her curls limp, plastered to her face and neck; she wore a white dress that would have been elegant but that the rain had ruined it, and it now clung to her body like a second skin. Fiona recognized her pitiful expression: it was the one she had seen on Annette the morning she left the convent, but it was even more potent on Leah's smooth white face.

Pierre hesitated where he stood then dragged his unwilling horse closer and caught Leah's face in his free hand, pressing his lips to hers. The gelding snorted and pulled at the reins, but his master was in no hurry; he held his wife so for a moment longer before jerking cruelly away and leading his horse to join the knot of riders that Fiona saw were waiting at the entrance to the courtyard. He did not look back again.

The moment he was out of sight, a harsh sob—a noise that Fiona had never heard from her mistress before—broke from Leah's throat, but the lady did not continue to stand weeping in the yard. Her face quivered for a moment as she forced down her tears, but then she turned dry-faced to the house again. Her footsteps were unhurried but not lagging, her chin was lifted slightly, and if the rain had not blurred her vision Fiona would have seen that only Leah's eyes revealed the torrent of emotion inside her. The latch clicked softly into place, and Fiona was left alone in the dreary day.

She hesitated awhile there, wondering if it was best to intrude on Leah's sorrow, but she was cold and wet and reasoned that perhaps the lady's happiness at seeing Fiona again would for a time dim her sorrow at her husband's departure. She came to the front door and rapped on it.

A maid whom she had never seen before cracked the door open and eyed her suspiciously. She consented to open it a little further when she saw Fiona's habit and said, still a little dubious, "Step inside, Sister. Do you want to see the lady?"

Fiona thought it best not to right her on the subject of her vocation. She only nodded, adding, "If you think it convenient."

The servant twitched an eyebrow and withdrew, letting Fiona stay behind in the foyer to drip and shiver. She looked about her as she waited and found little changed; all the tapestries were the same, and all she could see to be different was the addition of an English-made sword hanging over the entrance. "He must have won that in a battle," she murmured to herself, stepping back to see it better.

"Are you here to see Mother?"

Fiona dropped her eyes and saw a boy, young but sturdily built, standing before her in the entrance to the corridor. His expression was half curious and half wary, and the curve of his dark eyebrows made him look like a young replica of Pierre.

"You can't see my father just now," the boy went on, "because he's gone away. Who are you?"

"An old friend of your mother's," Fiona replied, not fully concentrating on what she was saying. She was enraptured by the youth and struck with how he, like the garden, had been utterly transformed by the passing of years. "You *are* Pierre?" she asked suddenly, frowning.

"Little Pierre," he corrected, looking not in the least ashamed of the nickname. "My father is Pierre. Did you come to see him?"

Fiona shook herself. "No. No, I came to see your mother; the maid went to announce me."

"Pierre? Pierre! Where are you, Pierre?" a child's mirthful voice echoed down the halls and presently a girl some years younger than the lad came running into view. "There you are!" she cried, screeching to a halt without even a glance at Fiona.

Pierre marched to the girl's side and put his hands on her shoulders proudly, presenting her with the words, "This is my sister, Jeannette."

Fiona looked at the child curiously, finding again more of Pierre in her face than of Leah; only her golden eyes were her mother's. "Do you have many siblings?" Fiona asked, directing the question at the boy.

"Her and Charles, but Charles is just a baby—he's only been walking for a year."

Jeannette was impatient with the talk, not knowing and not caring who this wet newcomer was. She grabbed young Pierre by the shirt cuff and tugged at it, urging, "Let's play at hiding again, Pierre; you have to hide this time. Don't hide too hard, because I never can find you when you do."

Fiona smiled as Pierre sighed and followed his sister off with the air of a martyr, reminding her of the games she and Giovanni had played in their childhood. That was a long time ago now, she reflected; nearly twenty years since they had both been young enough to romp about, carefree. It was strange to think of those times so far removed, when they could have been just yesterday.

"My lady wishes you to come to the nursery," the maid sniffed as she appeared by Fiona's side again. "If you will be so kind as to take off your cloak here; wouldn't want to drip all over the house." She cast a pointed look at Fiona's boots, in places caked in dried mud and laden with soft, gooey dirt in others. She hummed slightly and shook her head then reached out to take Fiona's arm.

"Never mind," Fiona assured her. "I know the way."

The maid looked at her as if to say, "Oh, you do, do you?" But she made no protests and merely shrugged her shoulders, withdrawing from the entry.

Fiona was in no hurry, and she wandered up and down the corridors in a state of suppressed bliss as she worked in the feel of the manor again. The place had not been home to her for long—certainly not as long as the convent—and yet it reached its arms out to her and called her name and welcomed her into it; here she had felt both needed and wanted, had been happy and sorrowful, had had the highest highs and the lowest lows. Gallandon was as much a home to her as the old manor under the Welsh mountains.

The nursery was worn with several uses, but it was still the peaceful little sanctuary that it had been when young Pierre was a baby. Leah was seated by the window, her hands idle in her lap and her head laid against the wall, watching her youngest child play with his carved men and fat woolly animals in the middle of the floor. Her embroidery was limp across one knee and her face was melancholy, but she caught up her sewing again as soon as she saw the door move and pretended to be hard at work, glancing up as though surprised to see the stranger.

Surprised she was after that first moment. Her doe-like eyes were huge and staring at the woman standing in the doorway, and her embroidery fell from her hands; the needle rolled away across the floor and little Charles, unaware of anything out of the ordinary, hurried to pick it up for his mother.

Fiona stepped in farther, half embarrassed now that she was seeing her mistress face-to-face again, and she wondered what Leah thought of her after having slipped away like an ungrateful wretch. She said nothing but waited for the other to move first.

The lady rose slowly and her gaze remained fixed for another moment longer, and then, all in a flash, joy swept across her face like a falling wave of emotion, and she flung out her arms to her old friend, and then they were embracing and kissing and crying over each other as women are wont to do. Little Charles stood with the needle in his fingers and looked at them both dubiously, as *men* are wont to do, and then retired to his toys again apparently with the decision that whatever had suddenly come over his mother, it was not his business.

When the first greetings had passed, Leah drew Fiona to a chair and made her sit down. She resumed her own seat and leaned forward, hands clasped, her eyes eagerly demanding the full story of all that had happened to Fiona since she left. The younger woman blushed and gave a short laugh, running her hands over her face. "There's so much to tell, I really have no idea where to start; and none of it is interesting, either."

But Leah frowned so terribly that Fiona sighed and spread her hands on her knees, amending, "Well, I shall tell you all, but do not expect a diverting story." And she did tell all, or at least all that had happened since she left; she told it clearly and succinctly and without much pathos in the relating of it. She concluded merely with, "And so I have been staying in the convent for about the past six years or more. But … well, I broke my promise to your husband to serve you faithfully for three years, and I felt I should come back and set things right. And I have grown so fond of this place."

Leah smiled and reached to squeeze Fiona's arm. They were quiet for a time, and the lady appeared to return to her embroidery as if nothing had happened, but Fiona felt her eyes watching her curiously even as the agile fingers wove the thread in and out of the fabric. To turn the conversation away from herself, the English girl cleared her throat and asked carefully, "Has your husband gone away, then?"

Leah only looked at her, but the expression was so rebuking that its message carried clearly.

Fiona dropped her eyes. "Yes, I did see him leave," she admitted. "I did not want you to think I was watching you."

Leah's lips twitched, half in a smile and half in a shrug. Fiona noticed now that there were shadowed hollows beneath her eyes, telling of sleepless nights and worry-filled days, and a muscle in the hollow where her throat met her shoulder twitched occasionally. "Has he been away often?" Fiona asked quietly.

Charles seemed to feel the air grow stale, for he raised his head and watched them both with very large, sombre eyes, two wooden soldiers lying forgotten in his hand. "Mother?" He had been silent for so long that the sound of his voice made Fiona start in her seat. "Mother, is Father coming home soon?"

Fiona watched the tears spring into Leah's eyes and her lip begin to quiver, and the younger girl hastily bent down to Charles's level and suggested, "Why don't you go and play with your brother and sister now?"

He gave no objection save for a sigh and laid down his toys, rising from the nursery floor and heading toward the door on his short legs. Once there he paused and turned back, his chin thrust high, saying with confidence found only in a child, "Father's coming back soon. I know he is. Father never leaves us for long."

"Of course he is," Fiona said stoutly as the child left in search of his siblings, but her tone could not be as assured as Charles's. She was too well aware of what happened in battles to give Leah much false hope; war was nasty and greedy, and it demanded many lives. She took Leah's cold hand in her own and repositioned herself comfortably, saying, "It seems as though I have been away for ages, for all the changes that have come about here. I can hardly believe that young Pierre is the same child that I christened." She shook her head, all the more incredulous as she expressed her disbelief in words.

Leah smiled faintly, a glint of pride in her eyes.

"You have been fortunate," Fiona added.

The lady nodded, understanding Fiona's meaning; infant mortality was so high that to bear three healthy children without mishap was a blessing from heaven. But Leah did not seem to want to stay on the subject of herself and her family for long, and she tipped her head to one side and eyed her companion critically, mouthing several words.

"I've changed?" Fiona blew a laugh through her nose. "Yes, I suppose I have. It's hard to explain without going back a long time; do you mind a long story?"

Leah settled back in her chair and picked up her work again, indicating for Fiona to continue.

"Well, then. Many years ago—almost a decade, now—I lived in my father's manor house in England. I won't bother to tell you just where, for it will mean nothing to you in any case, but it was a very beautiful piece of land. My mother died when I was little, and my poor father was very weak in mind, but I had an elder brother who looked out for me and filled their roles. I loved him dearly; I still do. But when the king—King Henry of England—launched his campaign against France, my brother felt called to join the army and cross the sea as well, and, in time, a messenger brought me news of his death at the Battle of Agincourt."

Leah flinched at this part in the tale, perhaps thinking of her husband and wondering if she would get similar news.

Fiona fell silent for a stretch of time, gathering her courage to go on. She turned her cross, more worn and smudged and tarnished than ever, over and over in her hands. "I was filled with bitterness," she went on, "and hate. The king had put a ban on merchant ships passing between France and England, but I crossed the Channel anyway and came to the continent in the wild hope of wreaking vengeance on my brother's killer. I was mad," she added with a little smile.

"In time I came here, but I could not be happy while living under a French roof. I ran away, and your husband was kind enough to let me go. I went to a convent near the Marne and stayed there, as I said, and while I was there, something happened to me. It's very difficult to explain; it was as though God spoke to me there. Not in a vision or a trance, but He came to me in some way or another and pardoned me—which was all the more amazing because I did not recognize that I had wronged Him at all, and that made my position all the worse. Well, He did—He pardoned me, and He gave me the peace I had been looking for since Giovanni died. It all happened so quickly; I could hardly tell you the date, much less the exact time.

"It was slower after that," she went on. "The learning and the realization of what exactly had occurred in its more minute details. I am not a very quick learner, and that was part of what made me feel inadequate to the role of a nun. But as I said, I had to come back here and tell you everything; I had hoped to speak to your husband as well, but it can wait until he comes back."

Leah sighed and shut her eyes for a moment as if to say, "If he comes back."

Fiona had deliberately left the cross-figurine out of her tale; it played a role that was to be kept unknown to all but Pierre and herself, for she had no desire to upset Leah with the news that her husband had killed her friend's brother. No, the cross was a secret—it was best that way.

ONCE AGAIN, FIONA BECAME the resident of the bedroom across from Leah's; once again, she helped the little lady with her children and household work, as well as translating for her to the servants. But she was not Leah's maid anymore, not even in word, only her friend and companion and a part of the household. The children grew to love her and called her *Tante*; Jeannette would make flower wreaths for her from the garden, young Pierre would gallantly offer her his arm when occasion dictated, and Charles, cheerful, loving Charles, would sit in her lap and put his arms around her neck with almost the same affection that he showed his darling mother. None of them asked where she came from or even cared to do so, and they were helpful to her beyond their imagination, for they helped her to lay aside the past and begin a new life.

Every evening when the children had been put to bed, Fiona and Leah sat up and read or sewed together to pass the time. The latter slept poorly when she did sleep at all, and she preferred to stay up rather than go to bed and be plagued by dreams. Fiona worried about her; it hurt her to see the lady's expression of longing as her gaze drifted from her thread to the window, as if willing Pierre to come home to her. Fiona knew the terrible pain of losing a loved one, and she would have spared Leah if she could.

One such warm, sultry night late in July, when the fire was dead and the casements were flung open to catch the barest scrap of a breeze, the two women sat by the windows and applied themselves in silence to their respective tasks. Fiona was going over the household accounts, but she was having difficulty in focusing her mind through the heat; Leah was painting on a small, square canvas, her brushstrokes languid. They both raised their heads often, the one to look searchingly out the window, the other to watch her companion. And then, quite suddenly and without any warning, Leah let out a shuddering breath and dropped her paint and her brush; they clattered on the wood and rolled away, the dark red liquid surging across the floor.

Fiona started up at the noise, staring in wide-eyed shock as Leah dropped her head into her hands. "Leah?" she heard her voice saying. "Leah, are you well?"

The lady pushed back her chair and stood, walking several paces away, her skirts rustling. One arm was clasped around her belly and the other hand was raised to her forehead; Fiona could hear her breathing from where she remained seated. Presently Leah looked up at the portrait hanging over the fireplace—a painting of her husband recently done by a Parisian artist. She looked at it for a long moment and in the space of time Fiona felt her skin crawl at the suddenly frigid atmosphere, and then the lady turned her head and looked pointedly at her friend. Her face was white, white as a star in a winter sky, and the utter anguish in her eyes made Fiona's stomach lurch: in that horrid moment of premonition, Leah had received a glimpse into the future, and she knew that Pierre would not be coming back.

As when her husband went away, Leah did not cry. She became like a cold, transparent goddess drifting silently through the days, her face drawn with sorrow and exhaustion, but she did not pull away into herself; she continued to work and to spend time with her children as though struggling to keep alive the barest glimmer of hope that she had been wrong and that the winter months would bring her husband home again.

All the children saw this change in their mother, but only Charles seemed to grasp some of its meaning. To Leah he no longer voiced the conviction that "Father is coming home soon," but he continued to whisper it to Fiona at night before he went to bed, his childish voice full of trust. And every night Fiona knelt by her bed and prayed to God that the little boy would be spared the grief of the father he adored being taken away from him so soon.

July slipped into August and all of Gallandon was on edge, trembling at the slowly approaching winter when the weather would turn foul and the war would come to a halt for the year, the men being allowed to return to their homes for the season. Long days were spent in the garden, and Leah waited by the gate where she could see and hear approaching horse hooves. At last, just before August gave way to September, there was a great clattering of equines approaching the gates.

Leah flew to the courtyard, dropping her embroidery in the mud as she did so, and Fiona followed close on her heels. The red flag of warning was waving in the latter's mind; something was not right. There were too many horses, and she could not see Pierre's face among the riders as they drew closer. She grabbed Leah's arm impulsively and dragged her to a halt, holding her back to await the approaching soldiers.

Every single detail of what transpired was engrained in Fiona's mind for long years afterward. She watched as the foremost rider, a man with a broad nose and sharp cheekbones, urged his bay closer and dismounted before them, bowing slightly. Leah did not curtsy in reply; she stared at him, lips parted, breast rising and falling unnaturally. Her hand sought out Fiona's and held it firm.

"My lady," the man greeted Leah in a horribly cheerful voice. "You are the wife of Pierre Charles, Lord of Gallandon, am I correct?"

"She is, my lord," Fiona answered, her voice cracked and dry.

The rider looked at her as if he did not see what business it was of hers then nodded sharply and twisted in his saddle, gesturing for something or someone. Another soldier, riding a dappled grey mare and leading by the reins another bay, came forward. There was a bundle thrown across the latter horse's back.

"The army under the Duke of Alençon and the Earl of Douglas suffered a heavy defeat at Verneuil in Normandy the week before last," the first man droned on. "The duke was captured by the English and the earl was himself slain, along with many good French soldiers."

Oh horrors! Fiona reeled and felt a long shudder run through Leah's body as both realized in the same moment that the bundle was a man's body, bereft of armour and clothed only in a long brown tunic that reached to his knees. He was limp and lifeless, his head dangling against the mare's barrel and nodding with every motion she made.

The man was speaking again, but Leah did not wait to hear more. She jerked forward with a suddenness that made the soldier's horse spook, throwing up its narrow head and shrieking a horse-curse at the lady as she skirted it and reached her husband's side. She took his head in both hands and raised it slightly, searching his face urgently as if she could instil life in him that way.

Fiona hurried to her side, taking one of Pierre's wrists in her hand to feel the pulse. She did not need to: the feel of his skin was enough to tell her what she wanted to know. "He's alive," she breathed, clutching Leah's hand again.

"Oh, yes, he's still alive," the leading soldier confirmed with a laugh of surprise. "They got him out of the fighting and staunched the wound before the battle was over. Still, it's a belly wound, so he's not likely to live much longer. The lady had best start looking for another husband soon."

"Shut your mouth!" Fiona snapped, whirling to face him. "If you had any scrap of decency, you would help us carry him inside and not sit there like a fool and a jackanapes!"

"Why, you are a regular vixen!" the man whistled, his eyebrows flyaway. "Well, Tomas, Henri, carry the fellow inside for the ladies. And be careful with him—no jerking him about."

The men obediently dismounted and unstrapped the sagging body, carrying him between them into the house and down the halls to Leah's chambers. Pierre looked white as death as they laid him on the bed; there was not the least bit of colour in his skin, not even in his lips. Leah and Fiona hurried to his side, and the soldiers drew back uncomfortably into the shadows, not much liking the flurry and bustle of females but feeling it impolite to leave without being told to do so. They waited like this until Fiona could distract herself enough to say, in a voice that was not very grateful, "Thank you for your help, sirs; please leave us now."

They were only too happy to oblige, trotting off like cheerful, obedient hounds to return to their sphere of comfort. Fiona soon heard the ring of horseshoes on the stones as the party withdrew, the men shouting at one another in good-natured banter until their voices faded into the distance; their humour was sickening to her.

Pierre had received an arrow wound to the left part of his abdomen, between his lowest rib and his hip, and when Leah unwound the bandage she revealed a red incision streaked in places by a whitish yellow. The arrow head had been removed but there had been no time to stitch the wound shut or purge out the infection, and neither woman had any clear idea if his bowels were still intact. They worked as if in a fever themselves, soaking the damaged flesh in hot water and herbs and laying yeast on it to draw out the infection, and once or twice Pierre stirred and gave a child's whimper, eyelids fluttering for a split second before he passed into unconsciousness again.

When the wound had been bound in clean cloth with herbs pressed to the open flesh and Fiona was able to tear herself from the task at hand, she sent young Pierre off for the physician. The other two children were left standing in the hallway by the door, listening and waiting with pale faces, casting wide-eyed glances at each other as if the other might be able to answer the horrible, dangling question, Would Father live? Fiona wordlessly led them to the nursery and left them there but not before hearing Charles whisper forcefully to himself, "He will live. He will live. He must live...."

The physician whom young Pierre brought back some twenty minutes later was Francis, now mostly bald but with silver hair bushing out from the sides of his head like downy thistle. He was also noticeably rounder at the paunch, which served only to make him slower and less hurried than ever, and even the explanation of Pierre's wound brought nothing more than the flick of a bushy eyebrow. He did not look upon Fiona with the slightest bit of curiosity as he entered the room; he crossed the distance to the bed and began methodically to unwind the carefully tied bandage, probing the wound.

"It is not a good one," he pronounced after a time, washing his hands in a basin. "At least one organ is punctured—maybe more. I suggest that you prepare yourself for the worst, my lady, and then if it does not come to pass, you may be pleasantly surprised."

Watching Leah's face crumple, Fiona reflected bitterly that it might have been easier for her if the soldiers had brought Pierre back quite dead; then Leah would have been spared the long, drawn-out waiting, the agony of not knowing what would come next. She looked at the face on the pillow, but there was no sign of life in it.

"There's nothing more I can do at the moment," Francis chirruped. He gave them instructions as to how to tend the wound, adding again his ominous prediction at the end, and then withdrew with the same rolling, toddling walk that had brought him in. He shut the door behind him, and as the latch fell into place Leah sat down heavily on the bed, dropped her head into her hands, and cried like a baby.

It was not the last time Leah wept like that; in the seclusion of her room with only Fiona and the unconscious Pierre nearby, she cried often in the days that followed. Usually her tears followed the moments when her husband's face would twitch and his eyelids flutter as if he would awake, and then he would drift off again in another restless slumber. Fiona and Leah lived and ate and slept—when they did sleep—by his bedside, hoping and praying that the soldier's words would be proven wrong and that Pierre would regain consciousness. Day became night, filled with the lonesome crackling of the fire, and night became day again, and the cycle went on as though it would never end.

As the third day drew on toward evening and both women sat sleeplessly in the darkening room, there was a change at last in Pierre's body. He convulsed twice, swallowed hard, and then lay still. Fiona crept closer and Leah sat as though paralyzed, looking down into the still face in fixed horror, and for a moment the two silently looked on. Then Fiona broke the silence with a whispered, "Oh God, say it isn't so."

Before the words were fairly out of her mouth, Pierre shuddered again and his eyes flew open. There was more white in them than usual, and there were lines of pain and confusion and fear, an expression that Fiona had never seen on her master's face before, underneath them and in the lines on his brow, but he was alert and stayed so. He stared hard into his wife's face, then rasped,

"Where am I?"

Fiona gripped Leah's arm hard, warning her against any display of emotion, and answered, "You are home, my lord."

His eyes shifted to look at her, and the furrow on his forehead deepened. "I'm dreaming. You went away; you're not right. This is just another dream—one more of those dreams that I always wake up from in the end. . . ." He shut his eyes briefly then reopened them with the expectation that the girl and the beautiful lady would be gone.

"I came back," Fiona explained gently, "and you are home. The soldiers brought you back injured from Vernueil."

A shadow of either humour or anger passed across Pierre's features. Then he shifted his head and searched Leah's face again, even raising one weak, shaking hand to caress her cheek. "You are warm," he breathed. "Warm and alive. Dearest Leah, am I truly home?"

She clasped his hand in hers, squeezing it for emphasis, and nodded. She mouthed that last word again, stroking his forehead.

Pierre gave a shuddering breath and managed something like a smile. "I dreamt of you often, but I always woke up and you were no longer there. The doctor said I was raving, but I knew you had been there—I could almost touch you, you were so near me. Ah. . . ," he sighed, letting his hand slip from Leah's face to rest against her arm, resting his weary limbs for a moment. When he spoke again his voice was still weaker than before and so quiet that Leah had to bend down near to his face to understand him. "I am sorry," he whispered; "I am not sure that I will get better from this."

"Of course you will," Fiona interjected. "You mustn't say that, nor think it, either."

He shook his head but did not pursue the subject. "The children—are they well?"

Leah nodded and Fiona began to move away, but Pierre stopped her with a half cry. "No, no, don't bring them; it would only vex them. If—when I get better, then they may come in, but not just now." He paused for a moment then asked slowly, "Has Charles asked about me?"

"He talks about you every day. He was ever so insistent that you were coming home."

Pierre's lip turned up slightly. "Dear child; so like his mother."

At this point Leah laid her hand across her husband's eyes to indicate that he needed to sleep, and after looking about him once more as if to assure himself that everything was as it should be, he complied. His wife continued to sit beside him, his hand held tightly in hers, and watch him as he slept. His face was smoother than before, but the colour had not yet returned; he looked too much like Giovanni had in death, and Fiona turned away.

Despite the words of gloom that Francis continued to shower upon them, Pierre improved. Sometimes he grew steadily more healthy, and sometimes he would lapse back into a spell of pain and exhaustion, but there was little doubt now in Fiona's mind as she watched the progress of the slowly-closing wound that, if complications could be kept away, the lord would not die. Four days after he returned to consciousness, he was well enough to sit half-upright in his bed and asked for the children.

Jeannette was the first to appear, crashing through the door and flinging herself upon his bed with confused words of rejoicing, and she had twice to be warned by *Tante* to be careful of her father's side. Young Pierre and Charles both followed; the former, who was usually fairly stoic, was close to tears as he came to the bedside. "We thought you were going to die," he told his father bluntly, slipping his hand into Pierre's larger one.

"I hope not," the other smiled, a trace of pain in the expression. And then he attempted to pull himself up and scanned the room for his youngest child. "Charles, won't you come to your father?" he asked weakly.

Charles did come but slower than his siblings had. When he came close Fiona saw that his lip was quivering, and when Pierre reached out and pulled him close, the child burst into tears and buried his head in his father's shoulder.

Fiona withdrew, leaving Leah with her husband and children and feeling, for the first time, truly happy for the little lady. She had her family back together again, and her pale, silent face was lit up from the inside with a beautiful light; the marriage that had begun as a disaster, Fiona reflected as she shut the door behind her, had become stronger and steadier than most of those built on transient beauty, wealth, or even a kind of emotion that young people flippantly refer to as love. On the poor, deceitful bringing together of two people God had let forth a deluge of mercy.

The next morning, when Fiona was standing by the open sliver-pane of window in her bedroom and looking out over the garden, a lesser servant brought her the message that Pierre requested her presence. It was the first time since his return that he had spoken to her as one individual speaks to another; before, he had said one or two things through her to Leah but had not really treated Fiona as if she existed at all. The young woman dutifully went to Leah's room, where Pierre continued to stay confined to the bed, and found him alone.

He glanced up as she entered, and his face was neither pleased nor angry but only very firm. "Shut the door, girl," he commanded, much of his old strength in his voice again. "And come nearer."

Fiona did so, trembling and uncertain, wondering what was to follow. She stood at the bedside and looked into Pierre's white, taut face, with its new lines and angles and the hollowness beneath the eyes, and at the same time felt the silver cross lying serenely on her chest. It was strange to see him again and to not feel hate or resentment toward him; strange to find herself instrumental in saving the life of the man who had killed her brother. Strange indeed, she reflected with something like a puzzled frown.

"So, the thief has come back," Pierre said, breaking into her thoughts. "Why?"

Fiona winced, and then replied slowly, "We had an agreement when I first came here that I would serve Leah—your wife, that is—for three years, and I broke that. I came back to set things right."

"I released you from that, though. It was not necessary."

"There were other reasons, too. I took Césaire from you, and though I cannot return him now, I am a thief for that. And I took this from you." She drew the cross and its chain from the confines of her dress and held it out, the blemishes and marks of age showing on the surface of the ornament but not obscuring its beauty. Her gaze followed it with longing and she thought of Giovanni, but still she continued, "You won this in battle, and it is yours. I should not have taken it."

Pierre also looked at the cross, brows creasing into a frown, and he lifted one pale, calloused hand to touch it thoughtfully. "It means a great deal to you," he observed.

Fiona gave a sharp nod and pulled her lip back to bite it; the cross wavered for a moment as her hand shook. "That man was my brother," she said, forcing her voice to remain clear. "And I loved him. He was all I had."

Pierre turned his gaze to her face and looked at her gravely. His face was wiser than she remembered it and kinder as well, as if the pain of his wound had taught him gentleness to others; he looked more than ever like Giovanni had. "Then I am sorry I took him from you," he said quietly. "Keep the cross; it is yours by right."

A flood of relief washed across her face; she did not object or take time to question him but drew her hand back quickly and hid the necklace away lest he change his mind. She gave him no thanks and it did not even occur to her to do so, but she was grateful all the same. "You don't need to explain," she added. "I understand: in battle, you don't think about who the opposing man is—you cannot. It is the way of things. I understand that now."

Pierre gave a slight smile in place of a nod and was quiet, lips turned out slightly, meditating on what to say next. "Is that all you came back for?" he asked in time, leaning his head back against the wood of the bed.

"And because I love this place. It has been a good home to me."

"And my wife? Do you love her enough to be a friend to her?"

"I do, and I would be. She is a beautiful lady; I can learn so much from her."

"She *is* a beautiful lady," Pierre agreed, pleased and satisfied. "I think it was not what Christopher had in mind when he tricked me into marrying her, that poor fool. If it were not for your sake I would be sorry I killed him, if only to see his disappointment with how his plans have turned out." He gave a full smile and a short laugh, which was no sooner out of his mouth before it changed to a wince and a groan of pain. "Ai, the wound's not fully healed yet," he hissed, drawing himself back down to a prone position; but when Fiona moved away, he made a negative gesture with his hand. "You say you cannot give me back Césaire. What happened to him?"

There was a sort of idle curiosity in the way he asked, but still Fiona felt a blush on her neck. "I…sold him, my lord."

"You sold him." Again Pierre shifted and grimaced. "Césaire was my best charger, girl! But I'll not ask why or for how much you sold him; you are my lady's friend, and thief or no, you will not be indebted to my house." He gave a fleeting smile—a very fleeting one indeed—and laid his head back to rest. "There: you may go now. Call my lady in."

That was the second of September. On that date, all was well with Pierre; his wound was improving and his limbs growing stronger, and there was joy in Gallandon as there had not been for many anxious months. But on the third of September, only the next day, there was a change for the worse. No one knew just how it happened—it might have been a stray draught or a trick of the fire or an evil spirit, for all they knew—but Pierre began first to cough and then to develop a catch in his breathing, and by nightfall his skin was hot with fever. Fiona and Leah stayed by him and the doctor came and went, but Pierre seemed to recognize only his lady, and that only when he was not shivering with chills.

Fiona entertained no hopes now. Such a regress could not be altered, and she knew it; as for Leah, though she was silent, her eyes spoke her despair. Once she raised her head and her gaze caught her maid's: it was stricken, and it reminded Fiona of the pain she had felt when she saw Giovanni lying in the cart. "Courage," the girl whispered.

Leah dropped her head again.

It was far past midnight and the candles burned low, casting small circles of light about them. Fiona left the bedside to replace one whose wick had disintegrated and fetch a taller one from the table near the window, and she stood for a moment with her back to Pierre as she lit it with tired, clumsy fingers. The light flamed against the darkness. There was a strangled noise from behind Fiona and a voice cried out, "Pierre!"

Fiona whirled, knocking down the candle and its brass holder with a crash; the flame sputtered out into no more than a thin wisp of smoke, and the candle rolled away from her feet. Leah was paler than her maid had yet seen her, with skin that seemed little more than a thin film stretched over her and eyes as wide as doors into her soul. She was standing, her hands and her entire body shaking like a dry leaf in a storm, and she cried out again.

It was strange that the first words Fiona ever heard her speak were given in such a pitiful, twisted scream. They exploded from her as if a door inside her throat had been opened by the strain, releasing the prisoner words that she had longed to speak for years. And yet it was fitting, Fiona thought briefly, that her first one would be her lord's name.

"Pierre! My lord Pierre!"

There were feet pounding in the corridor outside, voices being tossed back and forth. Then the door crashed open with a noise that sent another shudder through Leah's body and Francis, who had had the consideration to stay these past long days in case he was needed, trotted in. One glance should have been enough for him to know, but still he looked with his great owl-eyes at Fiona and asked, "Is he?"

"Yes," Fiona whispered, going and taking Leah's arm. "Yes."

THEY BURIED PIERRE THE next day. It was but slightly over a week since he had been brought home; he would be put on the list of casualties for the Battle of Vernueil. Leah stood like a small statue by the grave, shivering every now and then despite the warmth of the evening; she wore black and her face was covered, only her hands still bare and white as she clenched them together prayerfully. With her newfound voice she would whisper his name, punctuated by a quivering sigh. Fiona dared not try to lead her away, but after several long moments Leah turned away and walked toward the manor house.

"How are the children?" she asked softly. It was still strange for Fiona to hear her speak; it sounded more like a stirring in a spring wind than a human voice, so soft was it.

"It's not been easy," Fiona replied, taking the other woman's arm. "But they are only children; the pain will ease."

"Yes, and the memory as well." Leah sighed again, glancing back through her veil to the plot where Pierre now was. "He was a good husband, Fiona. He was so good to me, though I was mute and had no title; he only ever loved me. Oh, Fiona! Will you laugh at me if I tell you that I loved him as well?"

Fiona shook her head. "I will not laugh at you. You have been—God has blessed you. I would have been so happy if I could have had a man like yours."

Leah pressed her friend's hand, leaning on Fiona's shoulder as they passed through the courtyard and into the great house. She was silent again; there were no cries of pain, nor tears, nor sighs, and only the pinched look in her face showed her thoughts. The children had squirreled themselves away into their bedchambers, and the servants went about like ghosts, and even the dogs and the stray hog that rambled through the dining hall kept quiet. A hush had crept over Gallandon.

Leah did not retire for a long time that evening and spent her time standing by the half-open window listening to the rain begin to pitter-patter on the stonework outside. "Come to the fire, my lady," Fiona pressed her as the night drew on. "You'll catch cold. Come away."

Leah obeyed—silently, as usual. She sat in one of the massive, carved chairs next to Fiona, her body seeming very small and frail next to the thick wood, and picked up a piece of cloth that she had been embroidering with flowers. The needle slipped in and out of the fabric; the little pearly knobs in it turned slowly into rose petals drifting across her lap. Without raising her head, the lady spoke. "Will you be staying long, Fiona?"

Fiona turned her gaze from the fire with a start, blinking the pricks of light from her eyes. The question took her by surprise; she had not stopped to think of what she would do now, after having served out her years under Pierre and atoned, as much as she could, for her wrongdoings. "I would like to stay for a time," she said slowly, looking at her own embroidery in her hands. "And then—I would like to go back to England, I think."

"I thought you might." Leah nodded, continuing to loop her thread in regular patterns; but she sighed slightly. "I know that France can never be your home."

"I will always think of Gallandon as home," Fiona promised earnestly. "Truly. You and Pierre have taught me much; you showed me peace and joy and hope and love that I have never seen in anyone before—not since my brother died. I do not think I could ever fully explain to you why I ran away—"

"I do not ask." Looking up at last, Leah gave her a little smile. Then her eyes turned to the hearth and her work became idle, and her lips straightened into thoughtfulness. Presently she said, "God has arranged strange ways for some of us to find him. Sometimes He brings us on long physical journeys; sometimes He leaves us at home and makes the journey internal. Yours has been both. You have gone a long way and struggled a great deal, but I can see from your eyes that it was not for nothing. My own troubles were all inside." She sighed again, looking up at the ceiling for a long moment before continuing. "I am Bohemian, you know. I had an illness when I was young and lost my voice in the convalescence; I have not spoken in seventeen years.

"Before I came here to be my lord's bride, I sat under the teachings of a man named Jan Huss—a great man who taught us the Scripture in our own language. The first time I heard him speak, it was the most amazing thing I had ever heard; those incoherent Latin phrases, the mumbled words that made no sense, had suddenly shaped themselves into sounds I could understand." Leah's eyes seemed to brighten for a moment at the memory and her speech quickened, and she spread her hands out, palm up, as if with an offering. "Oh, he was a great man! No man, woman, or child who heard him speak could ever forget him. He taught us the words of God—truly taught us and made us comprehend them." Then the light in her face sank and she looked down at her hands. "They burned him at the stake as a heretic, barely months after I left Prague."

Fiona did not need to ask why. Even if the doctrines of Huss were in line with Rome's, the Church had seen too many heretical groups spring up through the past centuries—Albigensians and Waldensians, especially—to deal lightly with those outside the clergy who took it upon themselves to teach the Word. Translations of the Bible were especially despised. Fiona had nothing to say, and so she said nothing.

Leah took a deep breath and went on, "After my father died in Prague early in 1415, Christopher, my brother, decided that he must attach our family name (which was nothing at the time) to a greater one somewhere in Christendom. Anywhere would do. We left Bohemia and came here to France shortly after Agincourt, and Christopher attached himself to my lord Pierre like a leech. He claimed I was of noble Bohemian blood, invented a lineage and a family history—and I, mute as I was, could say nothing."

"Why did you not run away?" Fiona demanded. There were few things more shameful in her mind than gaining a husband through lies and cheating a man at so holy a sacrament as marriage.

"Did you not know Christopher? He was a devil, Fiona; you know it. He terrified me." She pulled her dress from her shoulder and turned so that the firelight showed up a thin line of puckered silver skin at the base of the neck, running diagonally across her collar bone and disappearing beneath the fabric. "He gave me that just an hour or so after our father died because he had been drinking and threw a silver platter at me. That was my brother. I dared not disobey him.

"I married my lord Pierre. Christopher fled; the story came out. I was fortunate in that my husband did not seek a divorce, but at the time that almost made it worse, for if he had I could have crawled away to a convent and shut myself up from the world. You know that things did not stay that way, by God's grace." She reassumed her needle and fabric with a partial shrug of her shoulder, adding, "And so by trickery I gained a better marriage than most women can boast."

"There is a certain amount of irony in that," Fiona murmured. They were silent for a long time, sometimes embroidering and sometimes watching the embers cracking and popping as they died down, until the English woman stirred and said, "It is best that I not leave with winter coming on. I'll wait until spring and warmer weather before I go; you will need help with the children until then, at any rate." Catching sight of the protest rising to the other's lips, she went on, "I know a man who will help me—if I can find him. He has helped twice before. It is you I am worried for; can you manage alone?"

Leah pressed her friend's hand. "Little Pierre is growing so quickly," she said with a little sigh. "He will be a man before we know it and ready to take care of the estates. Until then, my husband had a good steward. Yes, we can manage. But I will miss you; will you come back to us one day?"

"I do not know; only God does. But I would like to see Gallandon again." Lifting the silver cross from her chest and looking down at it, Fiona added quietly, "It will be strange to go back home again."

TEN YEARS AFTER SHE had left England on the old Welsh brig, Fiona returned just as clandestinely. It was night when her boat rattled against the dock and she stepped, shaking, onto firm ground again, but it was broad daylight when, several days later, she left her hired coach and went on foot the last mile to the manor house where she had grown up. The sky overhead was blue as aquamarine and laced with wisps of cloud as from a painter's brush, and the English hills were as green as she could ever remember them being. Quilted patterns of darker and lighter earth stretched before her as the road topped a hill, the house as out of place as ever in its farmland surroundings. Nothing seemed changed; the path winding up to the building was still chalk-silver, and the old apple tree was still growing in the meadow. Fiona went to it, drawn by a sort of companionship and affection for something that reminded her so keenly of careless summer days of long years before—of Giovanni's laughter and his clean-cut, honest face, especially.

The deep green leaves rustled welcomingly as she approached. When she came under the tree's outstretched boughs, a lone white blossom drifted down to her and landed in her palm, and the squirrels overhead chattered in what could have been laughter and could have been a warm reception. "It's been so long since I saw you last," Fiona whispered, putting a hand against the dark, cracked wood of the trunk. "You remember me, don't you? Do you see? I've brought back his cross, and much more than that. I've brought it back in *here* as well." She pressed the necklace to her heart and smiled up at the bits of sky that winked between the foliage. "I wanted to show you, old apple tree, because you were always such a friend to us. Dear old apple tree."

There was a sound behind her that was not part of the natural surroundings, and Fiona turned toward it. It was a man. He looked at her and she looked at him, both surprised and, on his part at least, a little amused. "I know you," he greeted her.

"And I know you," she replied. They always did seem to meet in this odd, chance-formed way, she reflected; if there was such a thing as chance. She did not think there was. Perhaps she had been praying that she would meet him and had not realized it herself.

David shifted to put his weight further on his left leg and to get a better view of her, his brow darkening in thought. "Yes," he went on, "the girl from London, though I almost did not recognize you. There's a difference in your face." He gestured vaguely at her but did not clarify. "It has been a long time since Reims. What do you here now? You do not look to be on your quest anymore."

"No, I finished that quest. This manor was once my father's and would have been my brother's if he had not died at Agincourt. I wanted to visit it again. Is it yours now?" Fiona looked away beyond the apple tree at the landscape, finding it strange, once again, to think of someone else working the fields and running the house.

"Ah. So it is; I bought it years ago, but I have had to travel a great deal. I recently came back for a visit." Again he looked at her and murmured as if to himself, "You look different—different from all the times I have seen you."

"All the times?"

"Four times; five, now. I knew your father, and I saw you twice when you were a little girl of nine or ten. That was when I was younger, myself." A grin cracked across his face for a moment, but then it melted and he narrowed one eye. "Have you never heard of me?"

Fiona thought she ought to have and searched desperately in her memory for a sight or a remembrance of him, but she could not find him. "No," she said at last, unwillingly.

"Indeed? I was a suitor of yours, once."

"A suitor? Of mine?" She looked aghast, bewildered not at the thought of his being her suitor, but at the thought of her ever having had one.

"Of a sort. I asked your father for your hand in marriage after—after your brother went away, but nothing came of it. Did you not hear of it at all?"

"No, indeed, my father never spoke of it. He was not as alert at that time as he had been. Perhaps he did not remember. I never remember seeing you before London."

David chuckled, putting his hands behind him and clasping them together. He moved to the bench on the other side of the trunk—new since Fiona had last been there—and sat down, and she, after hesitating a moment, sat beside him. He continued, "I knew who you were when I met you there. I'm afraid that is the only reason why I took you to Dover at all, for I had heard that your father was gone." He tipped his head to look at her, and the gesture let the sun hit an ornament on his chest: a small, almost tiny cross, the sight of which Fiona was growing almost used to. She observed it curiously as he continued to speak. "I heard about your brother's death later. I knew him myself; I was very sorry."

Fiona felt a moment's stab of pain, and then it subsided and she was able to say clearly, "Thank you."

"You're alone now. Have you come back to England to stay?"

She looked again at the landscape surrounding her. She thought of Leah across the Channel and missed her, but when she thought of France itself, she could not help but be keenly aware of how little she belonged there. In human terms, at least, she knew she never should have left the manor or England; though as she toyed with the cross around her neck, she knew also that her "quest," as David called it, had not been fruitless. She shook herself. "Yes, I'm here to stay now. Where, I'm not sure; I have little money. As usual," she added with a pathetic half-laugh.

David was silent for a time, and when he spoke he seemed to be desirous of changing the conversation. "I noticed your cross some time ago. You did not wear it in London or Reims."

"It was my brother's. An old family heirloom."

"You wear it for his sake, then?"

"And its own." Fiona was going to say no more, but, looking up at David's dark, sharply cut face, she found herself looking at someone who would understand. "I learned its meaning while I was away."

And David did understand. He said nothing in reply to that, but, not allowing another space of silence, spoke again bluntly. "As I said, you are still very much alone; you have no relatives, I take it? And, if you would be willing, my offer still holds."

Fiona had expected this. How, she could not say, but she had. She sat in thought for a time and mused aloud, with a slight nod toward David's cross, "We have things in common, I think."

"So." David shifted and crossed his arms, and when Fiona glanced up briefly she found his brows low over his eyes as he waited. Presently he added, "I suppose this is very sudden, but I would have had more time to prepare if I had known you were coming back."

She laughed then sighed, still smiling a little. "It is sudden, but I do not mind that. I—like you." Fiona was careful to state it in as modest a way as she could, but she meant it; she did like David, strangely enough, despite his mutilated foot and his brigand look and his gruff voice. She did not know him well, but that which she had seen had made her consider him kind and gracious—perhaps more so even than Pierre, who had been so devoted to Leah. She felt safe when she was with him, sheltered and protected. And there was his cross, which from a mere look of his she knew he understood, and that made up her mind. "I will marry you."

David sat back in satisfaction. For a moment his look softened, but only for a moment that Fiona could see. "You will not regret it," he said, in a voice quieter than she had ever heard him use before. He said no more but continued to sit beside her and watch the progress in the fields beyond the manor house. Nor did Fiona speak. But she was happy and content, content with her cross, and with the manor, and with David.

"So, Giovanni," she whispered aloud, just above silence, "I have both things you wished for me now."

THE END

About the Author

PEOPLE ARE STARTLED WHEN I tell them I was fourteen when I completed *The Soldier's Cross,* but considering how book-oriented my family is, it isn't so surprising that my love of reading and writing came early. I have been taught at home for all my schooling years, leaving more time for expanding into the fields of history and literature than I might otherwise have had; yet my inclination to write came primarily from reading my sister's early works. I loved the freedom she had in creating her own stories, and so when I was about nine or ten I ventured into the world of writing myself.

It was not until I wrote *The Soldier's Cross* for National Novel Writing Month in 2009 that I was able to bring together some of the things I love best—the written word, history, and, above all, my God—and complete a novel. The reasons for the first and the last are self-explanatory, but why the fifteenth century? I admit that the Middle Ages, as dark and gloomy as they were, are not my favorite centuries in history, but every story has a setting, and the one for *The Soldier's Cross* was Medieval France. It was the darkness and gloom themselves that shaped the storyline: the false security in which the majority of Christendom lay, like John Bunyan's Simple, Sloth, and Presumption. Though the Reformation did wonders to renew the cry of the Gospel to repent and believe, the danger of 'peace' outside of Christ is as present now as it was in Fiona's day—creating the theme of *The Soldier's Cross.*

For more information about Abigail, please visit her website:

www.scribblesandinkstains.blogspot.com

If you enjoyed *The Soldier's Cross* please check out Abigail's sister, Jennifer Freitag, and her historical fiction, *The Shadow Things*.

The Legions have left the province of Britain and the Western Roman Empire has dissolved into chaos. With the world plunged into darkness, paganism and superstition are as rampant as ever. In the Down country of southern Britain, young Indi has grown up knowing nothing more than his gods of horses and thunder; so when a man from across the sea comes preaching a single God slain on a cross, Indi must choose between his gods or the one God—and face the consequences of his decision.